PRAISE FOR *PAPER PRINCESS*

"A compulsively readable YA novel." *Kirkus*

"This generation's Cruel Intentions."—Jennifer L. Armentrout, #1 *New York Times* Bestselling Author

"Intense, haunting & hot—I can't stop thinking about Paper Princess!! The intriguing sexy characters draw you in and don't let go. A true must read!"—Emma Chase, *New York Times* bestselling author of the Tangled and Legal Briefs series

"Wickedly clever writing, deliciously provocative characters, & chilling final pages made Paper Princess impossible to put down! Confidently a 2016 Top Read!"—*Rockstars of Romance*

"Gritty, angsty, steamy, and rife with scandal and secrecy, Paper Princess is the kind of book you hope EVERY book will be when you open it. The kind you can't put down, can't forget about. This book consumed me and thanks to that crazy ending, I won't be moving on from this book for a good long while."—Jessica from *Angie & Jessica's Dreamy Reads*

"What a heady, indulgent and ADDICTIVE read..."—*Totally Booked Blog*

PRAISE FOR *FALLEN HEIR*

"Erin Watt is back at it again with more drama, scandals, and characters—new and old—you will love and love to hate."-Nissa, *of Pen and Pages*

"Fallen Heir has all the angst and heart I craved." - Angela, *Reading Frenzy Book Blog*

"The storyline and characters in Fallen Heir were great and I was addicted from page one." - Julia, *The Romance Bibliophile*

" This one is a great mix of fun and flirty moments but also angsty teen drama." - Beth, *Lustful Literature*

"As always Erin Watt has delivered a captivating and addictive read that has you begging for more." - *Lucie Lu's Book Reviews*

"Fallen Heir, in all of its humor and heartache, is an addictive read from start to JAW DROPPING finish and I. COULD. NOT. PUT. IT DOWN." - Jessica, *Angie & Jessica's Dreamy Reads*

CRACKED KINGDOM

erin watt

ALSO BY ERIN WATT

COPYRIGHT

To Lily,
Light of life.

CHAPTER ONE

Easton

EVERYONE IS SCREAMING.

If I weren't in a state of shock—not to mention drunker than drunk—I might've been able to hear the individual shouts, connect them to certain voices, make sense of the caustic words and angry accusations being hurled around.

But right now, it sounds like one unending wave of sound. A symphony of hatred, worry, and fear.

"...your son's fault!"

"Like hell it is!"

"...press charges..."

"Easton."

My head is buried in my hands, and I rub my eyes against my callused palms.

"...even here?...should have you taken out in handcuffs, you son of a bitch...harassment..."

"...like to see you try...not afraid of you, Callum Royal. I'm the district attorney—"

"Assistant district attorney."

"Easton."

My eyes feel dry and itchy. I'm sure they're bloodshot, too. They always get bloodshot when I'm wasted.

"Easton."

Something smacks my shoulder, and one voice breaks through the others. I jerk my head up to find my stepsister regarding me with deep concern in her blue eyes.

"You haven't moved in three hours. Talk to me," Ella begs softly. "Let me know you're okay."

Okay? How could I be okay? Look at what's happening, for fuck's sake. We're in a private waiting room at Bayview General—the Royals don't have to wait in the real ER waiting room with the rest of the peasants. We get special treatment everywhere we go, even hospitals. When my older brother Reed got stabbed last year, he was rushed into surgery like he was the president himself, no doubt taking an OR slot from someone who needed it more. But Callum Royal's name goes a long way in this state. Hell, the country. Everyone knows my father. Everyone fears him.

"…criminal charges against your son—"

"Your fucking daughter is responsible for…"

"Easton," Ella urges again.

I ignore her. She doesn't exist to me at the moment. None of them do. Not Ella. Not Dad. Not John Wright. Not even my younger brother Sawyer, who was just allowed to join us after getting a couple stitches on his temple. Massive car accident and Sawyer walks away with a scrape.

Meanwhile, his twin brother is…

Is what?

Fuck if I know. We haven't received an update about

Sebastian since we got to the hospital. His bloody, broken body was whisked away on a gurney, his family banished to this room to await the news of whether he's alive or dead.

"If my son doesn't survive, your daughter will pay for this."

"You sure he's even your son?"

"You goddamn asshole!"

"What? Seems to me like all your boys need DNA tests. Why not get all the testing done now? We're at a hospital, after all. It'll be easy enough to draw some blood and confirm which one of your boys is a Royal, and which one is O'Halloran spawn—"

"Dad! SHUT UP!"

Hartley's anguished voice cuts into me like a knife. The others might not exist to me right now, but she does. She's been sitting in the corner of the room for three hours. Like me, she hadn't spoken a word. Until now. Now she's on her feet, her gray eyes blazing with fury, her voice high and ringing with accusation as she lunges toward her father.

I don't know why John Wright is even here. He can't stand his daughter. He sent Hartley to boarding school. He wouldn't let her move back in once she returned to Bayview. He shouted at her tonight, told her she wasn't part of his family and threatened to send her little sister away.

But after the ambulances took Hartley, the twins, and the twins' girlfriend away, Mr. Wright was the first person to leave for the hospital. Maybe he wants to make sure Hartley doesn't tell anyone about what a piece of shit he is.

"Why are you even here!" Hartley screams out my thoughts. "I wasn't hurt in the accident! I'm just fine! I don't need you here and I don't *want* you here!"

Wright yells something back, but I'm not paying attention. I'm too busy watching Hartley. Since her car collided with the twins' Range Rover outside her father's mansion, she's insisted she's fine. Not to me, of course—nope, she hasn't looked my way even once. I don't blame her.

I did this. I destroyed her life tonight. My actions drove her to get into that car, at the exact moment my brothers were speeding around the curve. If she hadn't been upset, maybe she would've seen them sooner. Maybe Sebastian wouldn't be... dead? Alive?

Goddammit, why aren't there any updates?

Hartley keeps insisting she's not hurt, and the EMTs obviously concurred because they examined her and then let her come to the waiting room, but she doesn't look so good right now. She's swaying slightly on her feet. Her breathing is short. She's also paler than the white wall behind her head, creating a shocking contrast between her skin and jet-black hair. There isn't a drop of blood on her, though. None. It makes me weak with relief to see that, because Sebastian was covered in it.

Bile coats my throat as the scene of the accident flashes through my mind. Shards of the broken windshield littering the pavement. Sebastian's body. The red puddle. Lauren's shrieks. The Donovans already picked up Lauren and took her home, thank God. The girl didn't stop screaming from the second she got to Bayview General to the second she left it.

"Hartley," comes Ella's quiet voice, and I know my stepsister has noticed Hartley's ashen state. "Come sit down. You're not looking too good. Sawyer, go get Hartley some water."

My younger brother disappears without a word. He's been a zombie since his twin was taken away.

"I'm fine!" Hartley spits out, shoving Ella's small hand off her arm. She turns back to her father, still wobbly on her knees. "*You're* the reason Sebastian Royal got hurt!"

Wright's jaw drops. "How *dare* you insinuate—"

"Insinuate?" she interrupts angrily. "I'm not insinuating! I'm stating a fact! Easton wouldn't have been at the house tonight if you hadn't threatened to send my sister away! I wouldn't have come after him if he hadn't come to see you!"

That makes it my fault, I want to object, but I'm too weak and too fucking cowardly to do it. But it's true. I'm the reason this happened. I caused the accident, not Hartley's dad.

Hartley wobbles again, and this time Ella doesn't hesitate— she clamps a hand around Hartley's upper arm and forces her to a chair.

"Sit," Ella orders.

Meanwhile, my father and Hartley's father are staring each other down again. I've never seen my dad so pissed.

"You're not going to be able to buy yourself out of this one, Royal."

"Your daughter was driving the car, Wright. She'll be lucky if she doesn't spend her next birthday in juvie."

"If anyone's going to jail, it's your son. Hell, all of your sons belong there."

"Don't you dare threaten me, Wright. I can have the mayor here in five minutes."

"The mayor? You think that sniveling pencil-dick has the balls to fire me? I've won more cases in this godforsaken county than any other DA in the history of Bayview. The citizens would crucify him and you—"

For the first time in three hours, I find my voice.

"Hartley," I say hoarsely.

Mr. Wright stops mid-sentence. He whirls around to face me, daggers in his eyes. "Don't speak to my daughter! You hear me, you little bastard! Don't say a word to her."

I ignore him. My gaze is glued to Hartley's pale face.

"I'm sorry," I whisper to her. "This was all my fault. I caused the accident."

Her eyes widen.

"Don't say a word to her!" Shockingly, this comes from my father, not hers.

"Callum," Ella says, looking as astonished as I feel.

"No," he booms, his Royal-blue eyes fixed on me. "Not one word, Easton. Criminal charges could come into play here. And *he*"—Dad glances at John Wright as if he's a living manifestation of the Ebola virus—"is an assistant district attorney. Not another word about the accident without our lawyers present."

"Typical Royals," Wright sneers. "Always covering each other's asses."

"Your daughter hit my sons' car," Dad hisses back. "She is the only one responsible."

Hartley makes a whimpering sound. Ella sighs and strokes her shoulder.

"You're not responsible," I tell Hartley, ignoring everyone else. It's like we're the only two people in the room. Me and this girl. The first girl I've wanted to spend time with without getting naked. A girl I consider a friend. A girl I wanted to be more than friends with.

Because of me, this girl is facing my father's wrath. And she's wracked with guilt over an accident that wouldn't have happened if I wasn't in the picture. My older brother Reed used to call himself the Destroyer. He thought he ruined the lives of everyone he loved.

Reed's wrong. I'm the one who screws everything up.

"Don't worry, we're leaving," Wright growls.

I tense up as he stomps toward Hartley's seat.

Ella wraps one arm around Hartley's shoulder in a protective gesture, but my dad briskly shakes his head at her.

"Let them go," Dad barks. "Bastard's right—they don't belong here with us."

Panic lodges in my throat. I don't want Hartley to go. And I especially don't want her to go with her father. Who knows what he'll do to her.

Hartley obviously agrees, because she instantly balks when her dad tries to grab her. She shrugs off Ella's arm. "I'm not going anywhere with you!"

"You have no choice," he snaps. "I'm still your legal guardian whether you like it or not."

"*No!*" Hartley's voice is like a crack of thunder. "I'm not going!" Her head swivels toward my father. "Listen, my dad's a—"

She never finishes her sentence because in the next second she topples forward, crashing to the floor. The sound of her head thudding against the tile is going to live with me until I die.

A hundred hands seem to reach for her, but I get to her side first. "Hartley!" I yell, pulling on her shoulder. "Hartley!"

"Don't move her," my dad barks, and tries to shove me away.

I jerk out of his grasp but let her go. I lie down on the floor so my face is next to hers. "Hartley. Hart. It's me. Open your eyes. It's me."

Her eyelids don't move.

"Get away from her, you punk!" screams her father.

"Easton." It's Ella, and her voice is lined with horror as she gestures to the side of Hartley's head, where a thin stream of blood is spidering out. I feel like throwing up, and it's not just because of the alcohol still buzzing through my veins.

"Oh my God," Ella breathes. "Her head. She hit her head so hard."

I swallow my terror. "It's fine. It's going to be fine." I turn to Dad. "Get a doctor! She's hurt!"

Someone grabs my shoulder. "I said get away from my daughter!"

"You get away from her!" I spit at Hartley's father.

Suddenly there's a commotion behind me. Footsteps. More shouts. This time I let myself be wrenched away. It's like Sebastian all over again. Hartley's on a gurney, and doctors and nurses are barking orders at each other as they wheel her away.

I stare at the empty doorway, numb. Stunned.

What just happened?

"Oh my God," Ella says again.

My legs can no longer support my own weight. I drop into the nearest chair and gasp for air. What. Just. Happened?

Hartley was hurt this entire time and didn't say anything? Or maybe she didn't realize it? The paramedics cleared her, damn it.

"They said she was okay," I croak. "They didn't even admit her."

"She's going to be fine," Ella assures me, but her tone doesn't hold much conviction. We both saw that blood, and the purple bruise forming at her temple, and her slack mouth.

Oh fuck. I'm going to be sick.

Gotta give Ella credit—she doesn't jump away when I bend over and throw up all over her shoes. She simply strokes my hair and smooths it away from my forehead. "It's okay, East," she murmurs. "Callum, go get him some water. I don't know where Sawyer wandered off to when I sent him to get some. And you—" I assume she's talking to Mr. Wright, "I think it's time you left. You can wait for news about Hartley somewhere else."

"Gladly," Hartley's father says in disgust.

I know the moment he's gone, because the air in the room loses some of its tension.

"She's going to be fine," Ella says again. "And so will Sebastian. Everyone's going to be fine, East."

Rather than feel reassured, I throw up again.

I hear her murmur under her breath, "God, Reed, would you just *get* here already."

The waiting game begins again. I drink water. My dad and Sawyer sit in silence. Ella throws her arms around Reed when he finally shows up. He had to drive all the way from college and he looks exhausted. I don't blame him—it's three in the morning. We're all exhausted.

News of Sebastian's condition is the first to trickle in. His head injury is the biggest concern. There's swelling in his brain, but the doctors don't know how serious it is yet.

My oldest brother Gideon arrives a bit after Reed, in time to hear the part about Seb's brain. Gid throws up in the wastebasket in the corner of the room, though unlike me, I don't think he's drunk.

It's hours later when a different doctor appears in the

doorway. It's not the one who operated on Seb, and he looks incredibly uneasy as he glances around the room.

I stumble to my feet. Hartley. This has to be about Hartley.

CHAPTER TWO

Hartley

A BRIGHT LIGHT AIMED AT my face wakes me up. I blink groggily, trying to decipher actual shapes from the blobs of white in front of my eyes.

"There she is. Sleeping Beauty has awakened. How are you feeling?" The light flashes again. I reach up to wave it away and nearly black out from the pain that washes over me.

"That good, huh?" the voice says. "Why don't we give her another thirty milligrams of Toradol, but make sure to watch for bleeding."

"Yessir."

"Great." Someone snaps two pieces of metal together, making me wince.

What happened to me? Why am I in so much pain that even my teeth ache? Did I get in an accident?

"Steady there." A hand presses me back onto something soft—a mattress. "Don't sit up."

A mechanical whir buzzes and the back of the bed rises. I manage to unstick one of my eyelids and, through my lashes, I see a bed rail, the edge of a white coat, and another dark blob.

"What happened?" I croak.

"You were in a car accident," the dark blob at my side says. "When the airbag deployed it broke a couple ribs on the left side. Your eardrum burst. As a result of the vestibular imbalance along with some dyspnea—that's shortness of breath—you passed out and hit your noggin pretty hard. You have a concussion and some mild brain trauma."

"Brain trauma?"

I raise my hand toward my chest, wincing the whole way, until I can press my palm over my heart. I gasp. That hurts. I slowly lower my arm back to my side.

"It's still beating, if you're wondering." That's from the original voice. He must be the doctor. "You shorter girls need to try to sit as far from the steering wheel as possible. A deploying airbag is like getting punched in the face with a one-ton truck."

I let my heavy lids fall shut again and try to remember, but there's nothing in my head. It feels empty and full at the same time.

"Can you tell me what day it is?"

Day...I recite them one by one in my head. Monday, Tuesday, Wednesday—but none of them register as being accurate. "How long...been...here?" I manage to ask. My throat feels raw, but I don't know how an accident would cause that to happen.

"Here," the female voice says, pushing a straw against my lips. "It's water."

The water feels like a blessing, and I gulp until the straw's removed from my reach.

"That's enough. We don't want you getting sick."

Sick off water? I lick my dry lips but can't muster up any energy to argue. I slump back onto the pillows.

"You've been here for three days. Let's play a game," the doc suggests. "Can you tell me how old you are?"

That one's easy. "Fourteen."

"Hmmm." He and the nurse exchange a look that I can't figure out. Am I too young for the drugs they're giving me?

"And your name?"

"Sure." I open my mouth to answer, but my mind goes blank. I close my eyes and try again. Nothing. A big fat nothing. I glance at the doctor in panic. "I can't..." I gulp and give my head a fierce shake. "It's..."

"Don't worry about it." He grins easily, as if it's no big deal that I can't remember my own name. "Give her another dose of morphine and a Benzo cocktail and call me when she wakes up."

"On it, Doctor."

"But I—wait," I say as his footsteps fade.

"Shh. It'll be fine. Your body needs the rest," the nurse says, placing a restraining hand on my shoulder.

"I need to know—I need to ask," I correct myself.

"No one's going anywhere. We'll all be here when you wake up. I promise."

Because it hurts too much to move, I let myself be reassured. She's right, I decide. The doctor will be here, because this is a hospital and that's where doctors work. Why I'm here, how I got hurt—that can all wait. The morphine and Benzo cocktail—whatever that is—sounds good. I'll ask more questions the next time I'm awake.

I don't sleep well, though. I hear noises and voices—high, low, anxious, angry. I frown and try to tell the worried ones that I'm going to be all right. I hear a name on repeat—*Hartley, Hartley, Hartley.*

"Is she going to be okay?" asks a deep male voice. It's the one I've been hearing say that name—Hartley. Is it mine?

I lean toward the voice, like a flower seeking the sun.

"All signs point to that. Why don't you get some sleep, son. If you don't, you're going to be in the same bed as her."

"Well, I'm hopeful," cracks the first voice.

The doc laughs. "That's definitely the right attitude to have."

"So I can stay, right?"

"Nope. I'm still kicking you out."

Don't go, I plead, but the voices don't listen to me and all too soon I'm left with the dark, suffocating silence.

CHAPTER THREE

Easton

THE MARIA ROYAL WING OF Bayview General feels like a morgue. Every person in the plush waiting room is cloaked in their own fog of grief. The dark cloud is about to swallow me whole.

"I'm going to get some air," I mutter to Reed.

His eyes narrow. "Don't do anything stupid."

"Like putting my kid in a wing named after a mom who killed herself?" I mock.

Beside my brother, Ella sighs in frustration. "Where would you have put Seb?"

"Anywhere but here." I can't believe these two don't sense the bad vibes in this place. Nothing has ever gone right for us in this hospital. Our mom died here. Seb won't wake up from his coma, and my girlfriend's head nearly split open.

The two give me a dubious look and then turn to each other to engage in a silent conversation. They've been dating for over a year now, and their cycles have synced up or some shit. Of course, I don't need to be sleeping with either of them to figure out that they're talking about me. Ella's telegraphing that she's worried I'm going to lose it and Reed's reassuring her that I'm not going to do anything to embarrass the family. When she's not looking, he casts me a dark stare that repeats his earlier admonishment to keep my head screwed on.

I leave the grief room, the heavy automatic doors sliding shut behind me. I wander down one of the two wide, white marble halls of the hospital wing built with my dad's blood money. It's quiet here, unlike the emergency room on the first floor where kids are crying, adults are coughing, and bodies are in constant motion.

Here, rubber soles move silently across the tile as pristine uniformed staff dart in and out of rooms to check on their wealthy patients. There might be a new hospital wing lying in one of those beds, so they take extra-special care here. There are nicer mattresses, expensive sheets, designer hospital gowns. There are no interns or residents allowed up here unless accompanied by a full-fledged doctor. Of course, you pay for the privilege of being in one of these VIP suites. Hart's in one only because I threatened to raise holy hell if she was punted to the general admission population. Dad doesn't like it. He thinks it's tantamount to an admission of wrongdoing, but I threatened to go to the press and say it was all my fault. Dad told me he'd pay for a week. I'll fight him if she needs to stay longer, but I'm going to deal with one crisis at a time.

I locate my brother Sawyer slumped in front of a trash can.

"Dude, you okay? You want something to eat? Drink?"

He raises a set of hollow eyes in my direction. "I threw my cup away."

Does that mean he's thirsty? This boy is the walking dead.

If Seb doesn't wake up soon, Sawyer will be the next Royal in a hospital bed, not me.

"What was it?" I ask, peering into the can. I spot some fast food wrappers, the brown paper cartons from the VIP deli cart, and a couple of energy drinks. "A Gatorade?" I guess. "I'll get you a new one."

"I'm not thirsty," Sawyer mumbles.

"It's not a problem. Tell me what you want." If he even knows. He sounds delirious.

"Nothing." He struggles to his feet.

I hustle back to his side and put my hand on his shoulder. "Hey, tell me what you want."

Sawyer slaps my hand away. "Don't touch me," he spits out in a sudden burst of anger. "Seb wouldn't be in that room if it weren't for you."

I want to protest, but he isn't wrong. "Yeah, I got you," I say with my throat tight.

Sawyer's face grows pinched. He clenches his jaw to prevent his lips from trembling, but this is my baby brother. I know when he's seconds away from breaking down, so I haul him in for a hug, holding him even as he struggles.

"I'm sorry."

He grips my T-shirt shirt like it's a lifeline. "Seb's going to be okay, right?"

"Damn straight he is." I thump my brother on the back. "He's going to wake up and make fun of us for crying."

Sawyer can't reply. His emotions are filling his throat. He clings to me for a solid minute before pushing me away. "I'm going to sit with him for a while," he says, his face turned to the wall.

Seb likes to rescue baby animals and overuses the heart-eyes emoji, whereas Sawyer's the macho twin. The one who doesn't talk as much. The one who doesn't like showing emotion. But without his twin, Sawyer's alone and scared.

I squeeze his shoulder and let him go. The twins need to be together. If anyone can pull Seb out of his coma, it'll be Sawyer.

I make my way down to the end of the second hall where Hartley's room is. One of the near-silent nursing staff greets me at the door. "I'm sorry," she says. "No visitors."

She points to the digital display to the right of the door that has a private sign flashing.

"I'm family, Susan." I read her nametag. I haven't run into Nurse Susan before.

"I didn't realize that Ms. Wright had brothers." The nurse gives me a look that says she knows who I am and what kind of bullshit I'm trying to sell.

It's not in my nature to give up. I smile winningly. "Cousin. I just flew in."

"I'm sorry, Mr. Royal. No visitors."

Busted. "Look, Hartley's my girlfriend. I need to see her. What kind of asshole is she going to think I am if I'm not checking up on her? She's going to be hurt and we don't need to add any grief onto her plate, am I right?" I can see the nurse softening. "She's going to want to see me."

"Ms. Wright needs her rest."

"I won't stay long," I promise. When she doesn't give in immediately, I bring out the big guns. "My dad wants an update. Callum Royal? You can check the intake forms. His name is on there."

"You're not Callum Royal," she points out.

"I'm his son and his proxy." I should've asked Dad to put me on whatever form needed my name so I could come and go freely. This is the first time I've tried to get in without him, so I hadn't realized how much influence his name held. I should've, though. This wing was built with his money.

Nurse Susan frowns again but moves aside. There are advantages to having your last name on the side of the building.

"Don't wear her out," the nurse says. With one last warning glare, she leaves.

I wait until she's turned the corner before letting myself in. Yeah, I want her to rest, but she can sleep after I've seen her with my own two eyes and made sure she's okay.

Quietly, I make my way around the sofa and chairs in the sitting area of the suite. Like Seb, she's asleep. Unlike Seb, she's had moments of consciousness. The doctor told my dad this morning before he left for work that she'd probably be fully awake today or tomorrow.

I drag one of the heavy side chairs over to the bed and pick up her hand, careful not to dislodge the finger monitor. Seeing her motionless on the bed with tubes and wires snaking their way from her slender arms up to IV bags and machines makes my stomach roil. I want to rewind the clock, spin the world backwards, until we've returned to her apartment where I'm feeding her burritos from the corner food truck after she's worked a hard day at the restaurant.

"Hey, Sleeping Beauty." I stroke her soft skin with my thumb. "If you wanted to get out of going to class so bad, you should've told me. We could've just skipped or forged a doctor's note."

She doesn't stir. I peer up at the monitor above her head, not knowing quite what I'm looking for. The machine makes a steady beep. Her room is marginally less frightening than Seb's. He's got an oxygen mask, and the click of the machine as it winds up to breathe for him is scarier than the background music in a horror film.

I need Hart to wake up so she can hold my hand. I drag my free hand down my face and force myself to think of something positive.

"Before you showed up, I kinda wished I'd skipped my senior year, but now I'm glad I didn't. We're going to have fun. I'm thinking Saint-Tropez for Thanksgiving. It gets cold here and I'm tired of wearing coats and boots. And Christmas, we can go to Andermatt in the Alps. But if you ski, we could stay in Verbier. The high-altitude slopes are fucking awesome, but maybe you'd like St. Moritz better?" I vaguely remember some of the Astor girls not shutting up about the shopping there.

She doesn't answer. Maybe she doesn't like skiing at all. It occurs to me that, before the accident, we'd barely scratched the surface of getting to know each other. There's so much I don't know about Hartley.

"Or we could go to Rio. They have an awesome New Year's party. Pash went there a couple years ago and said it was like a two-million-person rave."

Actually. Maybe with her head injury, she won't want to party. *Fuck, East, you can be thick.* "Or we stay here. We could fix up the apartment. Or maybe find a new place for you and your little sister, Dylan, if you can convince her to come stay with you. Do you like that?"

I don't even get an eyelid twitch. Fear sweeps over me. I

can't take this, both Seb and Hartley unconscious. This isn't fair. The hand that holds hers begins to shake. I feel like I'm on the edge of a cliff and the ground's breaking away beneath my feet. The abyss is calling for me, promising me a dark peace after the free fall.

I drop my chin to my chest and bite the collar of my T-shirt as I try to get a hold of my emotions. I know exactly how desperate and lost Sawyer feels. Hartley showed up at a time when I was feeling my lowest. She made me laugh. She made me think that there was a future beyond drinking and partying and screwing. And now her light's snuffed out.

She's going to be okay. Nut up, boy. Sniveling into your T-shirt isn't going to change shit.

I take a deep breath and bring her hand to my lips. "You're going to be okay, babe." I say it to comfort myself as much as anything. "You're going to be okay, Hart."

She has to be okay—for her sake and mine.

CHAPTER FOUR

Hartley

HEART. HEART. THE WORD RUNS through my head. Something to do with my heart. *No. Hart. Hartley!* I pop open my eyes and croak. "Hartley. Hartley Wright's my name."

"Gold star for the pretty patient in blue," a familiar voice says.

I roll my head to the side and see the doctor there. We smile at each other—me because he's here like he said he'd be, and him because his patient woke up and said her name.

The cup of water and straw are shoved in front of me by Susan, per her nametag, a plump nurse who barely reaches the breast pocket of the doctor next to her.

"Thank you," I say gratefully, and this time it's not taken away, so I suck the paper cup dry. A whirring sound buzzes next to me as Susan raises the head of my bed into a seated position.

"Do you know where you are?" Doc asks, flicking a penlight at my eyes. His nametag says J. Joshi.

"Hospital." This answer is a guess, but given the doctor,

nurse, and ugly blue gown with pink flowers draped over my shoulders, I'm confident in my answer.

"Which one?"

"Bayview has more than one?" Nice. I even know where I am. I settle back comfortably. That blank space when I first woke up was entirely understandable. I'd been hurt bad enough to be hospitalized and was disoriented.

He knocks a fist against the wooden footrest. "Two out of three isn't bad."

"What happened?" Have I asked this question before? It seems familiar. But if I did, I didn't get an answer. At least, not one that I can't remember. When I close my eyes and try to recall how I got here, I see nothing but a black landscape. I hurt all over, so I feel like I must've been in an accident. Did I get hit by a truck? Fall out of a second-story window? Get bashed in the head while buying groceries?

"You were in a motor vehicle collision," the doctor says. "Your physical injuries are healing nicely, but from your other lucid moments you appear to be suffering from trauma-induced retrograde episodic memory loss suffered when you fell in the hospital."

"Wait, what?" Those were a lot of words he just fired out at me.

"You're suffering from memory loss that—"

"Like amnesia?" I cut in. "That's a real thing?"

"It's a real thing," Doc Joshi confirms with a small smile.

"What does that mean?"

"It basically means that the autobiographical memories that you formed, such as your first day of kindergarten or your first kiss or a bad fight with your boyfriend—those aren't likely to be retrieved."

My jaw falls open. He's kidding me. "I may never get my memory back? Is that possible?" I look around for the camera, for someone to jump out and yell, *"Surprise!"* Except no one does. The room remains empty but for Susan, the doctor and me.

"It is, but you're young and so it shouldn't be too traumatic."

I swing my gaze back to Dr. Joshi. "Not too traumatic?" I can feel hysteria burbling in my throat. "I can't remember a thing."

"That's how it feels now, but actually you remember many things. From what we've observed—when you were sleeping and just now as you and I talk—you've likely retained procedural memories. Motor skills that you've learned, along with developmental skills such as oratory abilities. Some of these skills you won't know you have until you do them. For example, you might not realize you know how to ride a bicycle until you hop onto one. What's important is that you're going to be just fine after a few weeks of rest and recovery."

"Just fine?" I repeat numbly. How can I be just fine if my memories are gone?

"Yes. Don't focus on the negative." He jots something down on the chart before handing it to Nurse Susan. "Now I'm going to give you the hardest bit of your recovery."

"It's a good thing I'm lying down if losing my entire memory isn't the hardest part of my recovery." I know I shouldn't be sarcastic, but damn, this is hard to swallow.

Doc Joshi grins. "See, you haven't lost your sense of humor." The smile fades as he grows somber. "And it's very possible you can regain your autobiographical memories. However, you need to keep an open mind when you interact with people.

Their recollection of events is going to be different than yours. Does that make sense?"

"No." The truth is the truth. None of this makes sense. How can I remember my name but not how the accident happened? How can I remember what a hospital is or that the tube running up my arm is an IV or that a harmonic series diverges to infinity but not my first kiss?

The doctor taps the bed rail to get my attention.

"Am I a doctor?" he asks.

"Yes."

"Why?"

"Because you're wearing a doctor's coat. You have the hearing thingy"—*stethoscope*, my mind helpfully supplies—"around your neck, and you talk like one."

"If Susan here was wearing my coat and the 'scope, wouldn't you think she was a doctor?"

I tilt my head up to look at the nurse. Susan smiles and frames her face with her hands. I dress her up in the coat and the metal stethoscope and see her exactly as he'd described—a doctor.

"You see, truth is a variable concept based on each individual's bias. If you saw Susan walking down the hall, you might have said that you saw a doctor, when it's really one of our very capable nurses. What your mother may remember about you borrowing a dress your sister promised you could wear is going to be different than your sister's memory. If you had a fight with your boyfriend, his memory of who is at fault might be different than yours.

"I've advised your family members and friends that they should avoid talking about your past to the best of their ability until it's confirmed that you've lost those memories entirely. I'll write you a note for school and you should warn your classmates about this. If they tell you things about the past, it can color your memories or even replace them."

My body chills as I attempt to absorb the doctor's warning. The whole "two sides to every story" thing is taking on scary implications.

"I don't like this," I tell him.

"I know. I wouldn't like it, either."

I'll just have to remember things on my own, I decide. That's the solution. "How long will it take for me to recover my memories on my own?"

Could I hide out until that time?

"It could be days or weeks or months or maybe even years. The brain is a big mystery for even doctors and scientists. I'm sorry. I wish I had a better answer. The good thing, like I said before, is that other than a few bruised ribs, you're physically in excellent condition."

The nurse pulls out a small vial and sticks a needle in it. I eye it and her with slight unease.

"Can you give me a drug to help me remember?"

"We are." She taps her needle.

"Can you at least give me a bare account of what happened?" I beg. "Did I hurt anyone else?" That's really the important thing here. "Was anyone in the car with me? My family?" I struggle to envision my family but can't come up with any clear images. There are shadows there. One, two…three? The doctor referenced a mom and an older sister, which would make me the youngest if my family is made up of four people. Or maybe my mom's divorced and I have three siblings? How can I not know this? Blood churns violently in my head. A sharp pain spikes behind my eyes. This not knowing may kill me.

"You were driving alone. There were three young people in another vehicle," Doc Joshi says. "Two were uninjured and the other, a male, is in critical condition."

"Oh God," I moan. This is the worst. "Who is it? And what's wrong with him? Was it my fault? Why don't I remember what happened?"

"It's your mind's way of protecting you. This often happens to trauma patients." He pats me on the hand before leaving. "I'm not concerned, so you don't need to be, either."

Not be concerned? *Dude, I've lost my mind, literally.*

"Are you ready for a few visitors?" asks the nurse after the doctor is gone. She injects the drugs into the plastic bag hanging on a hook next to my bed.

"I don't think—"

"Is she awake?" chirps a voice from the door.

"Your friend's been waiting for hours to see you. Should I let her in?" Nurse Susan asks.

My first impulse is to say no. I feel like death. My entire body aches, like even my toes feel bruised. The thought of smiling and pretending I'm okay, because that's what you do with people, isn't appealing.

Worse, every interaction with my friends and family might mean that the things I remember will be someone else's recollection, not my own. I've lost a part of myself and unless I remain completely isolated, I may never fully recover.

But I don't want to be completely isolated. Not knowing is worse than having incomplete information.

"Yes." I can piece things together. Compare and contrast

statements. When facts are confirmed by more than one source, that's the truth. I can deal with the physical pain; it's the uncertainty that's gnawing away inside. I nod and repeat, "Yes."

"She's awake, but be gentle with her," calls the nurse.

I watch as a girl with long, shiny blonde hair nears my bed. I don't recognize her. Disappointment pushes my shoulders down. If she's been waiting for hours, she must be a close friend. So why can't I remember her? *Think, Hartley, think!* I order.

Doc said I might not get some memories back, but he didn't mean I'd forget the people I cared about, did he? Is that even possible? Wouldn't the ones I love be etched into my heart, carved so deeply that I would always remember them?

I search the black void in my brain to see if I can pull up a name. Who am I close friends with? An image pops into my head of a pretty strawberry blonde with a face full of freckles. Kayleen. Kayleen O'Grady. After her name, a collage of images tumble into my brain—waiting in the park after school; spying on a boy; spending the night in her soccer-themed bedroom; going to music lessons together. I flex my hand in surprise. Music lessons? A picture of me bent over a violin appears. I played the violin? I'll have to ask Kayleen about that.

"Yeah, get over here, girl," I say, ignoring the pain the movement brings. Who cares if it hurts to move. I'm getting my memories back. Doc Joshi knows nothing. I smile broadly and reach for Kayleen's hand.

She ignores it, stopping about five feet from the bed as if I'm contagious. She's close enough for me to see she looks nothing like the snapshot in my memory. This girl's face is more oval.

Her eyebrows are sharply defined. Her hair is a light blonde and her face is freckle-free. Kayleen could have dyed her hair, but there's no way her face goes from cute with freckles to the chilly, unfriendly blonde with a vanilla complexion.

And her clothes…Kayleen's a jeans-and-oversized-flannel kind of girl. The person in front of me is wearing a knee-length cream plaid skirt with black-and-red striping. She's paired it with a cream long-sleeve blouse with lace at the sleeves and the collar. On her feet, she has a pair of quilted ballet slippers with shiny black caps and interlocking gold CCs finishing them off. Her hair is pulled back to one side and fastened with a barrette with the same interlocking letters, only these are studded with rhinestones—or hell, maybe they're diamonds.

She looks like an expensive magazine advertisement.

I frown, dropping my rejected hand to my lap. "Wait, you're not Kayleen." I squint. The girl looks vaguely familiar. "Is that you…Felicity?"

CHAPTER FIVE

Hartley

"In the flesh." The blonde tiptoes gingerly over to peer at the IV bag. "Hmm. Morphine. You're at least getting decent drugs."

Felicity Worthington is a girl I know more by reputation—like a celebrity of sorts—which explains why I remember her but not any specific interactions with her. The Worthingtons are big names in Bayview. They live in a huge house along the shore, drive expensive cars, and the kids throw massive parties that show up on everyone's Instagram feed and inspire the worst FOMO ever.

I can't envision a circumstance in which Felicity and I became friends, let alone close enough that she would sit in the hospital *waiting* to see me.

"I can't believe I'm the first one to see you," she says as she flips a curtain of blonde hair over one shoulder.

"Same." There's something vaguely unsettling about her.

She arches a perfectly plucked eyebrow. "I heard you lost some of your memories. Is that true?"

I'd like to deny it, but I have a feeling I'd be found out right away. "Yes."

She stretches out her arm and flicks a fingernail adorned with crystals against my IV line. "And your doctor told us that we shouldn't fill in your memory gaps because that would be too confusing for you."

"Also true."

"But you're dying to know, aren't you? Why I'm here? How we became friends? What's happened in your life? Those blank spaces need filling up, don't they?" She circles to the base of the bed and I watch her as carefully as I'd watch a snake.

"Why are you here?" Because I have this sense that we aren't friends at all. I think it's because of the way Felicity looks at me—as if I'm more science experiment or lab specimen than person.

"My grandmother is having hip surgery. She's in recovery two doors down." She gestures toward the door.

That makes sense. "I'm sorry. I hope she feels better soon."

"I'll pass on your well wishes," Felicity responds. She eyes me as if waiting for more questions.

I nearly bite my tongue through to keep them from coming out. I have a flood of them I want to ask, but I don't feel like Felicity's the right one to be giving me the answers.

She cracks first. "Don't you have anything you want to know?"

Yes. Lots. I sort through my questions to find a safe one.

"Where's Kayleen?" I crane my neck around gingerly, ignoring the shard of pain that spikes at each movement.

"Kayleen who?" Genuine confusion creases her brow.

"Kayleen O'Grady. Small redhead. Plays the cello."

At Felicity's continued blank look, I add, "She's my best friend. We take lessons with Mr. Hayes over at the Bayview Performing Arts Center." It seems like I'm not the only one with memory loss.

"O'Grady? Mr. Hayes? What century are you in? That pedo got run out of town two years ago, around the same time the O'Gradys moved to Georgia."

"What?" I blink in shock. "Kayleen lives next door to me."

A strange look passes over Felicity's face, and something I can't decipher sends a spider of apprehension skittering down my spine.

"How old are you, Hartley?" she asks, leaning over the footboard with something akin to glee sparkling in her golden-brown eyes.

"I—I…" The number *fourteen* pops into my head, but I feel older than that. How do I not know how old I am? "I'm fifte—seventeen," I hurriedly change my answer as Felicity's eyes widen.

She claps a hand over her mouth and then drops it. "You don't know how old you are? This is amazing." She whips out her phone and starts tapping. The screen looks new, but then Felicity always had the latest gadgets, designer clothes, expensive purses.

"Who are you texting?" I demand. It's rude but so is she.

"Everyone," she says, giving me a look that implies that my brain sustained more damage than the doctor has diagnosed.

I pick up the nurse alert button. "You can leave," I inform the girl. "I'm tired and I don't need to be treated like this." I can't believe the nerve of this girl to come into my room and then make fun of me because I injured my head. Tears of anger prick at the backs of my eyes and I blink rapidly to keep any from falling. I'm not showing an ounce of weakness in front of Felicity Worthington. She might have more money than me, but that doesn't mean I'm not entitled to some damned decency.

The coldness in my tone must have caught her attention. She lowers her phone, and pouts. "I'm trying to be helpful. I'm telling our friends that we're going to have to be extra careful with you."

I highly doubt that. I point to the door. "You can be helpful outside."

"Sure. I'll send your boyfriend in then."

"My what?" I half shout.

A malicious smile spreads across her face. In the distance, a warning bell rings, but I pay it little attention.

"My what?" I repeat, quieter this time.

"Your boyfriend. Kyle Hudson. You remember him, don't you? From the moment you laid eyes on each other, it was like a Disney romance." She clasps her hands to her chest. "You were all over each other. The PDA was *disgusting*, but then *that* happened."

She dangles the bait, and against my better judgment, I ask, "What happened?"

"You cheated on him with Easton Royal."

"Easton Royal? Cheated?" There's so many things wrong with Felicity's statement that I start laughing. "Okay. That's hilarious. You can go now."

If she's going to make up stories, she should craft believable ones. The Royals make the Worthingtons look like poor white trash. The Royal mansion on Bayview Shore is so big you can see it from a satellite image. I remember exclaiming over it when I was in...what grade was I in? Sixth? Seventh? Kayleen and I talked about how even though there are five Royal brothers, the house is so big that they probably don't see each other for days. There's no way I've ever run into Easton Royal, let alone been in a situation where the two of us would hook up.

I don't know why Felicity is telling these ridiculous tales. I guess she's bored from waiting for her grandma to get better. I settle on that reason. It makes sense to me.

"It's true," she insists.

"Uh huh." My instincts regarding Felicity were spot-on and I take comfort in that. Soon, all the details of my past will come into sharp clarity.

"Then what's this?" She shoves her phone in front of my face.

I blink. And then blink again. And then do it a third time because I can't quite believe what I'm seeing. Against the backdrop of a neon-lit pier, a gorgeous dark-haired boy is standing in front of me. His hands are twisted in my hair. My arms are around his waist. Our lips are fused together in a way that almost makes me blush. Under the picture, there's a number of hashtags and what I assume is Easton's online handle: #couplegoals #EastonRoyal #justRoyalthings @F14_flyboy.

"No." I shake my head.

"Yes. Pictures don't lie." She takes her phone away and sniffs as if I mortally wounded her feelings. "Poor Kyle. You don't deserve him, but he forgave you for cheating on him. He's here waiting for you but was afraid to come in. I told him I'd come in first. I know it's hard, but try to be a decent person when he visits." She gives me a scathing look before spinning on her ballet slipper shoes and heading toward the door.

I let her go because I'm reeling from the information she just spat out. Boyfriend Kyle? Cheated? Easton Royal? My brain stops at his name and my heart flips over. I take a shaky breath. Am I feeling like this because I have feelings for Easton Royal or because the picture Felicity showed me was so damned hot? It doesn't seem possible that I would've been in a position to kiss any Royal, let alone one that looked as fine as the boy in the picture.

The Royals own this town. Their wealth puts Felicity's to shame. Atlantic Aviation is one of the biggest employers in the state. The likelihood that I'd ever hook up with Easton Royal is as low as me winning the lottery. What did the doctor say? That truth varies based on the person who tells it? But like Felicity says, a picture can't lie, can it?

The door squeaks as it opens. I turn toward the sound and see a stocky guy with wheat-brown hair, small eyes, and thin lips. This must be Kyle Hudson. He looks like he'd rather be anywhere other than my hospital room. He drags his feet past the sitting area, stopping a few feet away from the end of my bed. I finger the nursing station call button.

Stop being such a baby, I chide myself. "Hey, Kyle."

His name tastes unfamiliar. I wrack my brain for a memory or feeling, but nothing comes up. How can he be my boyfriend? If I'm with him, wouldn't I at least have some kind of response toward him instead of this dark, blank void? Why did I cheat? Were we fighting? On a break? Was I drunk? Am I just a bad person? I don't feel like a bad person, but then, really, how does a bad person feel?

"Hey," he answers, busily inspecting the tile floor.

"You doing okay?" I ask. Maybe he's afraid of hospitals and being in one makes him supremely awkward. Still, it's weird that I'm asking him if he's all right, while I'm the one growing bedsores from lying on my back in this bed for so long.

"Yeah. Great." He sticks his hands under his armpits and throws a glance toward the door as if waiting for someone to save him. When no one does, he returns his eyes to the floor and mutters, "I'm, uh, excited to see you."

If this is his enthusiastic mode, I'd hate to see the bored one. I dated this guy? It was love at first sight? We were all over each other? There's less chemistry between us than I'd have with a rock. Maybe we didn't even date, but we were just hanging out and realized we liked other people.

But Easton Royal? There's no way we dated. No way. How would we even meet each other? He's a rich kid, which means he attends Astor Park Prep, and I'm sure I go to North.

I wait for Kyle to say something else, but when he remains silent, I just blurt out, "I'm sorry, but I don't remember you."

"Yeah, I know." He finally swings his gaze up to meet mine. His eyes are a muddy blue-brown, I note, and they don't hold any warmth for me. "It's okay. Felicity filled me in."

"What'd she fill me in on, exactly?"

"That you lost your memory because you fell. You got some stitches under that bandage?" Talk of my injury animates him. That's not freaky.

I lift my hand to the gauze taped to my forehead. "A few."

"Anything else wrong with you? Like, can you count and shit?" He crosses his arms and inspects me with narrowed eyes.

I prefer when he's staring at the floor. "Yes, I can count and talk and everything else. I just can't remember some things."

Like that you and I hooked up and went out. Did we kiss? Did he see me naked? That's a disturbing thought. I pull my thin hospital blanket up higher.

Kyle not only notices, but also reads my thoughts as if they were flashing on a sign above my head. "Yeah, we fucked, if that's what you were wondering. You like giving head and are always on my jock. I can't take you out in public because you're too handsy. It's embarrassing. I had to tell you to back off more than once."

I feel my face turn beet red. I didn't realize how humiliating not having a memory would be. "Ah, I'm sorry."

Kyle's not paying me attention. He's on a roll now. "You got mad at me once and tried to hook up with Easton Royal to get back at me, but I forgive you for that."

I got mad. Hooked up with Easton. Kyle forgives me. I try to process all of this, but it's hard. "Did we fight?"

"Nah, you're just a slut. You've probably whored yourself around to more Astor guys, but Easton's the only one Felicity told me about—I mean, that I know about."

Half of me is consumed by embarrassment at the idea that I *whored myself around* and the other half is angry at my own boyfriend slut-shaming me. I'm also real disappointed in myself for having shit taste in men. And did he say that his sole evidence is that Felicity told him I cheated on him?

"How do you know that Felicity is telling you the truth?" I challenge. Truth is a variable concept, right? And so Felicity's truth could be very different than what really happened. Maybe she saw someone else with Easton…although, that picture was definitely me.

"Why would she lie?"

There's something odd about how he says it, but I don't have an answer for why Felicity would even know of my existence, let alone want to make up malicious rumors about me.

"I don't know. Tell me what happened, then," I press. If I truly am not going to remember these things like Dr. Joshi suggested and I'm not going into a sensory deprivation tank until all my memories come back, then the only recourse I have is to collect as much information as possible.

Kyle's smirk turns to a sneer. "You want details? It's not like you did him in front of me. He got jealous because I slept with his ex once, so to get back at me, he took you to the pier and got pictures of the two of you making out. I don't know if you two screwed. You probably did because you're kind of a whore and that guy's seen more pussy than a gyno. He breathes in your direction and you girls fight to drop your shorts. You should be happy because I forgave you. You begged me nice and pretty." He points to the floor with three fingers, clearly implying that I gave him not one apology blowjob, but three.

Gross.

"Why'd you take me back?" If I were in his position, I wouldn't have wanted such an awful girlfriend. My blowjobs can't be that good.

"Because I'm a good guy and good guys don't dump broken pieces like you." He gestures toward the bed. "You can pay me back when you're better." The leer he sends my way tells me exactly how he's going to extract payment.

I see myself being sick for a very long time.

"So Hart-*lay*, when are you getting out of here?" He mispronounces my name and I can't tell if it's intentional or, God forbid, his pet name for me. I cringe inside.

"No clue."

"Great." He doesn't know what I said nor does he care. "Call me when you get out. We'll hook up again."

That will be a hard no from me, but I figure I don't need to tell Kyle that. He'll get the message soon enough when I'm back at school and not calling him. I'd rather be a nun than get on my knees in front of this jerk. He doesn't require a response. Already, he's threading his way past the sitting room and slipping out the door.

Man, pre-memory loss Hartley had some shitty taste—in girlfriends *and* boyfriends.

CHAPTER SIX

Easton

AFTER AN HOUR OF COOLING my heels near the nurses station, I finally spot my prey approaching. I shove my hands into my pockets and saunter casually up to the counter, trying not to look as desperate as I feel.

"Doc Joshi, do you have a minute?"

He breezes straight past me, the white coat flapping against his blue scrubs. "Watch room two-oh-five's liquid intake and report any signs of stomach pain or increased fever." He hands a chart over. "When does Doctor Coventry arrive?"

"In an hour, sir." The round-cheeked nurse makes a note.

The doctor frowns. "That late? I need to eat now."

"I can grab you a burger," I offer in a bid to grab his attention. It works, because he turns to me.

"Who are you?"

I open my mouth to answer, but the nurse pipes up before I can get anything out. "It's Easton Royal, sir. Of the Maria Royal Royals," she adds.

Thank you, pretty nurse. I'm buying you flowers later.

"Easton Royal, eh?" He scratches his head with a pen while the light bulb turns on. "What is it?"

"I'm wondering about Hartley Wright. My sister said that you came and talked with them about her? I was sitting with my brother. I wondered if you could repeat it. Hartley's my girlfriend and I want to make sure I don't screw up." I smile—or try to, anyway.

"Your girlfriend, eh?" He sighs and tucks the pen in his pocket. "That's tough. When your girlfriend fell, she struck the front of her head the hardest and that knocked around her frontal lobe. There's no obvious damage from the CT scan, but we can't see everything." He shrugs. "What we can ascertain from the patient is memory loss, mostly autobiographical ones—which means she can't remember actual events such as how you asked her out for prom, your first kiss, that sort of thing. She may not even recall that the two of you are dating. We don't know how far back her memory loss goes, but…" He pauses as if there's worse news than the stuff he's already punched me in the face with.

I stiffen my watery spine. "But what?"

"But yesterday she said she was fourteen, so it looks like about three years or so of memory loss. Have the two of you been dating since then?"

Numb, I shake my head. Seb won't wake up and Hartley lost her memories. I can't believe this shit.

"Tough luck, son. She might regain her memories. It's early yet, so my recommendation is that you wait a bit before you start telling her about all the great times you had. And if you had some bad moments, well, this memory loss is a good thing. I wish my first wife suffered it. I might have ended up better after the divorce." He winks and jabs me in the shoulder. "Any other questions?"

"Is she awake?"

"She was when I checked on her a few hours ago. You can go see for yourself. Put in a good word for me with your dad, will you?" Doc says way too cheerily and walks off.

I drop my head to my chest and start counting backwards from a thousand so I don't chase after him and bash his head against the tile.

Beating up the doctor isn't going to bring Hartley's memories back sooner, says my better half.

No, but I'll feel better, I retort.

I pinch the bridge of my nose in frustration. All the time I'm spending here in this tomb-like quiet with nothing but hushed voices and mechanical beeps and clicking machines is driving me crazy. I want to leave, yet the moment I step outside I grow so anxious I want to peel my skin off. Nope. I've got to stay here—close to Seb and Hartley.

I make my way to Hartley's room, knocking lightly as I open the door.

"Mom?" Hartley's voice calls out weakly.

"Just me, babe," I reply, rounding the set of sofas and chairs separating the hospital bed from the rest of the suite. My gut clenches again at the sight of her looking small and vulnerable under the white sheets. I crouch down next to the bed and pick up her hand, careful not to dislodge the monitor on her finger.

"Um…" She stares at our connected fingers and then up at my face.

The blankness there rocks me. She has no clue who I am.

The doctor warned me, but I wasn't prepared. What he'd said about her loss of memories hadn't sunk in. It had floated on the surface of my brain like some random factoid that I knew but didn't absorb, because it wasn't important. Had it been because I was so arrogant to believe that she'd remember me regardless? No, it's because I hadn't wanted to accept the truth. But now that it's clocked me in the face, I can't ignore it.

"It's me, Hart. Easton."

Her eyes widen and recognition creeps in. Wait, she does know me. I let out a long exhale. I can breathe finally. Somehow just being in her presence calms me down.

"Fuck, Hart, I'm so glad you're okay."

"You keep calling me Hart." She's staring at me. "Is that my nickname?"

I pause for a second, because I realize I've never heard anyone else call her that, and I didn't start doing it myself until after the accident. I guess…well, I guess it makes me feel closer to her to call her that, like she's more than just Hartley to me. She's Hart, and she's my heart.

Christ. That's the cheesiest thing I've ever thought in my life. No way am I going to say that to her.

So I shrug and say, "It's my nickname for you. Not sure about anybody else." Then I lace my fingers through hers, lifting them both to my lips. Her fingertips are pink, like mine. She must be feeling healthier. A couple of her nails are shorter than the rest. She must've broken them in the accident. I run the stubby ones across my bottom lip. "These past few days have been a nightmare, babe. It could've been worse, though. That's what I keep telling myself. It could've been so fucking worse. So how do you feel?"

There's a prolonged silence and then the only fingers against my mouth are my own. I glance up to see her wide eyes staring at me with genuine alarm tinged with…is that fear?

"Hartley?" I ask uncertainly.

"Easton…Royal?" she says as if she's never said my name out loud before.

Fuck. *Fuck.*

She really doesn't remember me.

Her pink skin turns white enough to match the sheets on her bed. "I'm going to be sick," she croaks, and starts to gag.

I spin around and look for something she can barf into. I see nothing but a discarded lunch tray with most of the food uneaten. I shove it on her lap just in time. She tries to retch onto the tray, but it gets messy. Tears stream down her pale face.

I curse and press the call button. "Hartley Wright needs some help in here."

I dart into the bathroom and grab some towels that I use to wipe her face with. She cries harder.

"What can I do?" I plead. "Do you want some water? Should I carry you to the shower?"

"Go. Just, please go," she gasps out.

The door to the room bursts open as the round-cheeked nurse rushes in. A serious expression has replaced her jolly one. She spears me with a heated look. "You can leave now, Mr. Royal."

The nurse calls for backup and soon the room is filled with people pushing me out of the way as they try to help Hartley. I stand there like an idiot, with wet towels in my hands as sheets are pulled off and washcloths are applied. An orderly grabs me by the shoulder. "Sorry, buddy, but we're going to have to ask you to go. Patient needs some treatment."

"But I—"

"Nope." He doesn't let me finish, and somehow I find myself in the hall staring at the closed door with the dirty towels still in my hand.

"Did you have a nice visit with your girlfriend?" a viper says behind me.

I spin around and scowl at Felicity Worthington. "What are you doing here?"

She shoots me a fake smile. "My grandmother broke her hip and she's here recovering from surgery. She might die because of her old age and brittle bones, but thanks for asking."

"Sorry," I mutter. Of course, I'd mess this up too. I shift uncomfortably, and the odor of vomit rises up between us.

"You smell like you took a bath in day-old moonshine and puke. Haven't you showered since the accident?"

I take a sniff. Shit, I do reek. Is that what made Hartley sick? I ball the towels up. There are showers next to the waiting room. I might as well make use of those. Then I can go back and apologize to Hartley.

"What have you been doing?" Felicity dogs my steps.

"Thanks for your non-genuine concern, but I've been worried about Hartley and my brother."

"When he does wake up, he'll be sent back into his coma the minute he catches wind of you." She waves a hand in front of her face. "I can't believe I seriously considered you boyfriend material. You're foulmouthed and foul-smelling. Gross."

"You're mistaking me for someone who gives a shit."

She wrinkles her nose and drops back. "I'd tell you to

shower before you go see Hartley again, but it probably won't matter. She still won't know who you are." She gives me a smirk and starts to turn away.

How the hell does Felicity know what went on in Hartley's room? I grab her by the shoulder and spin her around. "What the hell is that supposed to mean?"

"Ugh, stop touching me." She shrugs my hand off.

"Repeat what you just said," I demand.

"You didn't hear?" she asks with saccharine sweetness. "Your girl has amnesia. She doesn't remember a thing, including how your entire family would like to see her blotted off the face of the earth. But don't worry, sugar, because I set her straight."

"You set her straight?" I seethe. If Felicity so much as stepped foot in that room to fill Hart's head with a truckload of lies, I'm going to choke her until all her diamonds fall off.

"Are you still drunk? My God, I bet you are. This is hilarious. I bet you scared the pants off of her. A big, stinking hulk like you in her room declaring your undying love." As I grind my back teeth into fine dust, Felicity laughs with genuine, evil delight. "I didn't realize Santa was bringing one of my Christmas presents early." She skips down the hall, her long hair waving like a flag behind her.

The fucking injustice of it, I seethe. I haven't drunk since the night of the accident. As I rein in the urge to go tackle her, I hear the doors behind me open and close. I twist and catch a glimpse of an angry nurse stomping down the hall. I run after her.

"No visitors right now," she says, anticipating my question.

"Fine, but what's wrong with her?"

"She's suffering from short-term memory loss, and

whatever the two of you were talking about in there triggered a vestibular disorder that caused her to vomit. Doc Joshi told you to let her remember at her own pace."

"I didn't say anything..." But I trail off, because I did. I held her hand. I kissed her fingertips. I told her that I'd been worried out of my skull for her.

The nurse pounces on my hesitation. "Whatever you did say made her sick, so be careful next time or we won't be able to keep letting you into her room."

"Right," I grit out and let her go. I want to shout, but the nurse already dislikes me, so I can't give her more reasons to keep me out of Hart's room. I try to gather my thoughts and focus. First things first. Hart's ill. She needs me to be strong for her. Seb's in a coma. He needs me to keep it together. I tell myself to breathe. I've got to focus on the positive. Everyone's alive. Sure, they're banged up, but they're all breathing. This is going to work out.

I return to the VIP lounge and head for the back where the showers are. After toweling dry, I put my old clothes back on and make my way to Seb's room. As quietly as possible, I depress the latch and walk in.

Sawyer's slumped over the end of the bed. He's been in here since Seb came out of surgery. I don't think the kid has eaten or slept. He's going to join his brother if he doesn't take better care of himself. Knowing the twins, I wouldn't be surprised if that was Sawyer's goal. The two are inseparable. They even date the same girl.

I cross the room and place a hand on my brother's shoulder. Sawyer jerks up. "Is he awake?"

"No, but I'll watch him. Go get some sleep in a bed."

Sawyer shrugs my hand off and glares. "Piss off. We don't want you here. It was your girlfriend that did this." He jerks his thumb toward the bed.

"Seb was driving seventy around that corner," I snap.

"Fuck you," he spits out. "Fuck you and your girlfriend. If it wasn't for her, he wouldn't be here. We've driven that route a million times and never once had an accident."

"You guys almost ran me over the first time I went there," I argue without thinking.

"Are you saying this is Seb's fault?" Sawyer's suddenly on his feet and in my face. "You saying he put himself in that coma? It was that bitch. That bitch!" he repeats, red-faced and furious. "I hope she fucking dies."

I spin on my heel and walk out. It's either that or deck my grieving brother.

Outside the room, I slump against the wall. This is a horrible fucking mess. Hartley wasn't playing back there. She legit didn't remember me for a moment, and when she did recall my name, it made her sick enough to vomit. My youngest brother is lying in a coma and his twin is praying for my girl's death.

I don't need anything from you. You've caused me nothing but trouble from the moment I met you. All you do is break things.

Hart's words, the ones she said right before the accident, haunt me. This is my fault. Drunk off my ass, I thought I could solve everyone's problems, but instead I made them worse. I drop my head into my hands. If anyone deserves to be in a hospital bed, it's me.

CHAPTER SEVEN

Hartley

"Is there a medical diagnosis for not remembering things that happen right now?" I ask Nurse Susan as she helps me back onto the bed with its freshly changed sheets.

Her cheeks plump up as she smiles. "It's called anterograde amnesia."

"Can I self-induce that? Like sticking my finger down my throat to throw up, only this time I poke myself in the eye?" I want to crawl underneath the bed and hide in embarrassment. I just threw up on the lap of the most beautiful boy to walk the face of this earth. "Alternatively, do you have a special machine where I can make everyone lose their memory?"

"There, there, Ms. Wright. You got a little sick to your stomach. That happens to everyone. It's a very normal occurrence. Lightheadedness, dizziness, loss of balance are all things that you might suffer from as a result of hitting your head."

"Wow, it's a basket of horribles." I throw my arm over my forehead to block out the light.

"You're doing very well," she assures me, hooking me up to my tubes and monitors. "In fact, so well that Doctor Joshi believes you'll be able to go home tomorrow. Won't that be nice?" She pats me on the arm and shuffles out.

I don't know if it will be nice. Whenever Mom and Dad have shown up to the hospital, there's been a faint air of disapproval, as if they're mad that I got injured. I wish someone would tell me exactly how the accident occurred— or some version of how it went down. I wonder how that other person is. What does it mean to be in critical condition? What condition am I in? I should've asked Nurse Susan that. Maybe Felicity or Kyle knew. Why didn't I press them for that information instead of the irrelevant crap like who I did or did not sleep with—although having seen Easton Royal, I figure both of them are full of shit.

There's no way Easton Royal ever took an interest in me. I'm plain. I have plain black hair and plain gray eyes. I have a plain face with a small nose, a nonexistent bridge, and the occasional zit. I'm average height and wear a very average bra size: 34B.

Easton Royal has hair so dark and rich, it could be on the cover of a hair dye box. His eyes are so blue I swear I could hear the ocean waves crashing against the beach when he blinked. *He's* the one suffering from memory loss, wandering into my room, pressing his kissable lips against my fingers.

I lift my fingers to my own lips. The smell of the hospital's medicinal soap fills my nostrils and I fling my hand down in disgust.

Kyle was right about one thing. I definitely liked Easton Royal. And that's depressing, because first, that means Kyle might be right about other things, and second, me liking a boy of Easton Royal's stature is as dumb as anything I could do.

Where could I have possibly met Easton? Or Felicity, for that matter? Kyle, on the other hand, he looks like a North kid. If I had to guess, Kyle and I somehow snuck into an Astor Park party and we got into a fight. Easton was feeling charitable and decided to let me maul him?

That scenario doesn't feel right, but I can't think of another realistic explanation.

I let out a small, frustrated scream. I hate this not knowing. It's terrible. All these people out there know things about me. It's unfair. What I need is pictures. Although...Felicity's quickly shared image only served to confuse me more. It *was* Easton and me in that picture. We *were* kissing. Why? How? When? Those are all unknown. I need to do my own research, which means I need my phone, a computer, and my purse—and not necessarily in that order.

I'll ask my mom when she comes to visit.

"How's MY FAVORITE PATIENT?" Doc Joshi sings as he walks into the room the next morning. His ever-present smile is stretched across his angular face.

"Good." I struggle into a seated position. "Have you seen my parents?"

Mom never showed up last night. I slept awful because I kept worrying that I might miss her.

"They didn't come last night?" Doc Joshi looks mildly surprised.

"I...maybe I missed them."

"Probably."

But I don't think I did. They must be angry with me, but I don't know why. Was it the accident or something? A hollow feeling inside my chest has developed. It generates a different kind of ache than the physical one. Worse, guilt is eating me alive. I really, really need to know how that other person is doing. Maybe Dr. Joshi will help me out if I ask.

"Doc," I say to get his attention.

"Hmmm?" He's engrossed in my chart.

"How's the other person? The critical patient?"

"Mmmm, I can't really say, Hartley. Privacy rules and all." He pulls out a flashlight and points it into one of my pupils. "How's the memory today?"

"Great."

"You're not lying, of course."

"No."

He hums again as he inspects my other eye. I don't think he believes me.

"Is the critical patient still critical?"

"No. He's stable."

He. Right. I was told that before. "Does he have any broken bones? Any memory loss? Where exactly was he hurt?"

Doc Joshi straightens and shakes the flashlight at me. "No broken bones, but that's all you're getting out of me." He pockets the light and makes a note on my chart.

I arch my neck to see if I can read it, but it looks like a bunch of chicken scratching. I ask a different question. "Is he ever going to get better?"

"I can't see any reason why not. Now it's time you focus on making yourself better. Can you do that?"

I relax on the pillows, allowing Doc Joshi's confidence to comfort me. "Yes."

"How are you feeling today?"

"Fine."

He pokes my chest. I wince. "Okay, I hurt some," I revise.

"Doctor Joshi."

My mother's voice sends a surge of happiness through me. "Mom!" I exclaim, thrilled that she's actually here.

Of course she is, a little voice assures me. *Where else would she be?* Right. And she must have come last night, too, during one of the times when I was resting my eyes. She probably poked her head into the room and thought I was sleeping and didn't want to disturb me—

"Hartley." Her tone is clipped.

Doc looks around and greets her. "Mrs. Wright, good morning to you."

The smile on my face wavers as Mom takes a step forward. She's not even looking at me, only at the doc. What's going on? Why isn't she coming to give me a hug, or a kiss on the cheek, a pat on the arm? Anything.

"Good morning. I spoke with the nursing staff and they said that Hartley can be discharged today. I'd like for her to go back to school tomorrow. She has finals approaching."

I gawk at her in surprise. My head aches, my chest feels like a concrete truck ran over it—twice—and I still have no memory of the last three years. Don't I need a few more days off before I throw myself back into school?

Doc frowns. "I discussed the possibility of discharging her, but now that I've seen her this morning, I think she should stay for another twenty-four hours. We can see how she's progressing tomorrow."

"I think today's fine." Mom sounds surprisingly firm. "The nurse said her vitals have been stable for the last twenty-four hours. She no longer needs an IV drip as she can take the oral painkillers. There's no reason for her to be here another day." She backs up, reaches through the doorway and pulls my father into the room

My heart does a little jump at the sight of him. At first I think it's a jump of joy, but...I'm not sure that's quite it. It's nervousness, I realize.

Why would I be nervous at seeing my dad?

His phone is glued to his ear, but he slides it halfway down his cheek to address us. "What's the problem here?"

"John, they want to keep Hartley here another day." Mom's agitated. Why is me staying at the hospital another night such a problem?

"So? Let them keep her." He puts the phone back to his ear and turns away.

"Okay then." Doc makes a notation.

Over his back, I see Mom move to Dad's side and tug on his arm. He glares at her, but she's not deterred. There's a whispered conversation that I can't hear, but I see Mom rub her fingers together. Dad's glare shifts from Mom's face to my doctor's back.

He disconnects his call and walks stiffly over to stand by the doctor. "This is still on Callum Royal's dime, correct?"

Callum Royal's dime? My eyes widen. Why would Mr. Royal be paying for my hospital bills?

Doc's eyebrows go up. "I have no idea. You'll have to talk to Billing about that."

"How do you not know?" Dad demands. "This is how you earn your money."

I didn't die from the injuries from the car crash, but embarrassment might do me in. Doc senses my unease. He winks at me and tries to lighten the mood. "I'm in charge of making sure your girl gets better. Another night should do it." He grabs my big toe and wiggles it. "You like it here at Bayview General, don't you? New sheets every day and lots of one-on-one attention."

If I never see another nurse in my entire life, I'll be thrilled.

"The food's great, too," I add wryly.

"We aim to please." He hangs the chart back on my hospital bed.

He nods at both my parents as he walks out. Mom barely waits for the door to shut before rushing over to my bed and pulling on the sheets. "Let's go."

"Let's go where?" I ask in confusion.

"We're leaving. You are not spending another night here. Do you know what this room costs?" She pulls the finger monitor off and tosses it to the side. "A small car. That's how much a private room is for one night here at Bayview."

She tugs me to my feet and hands me a small bag I hadn't realized she was carrying.

"John, go and talk to the nurse and find out how to get her discharged. We'll take her regardless."

"I'm calling the billing office," Dad grouses.

"There's no point. I received the call this morning that the Royals were refusing to pay Hartley's medical bills because they believe she is at fault for the accident." Mom turns to me in anger. "I can't believe you hurt a Royal! Do you know what this is going to do to us? We're ruined. Ruined! What are you doing? Get dressed!" she snaps, a feral look in her eyes.

I can't move, though. The news that Mom just blurted out has frozen me in place. Mr. Critical is one of the Royal boys? Easton's brother? No. That can't be. Why would Easton come into my room and hold my hand if I'd hurt his brother?

"Would you go!" Mom screeches.

I jump up from the bed and nearly vomit when pain crashes over me. Mom grabs my arm and shoves me toward the bathroom. I brace myself on the sink and lean over the toilet to spit up the five bites of oatmeal I'd managed to swallow for breakfast.

Oblivious to my condition, Mom continues to rant. "When you go to school tomorrow, you need to make sure that you're nice to everyone. Do not cause any drama. Do not get into any conflict. If you do, you could ruin this family. Your dad could lose his job. We could lose the house. Parker's husband could leave her. You and your sister would have to be sent to MawMaw's home and not that fancy boarding school up north."

MawMaw? That old crone? She beats people with a spoon. I turn on the faucet and wet a paper towel. Mom's overreacting, I decide as I wipe down my face. She has a tendency to do this. If someone spills punch on the floor, even if it's on tile, Mom's crying about how she's never going to get the stain out and her floor is ruined. Or if the turkey is slightly overdone at Thanksgiving, the entire bird is inedible. She always uses the threat of sending us away to keep us in line and she's never followed through—I pause, holding the towel against my lips as the last thing she said finally registers.

And not that fancy boarding school up north.

CHAPTER EIGHT

Hartley

MOM DOESN'T MAKE ME GO to school the next day as she threatened. Doc Joshi released me with the promise that I'd stay home for a week. I didn't expect my parents to follow his instructions, but they did.

The last six days haven't been a boatload of fun. My physical injuries are healing fine. It doesn't hurt to breathe anymore. I can walk around. But although my health is getting better, I feel like things in my house are getting worse. I don't understand what's going on. My dad barely looks at me. My mom is always criticizing me. My little sister Dylan hardly speaks to me. And my older sister Parker hasn't even come to see me. I was in the hospital for a week, recovering for more than that, and Parker can't be bothered to visit?

Tomorrow I go back to school, and I don't even want to know what kind of response I'll get there, if I'm to go by my family's not-so-warm welcome.

It's Sunday night, and I'm spending it wandering around my house, which is both familiar and foreign at the same time. My room smells stale—as if it had been closed up for the entire three years I was at boarding school. The bedspread looks unfamiliar, as does the white laminate desk in the corner, along with the small collection of uniforms, shirts, and sweaters in the closet.

The stark white walls are bare. The only splashes of color are the purple-and-blue ombré bedspread and the matching curtains that still have creases in them from the cardboard inserts they were folded around.

I push the hangers on the closet rod from one side to the other. I have a tiny amount of clothes. Two expensive dark wool blazers with a red, white, and gold patch sewn over the breast hang in the middle. There's a balled-up Kleenex in one of the blazer's front patch pockets. To the left is a row of white button-down dress shirts: three long-sleeved, two short-sleeved. A zip hoodie and a navy sweater hang beside them. On the floor are a pair of bright white tennis shoes that look—and smell—brand new, and a pair of scuffed black loafers.

For bottoms, I have three pairs of jeans, two pairs of yoga pants, and two ugly green-and-navy tartan pleated skirts. The latter must be part of my school uniform. Mom informed me that I attend Astor Park Prep, the most exclusive—and expensive—prep school in the state. That solved the mystery of how I know Felicity and Easton and, I guess, Kyle, although nothing makes complete sense to me.

Mom provided no explanation for why I attend Astor Park or why I was at a boarding school in upstate New York for three years. She didn't warn me that my bedroom had been turned into a storage room while I was gone and that all of my personal belongings had been given away to Goodwill. When

I asked where my purse and phone were, she told me that both had been destroyed in the accident. That bit of news was such a punch in the gut that I stopped asking questions. I'd hoped that I could piece together parts of my life from my phone—my photo roll, my messages, my social media accounts—but that opportunity had been ground up in the accident.

The rest of the closet is empty. In the small dresser across from my bed, I find underwear, plain bras, and a couple of cute hoodies. My current style is spare, I guess. I have a hard time believing that these are all the clothes I own. I vaguely remember this closet bursting with shit I picked up at Forever 21 and Charlotte Russe. It was cheap, but fun and colorful.

I guess when I was in boarding school, my tastes evolved into something as bland as white toast. Is this progress? I can't tell. I rifle through my desk, searching for clues to my past, but there's nothing there. There aren't any old cards or pictures or even used pencils. Everything in the drawers is new. Even the notebooks are pristine, as if tomorrow is my first day of school instead of the third month of the semester.

A list of my classes and a small map of the campus is tucked inside the first notebook. I pull it out. Calculus, Feminist Thought, Music. I glance around the room but don't see my violin. Is it at school?

I trot over to the door and call for Mom.

"What is it?" she asks, appearing at the bottom of the stairs with a dishrag in her hands.

"Where's my violin?"

"Your what?"

"My violin. I still play that, right? I'm taking music." I hold up my class schedule.

"Oh, that." She gives a sniff of disdain. "You barely play it anymore, but you're required to take an elective and so we signed you up for music. You play a school one."

She walks off. I have an answer, but it doesn't feel complete to me. I rub my wrist again. As I return to the bedroom, the pictures on the hallway walls catch my eye. There's something off about them. I walk over slowly, inspecting each one. There are pictures of Parker, my oldest sister, from birth to her wedding. The photos of Dylan, my younger sister, stop after the ninth one, which means she's currently in eighth grade.

At the end is a picture of the family. It must be a recent one because I'm not there. They're at dinner in a hotel or something. There are tall ceilings and large paintings with gold gilt. The chairs are upholstered in what looks like velvet. All of them are dressed up—Dad in a black suit, Mom in a red dress with sparkles, Parker wearing a simple black dress with pearls around her neck, and Dylan in a sweater and purple skirt. Everyone is smiling—even Dylan, who sneered a whole "It's you" when I arrived home and then disappeared into her room and has avoided me ever since.

It's the family picture that reveals the answer to the riddle of what is wrong with the hallway setup. I'm not in any of them.

My family literally erased me from my home.

What exactly did I do three years ago? Did I set the house on fire? Did I kill the family pet? I search my memory but come up blank. I don't even recall being sent away. The clearest recollection I have is of my sister Parker's wedding. That happened four years ago. I remember being vaguely annoyed I didn't get to have champagne during the wedding toast, and sneaking some anyway with a tiny brown-haired girl who my memory says is my cousin Jeanette. We both got sick off one glass each. I should call her. Maybe she can fill in the blanks because no one in this house will.

I heave myself down the stairs to find Mom. She's washing dishes, a denim-colored apron tied around her waist and a faint frown stretched across her mouth.

"What is it?" she asks, irritation in her voice.

"Can I use your phone?"

"For what?" Irritation morphs into suspicion.

I clasp my hands behind my back and try not to look guilty, because what's wrong with wanting to talk to my cousin? "I was thinking of calling Jeanette."

"No, she's busy," Mom replies flatly.

"It's nine at night," I protest.

"It's too late to be on the phone."

"Mom—"

The doorbell rings before I can mount an argument. Mom mutters something that sounds suspiciously like "Thank goodness," before she sets the pot she'd been scrubbing onto the drainer and hurries to the front door.

I eye her purse. Her phone is sticking out the top of it, taunting me. If I borrowed her phone for, say, ten minutes, would she figure it out? I inch along the counter. If she catches me, what's the worst thing that happens? She can't take my phone away, I think, feeling a mild hysteria creeping over me.

"Your boyfriend is here to see you," Mom announces. "He's an Astor boy," she whispers as she grabs my arm.

I'm about to ask how she knows, when I see him—Kyle Hudson—standing near the front door looking around my house with curious eyes, as if he's never once stepped foot inside. He's wearing skinny jeans that are too tight on his stocky frame and a dark blue letter jacket with a patch over the left breast that matches the patches on my blazers upstairs.

"I, ah, stopped by to see how you were doing," he says, not quite meeting my eyes.

"I'm fine." This is the first time he's checked in on me in a week.

He rubs his foot against the tile.

Mom pinches me in the side. "What Hartley means is that she's so happy that you stopped by. Hartley is shocked that she has such a caring boyfriend. Have a seat." She gestures toward the living room sofa. "Can I get you anything?"

Kyle shakes his head. "I thought I'd take Hart-*lay* over to the French Twist. Some Astor kids are meeting up there."

I grind my teeth together. I hate how he says my name.

"Of course," chirps my mother. "Let me get some money."

Only she doesn't move right away, waiting for him to stop her. Instead, he raises his eyebrows in anticipation.

"Actually, I'm tired." I pull out of Mom's grip. "I'm not up for going out."

"We aren't clubbing, Hart-*lay*. It's a bakery."

Yeah, he's real caring.

"She'll go. Why don't you change," Mom suggests and then hurries off to get the money.

I look down at my dark-washed jeans and navy hoodie with the white stripes on the sleeves. "What's wrong with what I have on?"

"Everything," Kyle answers.

I lift my chin. "I'm not changing."

"Fine. Your funeral. Don't cry to me when you get made fun of."

"Made fun of? Are we in middle school? Why would anyone care what I wear?" I shake my head in annoyance. "Also, I can drive myself," I add, because I don't want to get into whatever death trap he's motoring around.

"You can't. We don't have your license," Mom says, returning with her wallet. "It got lost with your purse," she reminds me.

That complication hadn't occurred to me. "But, Mom—"

"Don't *but, Mom* me. Here's twenty dollars." She shoves a bill in my face. "That should be enough."

Kyle makes a face.

"Yeah, that's enough," I declare and pocket the twenty.

"Great. You two have a nice time tonight." She practically shoves me out the door.

As soon as it shuts behind me, I turn to Kyle. "I don't believe we ever dated. You treat me like trash and I have zero warm feelings toward you. If we didn't break up before, let's do it now."

"You're an amnesiac. What do you know? Let's go." He jerks a thumb toward an SUV parked crookedly in our driveway. "Felicity's waiting."

"I don't want to go. How many times do I have to tell you that?"

He stares at me and then at the sky and then at me again. Annoyance is written on his face—in the straight line of his mouth, the deep lines in his forehead, and the dark expression in his eyes.

"I'm trying to do you a favor here. You don't remember shit, right?"

I nod because there's no point in denying it.

"Tomorrow you're going back to school, right?"

I feel like I'm on the bad end of one of my dad's cross examinations, but I nod again.

"Then do you want some answers tonight or do you want to bumble around like a fool tomorrow and for the rest of your days at Astor?"

I glance over my shoulder to see my mother waving at me from the front door, and then return my gaze to Kyle. The carrot he's dangling in front of me is too sweet to pass up. I don't know what's waiting for me at the bakery, but he's right. Meeting people tonight in a casual setting is better than going to school tomorrow blind.

"I want answers tonight," I finally mutter.

"Then let's go."

He walks off toward his SUV without waiting for me. I scurry to catch up, grabbing hold of the door handle and hauling myself into the passenger seat.

"We're still breaking up," I tell him as I buckle in.

"Whatever." He jams his finger against the engine's start button. Country music blares out of the speakers.

I reach over and turn it down. He sends me a look of death, but I keep my hand on the knob. I'm going to win this battle.

"How long did we date?" I ask.

"What?"

"How long did we date?" I repeat. If tonight's going to be about answers, they might as well start now.

"I dunno."

Felicity had suggested it was from the moment I got to school. I'm guessing that school started at the end of August and it's nearing Thanksgiving, so the longest we could have dated is three months or so.

"I'm not asking for our anniversary date, just a general timeframe."

He hunches uncomfortably over the steering wheel. "Weeks, I guess."

"Weeks?"

"Yeah, weeks."

He's either got a bad memory or is bad at math. Maybe both.

"Did we have sex?" The idea makes me sick to my stomach, but I have to know.

"Yeah." He smirks. "That's the only reason I agreed to go out with you. You were begging me, you know. Following me around in the halls, sitting by me at lunch. You left your panties in my locker." He's animated for the first time. "So I let you slob on my knob."

"Wonderful," I say faintly. Could I be more disgusting? Could he? I guess we were a perfect match.

"Any more questions? Do you want to know when and where we got down?"

"No thanks." The Diet Coke I drank after dinner starts churning in my stomach. Sometimes amnesia can be a good thing, I decide. Too bad these are the memories I'm regaining. I crack the window open and raise my nose up to the breeze.

"You gonna be sick?" Kyle asks in a panicked voice.

"I hope not," I say noncommittally.

His response is to press the gas to the floor. *Honey, I want to get away from your company as fast as you want to get away from mine.*

CHAPTER NINE

Easton

THE LOCK ON HARTLEY'S APARTMENT door is so flimsy, I don't even need to pull out the key that I just obtained from the landlord downstairs. A few jerks of my wrist and the wooden slab swings open.

It's empty, as he said it would be, but I'm still surprised and more than a little devastated. I wanted it to be full of Hartley—her things, her scent, *her.* Instead it's an empty shell. There's no ten-year-old sofa with tears in the arms. The cupboard doors hang open, revealing their empty shelves. Even the crappy table that I was always afraid was going to collapse when Hartley put so much as a paper plate on it is gone. *She's* gone. Or at least that's how it's felt for nearly a week now. Her parents whisked her out of the hospital, and I haven't seen or heard from her since.

It's been torture. I've texted her. I've tried calling. I even drove past her house like a stalker hoping to catch a glimpse of her through one of the windows. But no such luck. Hartley's folks are keeping her out of sight, I guess.

I just hope she's all right. One of her nurses admitted—after a bit of coaxing—that they might've discharged her too early, and worry has been gnawing at my gut ever since hearing that.

Why won't she call me back, dammit?

The need to feel close to her, at least in some way, is what brought me to her old apartment tonight.

I toss my backpack onto the kitchen counter and take a peek inside the refrigerator, where I find three cans of Diet Coke. I pop one open and bleakly survey the small space. I'd hoped if I brought her here, it'd jog her memories, but her parents have wiped the space clean.

It doesn't look like anyone lived here. Even the dingy carpet is gone, replaced with cheap terracotta-colored linoleum. Helplessness fills my throat, choking off the airways. The room spins and the bottle in my backpack calls to me.

I clench and unclench my jaw. My heart pounds. My mouth is as dry as a desert. A siren song fills my ears. Drinking and pills have always been my go-to problem solver. Mom offs herself, pop a pill. Fight with the fam, swallow a bottle of Jack. Disagreement with the girl, do both and forget everything until morning.

The metal can in my hand crunches as the sides cave in.

All you do is break things.

With deliberation, I set the crushed can in the sink and pull out my phone, flicking to the notes app where I wrote a list of the places we went:

- Beach
- Pier

- Apartment
- School
- Practice room
- My house (media room)

Ironically, for a guy whose primary purpose in life was to bed every available girl up and down the coast, I never once took Hartley to my bedroom. I don't know if I should give myself a gold star for being patient or kick myself for not inviting her deeper into my life. I wish she'd imprinted all over it so that everywhere we went, she'd see how the two of us fit together.

All you do is break things.

I can't have that memory be the one she recalls. I need to make her see what we had before Felicity stuck her hands into the mess, before her father's threats scared her, before my drunk ass screwed things up.

We were friends. Hell, she was the first female friend I ever had other than Ella. We enjoyed each other's company. I made her laugh. She made me…well, she made me want to be a better person.

I can't lose her. I won't.

Hartley's living at home again. Dealing with her sisters, her mom. Her father, that son of a bitch who… Worry jolts through me. I sit up and send another text.

I'm here for you. No matter what.

I stare at the phone, willing her to text me back. She doesn't, of course. I remind myself she's sick and probably heavily medicated. That's why she's not responding. Fuck. I hate this. If I dwell on it, it's only going to make me crazier.

Before she was sent to boarding school, her dad had broken her wrist after she found out he was taking bribes for his job. She told me that her wrist was broken as an accident and I have to believe that. Besides, only a sicko would beat his already injured daughter.

I open another app and start making a list of everything I'm going to need. First off, another dark blue sofa. I add two folding chairs and a small wooden table. The chairs were plastic and the table was…light. Some kind of light-colored wood. Maybe pine?

She had nice hand towels. I close my eyes and try to remember the color. Was it gray? Or pink? Or purple? Shit, I don't recall. I'll buy all three and keep the ones she likes the best. She also had a pretty quilt. That was white with flowers.

Feeling better now that I have a plan, I allow myself to unpack. The bottle of Ciroc is at the top. I debate pouring it out but opt not to. Hart might need it, so I stick it into the cabinet next to the fridge.

The picture of the two of us at the pier, I lay on the counter. I need a frame or a magnet. Frame, I decide. I'm going to hang it on the wall. In fact, I think I'll blow it up so all she sees when she comes home is a giant-ass picture of the two of us kissing like the legends we are. I grunt with approval at my own genius and add that to the bottom of my to-do list.

A change of clothes and two bottles of cheap vodka are all that remain in my backpack. I'd planned to sleep here, but as I stare at the bare floor, I wonder if that's a good idea. I check out the bathroom. The shower still works and the water pressure is decent. The landlord said that the place had been repainted and the flooring is new.

I toss my joggers and hoodie on the floor and bed down, placing my head on my backpack and folding my hands across my chest. Tomorrow I'll ask Ella where to buy all the shit I need.

There might be nothing here that can help Hartley regain her memories, but I still have mine. And we can create new ones, happier ones—ones with her sister, ones with my brothers.

I cling to the hope that tomorrow's going to be better. Ella told me that once. That if today's a shit day, I should be glad because even if tomorrow's another hellish experience, you know that you can make it.

The Ciroc bottle is still sealed. I wanted to drink but I avoided it. That's a win for me.

Tomorrow's going to be better.

CHAPTER TEN

Easton

A TEXT FROM PASH FLASHES across my phone at a quarter to ten. I sit up and stretch. The floor is killing my back. First thing tomorrow, I'm getting a bed sent over here.

Kyle Hudson. U kno him?
Nvr heard of him. School?
Astor
No clue.

A picture pops up along with another message:

He's sitting w ur girl and Frank at FT

I zoom in on the image. Both students are sitting with their backs to me. While I can't make out the thick guy with no neck, I'd recognize that waterfall of blue-black hair on the girl next to him anywhere.

I shoot to my feet. What in the hell is Hartley doing with this guy? Across from both of them is the snake, Felicity. Pash has taken to calling her Frankenstein because she's a scary motherfucker who's more monster than human. Hell, calling her Frank's probably an insult to ol' Frankenstein.

I haul my jacket onto one arm while trying to text Pash at the same time.

Go over there and make sure she's ok.

I'm sitting right behind them w Davey. Davey says Kyle and Hartley are a couple?

The hell they are.

What lies is Felicity feeding Hartley? This is bad. Very bad.

I call Pash instead of texting. "Dude, go over there and interrupt," I order before my friend can bleat out a greeting. "Her doctor said that if we tell her stuff before she remembers on her own it can mess her up."

"What am I supposed to say?" he cries.

"I dunno. Tell her a story about how great your castle is in Kolkata." Pash comes from an old and very wealthy Indian family. A couple of years ago, his grandfather decided to build a new compound, and from all the pictures on Pash's Instagram feed, the joint looks big enough to house Astor Park and every one of its students. He could waste an hour just going through the first floor.

"Davey's giving me the eye. If I get up, she's going to kill me."

"If you don't get up, *I'm* going to kill you," I threaten.

"Yeah, but I'm not having sex with you. Sorry, gotta go."

The weak-kneed asshole. I throw myself into my truck and step on the gas. It's a twenty-minute drive from this side of town to the French Twist. It's too bad Ella doesn't work there anymore, or I could've gotten her to step in. Unlike Pash, she knows the meaning of *loyalty*.

I make it in twelve minutes, sweating like a pig from the fear that I would be pulled over by a cop and waste even more time. I throw open the door and scan the small bakery for Hartley, but only see Pash and his new girlfriend chatting over coffee.

He jumps to his feet and waves me over.

"Where are they?" I growl.

"They left like five minutes after I called you."

"Fuck!" I turn on Davey, who blinks her brown doe eyes up at me. "What did you hear? Word for word. I want every detail. Don't leave anything out."

"I didn't hear much," Davey admits. "They were talking low. The only thing I heard really clearly was Hartley telling Kyle that they were broken up."

"I didn't know she dated anyone but you," Pash puts in.

"She didn't," I say in frustration.

Has everyone's memory been wiped clean? Did the Men in Black come in here and zap everyone? Hartley dated zero people. She didn't hang out with the Astor kids. She worked at an all-night diner on the east side of town during her free time, sometimes even skipping class to take a shift. When she wasn't delivering trays of food and drinks, she was sleeping. Life was serious for Hartley.

I turn back to Davey. "Who was doing the talking?" I demand.

"Mostly Felicity."

"Who's this Kyle kid?"

"I don't know. He doesn't hang with us."

"Why was Felicity here?"

"I don't know," Davey cries, throwing her hands up as if to fend off my barrage of questions.

Pash half rises from his seat. "Come on, man. Ease off. Davey's being as helpful as possible."

"I am." Davey pouts.

Pash scurries over to throw a comforting arm around his girlfriend of ten days. "Are you done?" he asks me in a frosty tone.

I drag a hand down my face. The amount of damage that this kid Kyle and Felicity could've done to Hartley makes me sick to my stomach, but yelling at Pash and his delicate girlfriend won't result in anything but my friend being pissed at me.

"Yeah, I'm done. Call me if you hear anything."

"Yeah, yeah." Pash slides back into his chair. "Do you need another bubble tea, baby?" he coos. "Or maybe I should buy you that bracelet from Chanel. That'd make you feel better, right?"

I stalk out of the bakery before I ram my foot through one of the glass display cases in frustration. Pausing on the sidewalk, I consider my options. There's only one that appeals to me. I know I won't be welcome at her house, but I have to see if she's okay.

My foot is off the curb when I hear someone stutter my name.

"E-Easton?"

I spin around. "Hartley?" I search the front of the store for her, not seeing her. Maybe I'm hearing things. Maybe I've spent so many hours thinking about her that my mind is gone. Soon I'll be talking to a pretend Hartley, shutting my eyes and—

"Over here."

My gaze drops to a figure crouched on the curb about twenty feet away. The figure rises and morphs into Hartley Wright.

"What happened?" I ask, crossing the space between us in about two seconds. I grab her shoulders, drag her into the light, and inspect her from head to foot. "You okay?"

She looks beautiful in the lamplight, her long black hair a silky curtain framing her face. She's covered up in one of her trademark oversized hoodies and her legs are sexily displayed in her dark skinny jeans. Her gray eyes look almost black as she stares solemnly back at me.

"I think so."

"What are you doing out here?"

"I was waiting for the bus." She points to the sign above her head.

"It doesn't come this late. The bus service stops at like ten." I only know this because Dad arranged for a stop to be placed here back when Ella used to be an employee. Despite having a car of her own, she prefers being driven around even if it means riding with thirty other strangers.

"Oh." She rubs her arms and shivers. "They didn't tell me that."

I swing my coat off and around her shoulders. I'm guessing *they* refers to Kyle and Felicity. "What were you doing with those two?"

She gazes at me with troubled eyes for a second before shifting her gaze to the dimly lit parking lot and the darkened pavement. "They were telling me things," she admits finally. Despite my coat, she shudders again.

Fear curdles in my stomach. What the hell could they have said? Actually, it's the breadth of lies they could've told her that scares the shit out of me, starting with the one where she's Kyle Hudson's girlfriend. Is that sick fuck trying to con her into bed with him? Bile crawls up my esophagus.

"Like what?" I croak.

"Things…" She licks her lips. "Bad things."

"About you? There's nothing bad about you. They don't even know you."

"No. About you," she says quietly.

I rear back. This I don't expect. I know Felicity hates me. She hates me because one drunken night I promised her I'd pretend to be her boyfriend so she could be in some photo shoot. When I sobered up, I told her that the promise was void, and apologized. Then I took Hartley to the pier and she kissed me for the first time.

Felicity decided that we were mortal enemies, got Hartley suspended for cheating, and told me that she was only getting started.

"Look, whatever she told you was a big fucking lie."

"She said you slept with the girlfriends of your two older brothers."

My protest dies in the acid pooling at the back of my throat. "They were ex-girlfriends."

Except for Savannah. She and my oldest brother Gideon had a love-hate relationship for years. During one of their breakups, I convinced her that we could console each other—with our clothes off.

Guilt seeps into my gut.

A faint look of disgust flickers across Hart's face. Shit. Of all the things about me she's going to remember, this is it.

"That was before you," I argue.

Her jaw tightens. "Kyle said you slept with his girlfriend while they were dating."

"I don't even know who Kyle is," I grind out. Is this how Scrooge felt when all his sins were being thrown in his face by the Ghost of Christmas Past? At what point do I get a break?

"He said you'd say that. Because he's not rich enough or popular enough for you to notice him, but he had a pretty girlfriend and one night at a party at Jordan Carrington's house, you had sex with his girlfriend in the pool while Kyle watched."

My stomach sinks to my feet. Fuck, I could've done that. I've definitely had sex in the Carrington pool. I've had sex in a lot of pools with many girls and a few adult women. Did I knowingly screw them while they were dating someone else? No. I wouldn't do that. But at a party when you're drunk and horny, it's not like I fished out a questionnaire and asked about their dating status. I assumed if they were ready to ride my dick, they were free to do so.

But explaining that to Hartley, a girl who I want to take me seriously, a girl who I have some strong feelings for, a girl who I want to *like* me? That's an impossible task.

I run an agitated hand through my hair. "I partied some. I had sex with girls, but after I met you, I never touched anyone else. Hell, I didn't even make the first move on you—" *That's shading the truth*, I think. *Shut up!* "You kissed me."

She nods slowly. "Yes, I guess I could've, but it seems like the question is, *should* I have?"

"Hart."

She doesn't respond. The blood's pounding hard in my ears. There's a thickness in the air—a swampy, soupy heaviness that's weighing everything down. I fight through it and step off the curb to position myself where she can't avoid looking at me.

"Hart," I say softly. "I did shit things in the past. Not gonna lie, but I'm different now."

When she finally raises her eyes to meet mine, they are full of pain. "They said you like girls you can't have. Like your foster sister, Ella. And when you couldn't have her, you turned your attention to me. That I'm going to be the most exciting forbidden fruit ever dangled in front of you because I hurt your brother and your family hates me. Are you telling me that it's all untrue?"

It was that bitch. That bitch! I hope she fucking dies.

I could tell her the truth, but she's in so much pain. Besides, once Seb wakes up—and he will—Sawyer's not going to be mad anymore. Ella and me are so far in the past that I can barely remember why I kissed her that one time in the club, other than I was lonely and she was lonely and I enjoyed taking the piss out of my brother Reed who was watching the whole time.

The truth will only hurt Hartley more.

"I'm telling you that Felicity and Kyle aren't saying these things to help you out."

"I know that. I just want one person to be straight with me. Is that you?"

The reply sticks in my throat.

"Ask me no questions and I'll tell you no lies, huh?" She exhales heavily, reading me all too well. "I guess since there's no bus, you're my ride home." She tugs my jacket around her shoulders.

She'd rather walk ten miles than get into my truck, I think, but climbs into the cab anyway. Her choices have been narrowed down to bad and worse. I'm the bad option so I win by default.

She's quiet on the drive, and since I'm afraid of answering any more of her questions, I keep my own mouth shut. When we arrive at her house, I opt not to walk her to the door. If her dad sees me, all hell will break loose and she doesn't need that.

Halfway out the door, she turns. "Thanks for the ride."

"Tomorrow, wait for me outside in the morning. I'll walk in with you. Astor's not the easiest place to navigate." The students there love preying on the weak. And right now, Hartley's as fragile as they come.

A sad smile crosses her lips. "Funny. That's the same thing that Kyle said. I guess he didn't lie about everything."

And with that disturbing last word, she slams the door shut and runs into her house.

DAD CALLS ME INTO THE office the next morning. I lumber in, a bowl of hot oatmeal in my hand and a spoon poking out the side of my mouth. "What's up?" I ask.

"I'm glad you're up early." He scrambles around his den, throwing papers into his flight bag.

I'm early because I never slept. Last night, I kept turning over the Hart, Kyle, Felicity scene in my head. I vaguely remember Kyle. Scratch that—I don't remember him at all. Obviously, we go to school together, but I can't think of a single instance where we exchanged so much as a *hello*. But he's got a beef with me, and if I did screw his girlfriend, he clearly hasn't gotten over it. Why else would he risk the Royal wrath by messing with a girl that belongs to one of us?

Not that Hart *belongs* to me.

Yes she does.

Fuck. Fine. Okay, I do see her as mine. And I don't want Kyle Hudson and his nonexistent neck anywhere near her.

Felicity's motives are equally easy to guess. She hates me, period. She's out for revenge. And though I have zero interest in making amends with that bitch, I realize in dismay it might come down to that. I can't have Frankenstein and No Neck screwing with Hartley's head. She's confused enough as it is.

My dad hurriedly shoves a file folder into his bag, interrupting my thoughts.

"You going somewhere?" I say in between bites.

"I have to go to Dubai today. Ben El-Baz contacted me about an order for ten of the new jets. I need to close this deal in person."

"What about Seb?"

"He's in stable condition. If he wakes up, I'll be home before you know it. Now, I'm counting on you to take care of the rest of the kids while I'm gone. You're the oldest and I don't want Ella to worry about the twins. She has a meeting with the DA's office over her testimony."

"Fuck." Ella has to testify against her father, Steve O'Halloran, in his upcoming trial. I hadn't realized that was approaching, but I guess the February trial date isn't too far away.

"Exactly." He hands me a slip of paper. "I've obtained permission for you to skip school for the rest of this week and possibly the next, depending on how long this transaction takes." He zips closed his flight bag.

"Skip school?" I need to be at Astor to protect Hartley. "I've already missed the last two weeks."

Dad tilts his head. "Who are you and what have you done with my school-hating son, Easton?"

I shift uncomfortably under his fatherly gaze. I can't tell him why I need to go to school in case he's got a hate-on for Hartley like Sawyer does. "I don't hate school. I just choose not to go some days because I've got better things to do."

"And this week you have better things to do." He claps his hand on my shoulder. "Ordinarily, I wouldn't trust you to be responsible for a minute, let alone a week, but these are your brothers and I know you love them." He grabs his bag and walks briskly out into the foyer where Durand, his driver, waits. "Make sure Sawyer's eating and getting some rest. Call me if there's any change in Sebastian's condition, and be there for Ella if she needs a shoulder to cry on. I'll see you in less than a week." He gives me a salute and takes off.

Fuck.

I grab my phone and text Hartley.

Change of plans. My dad's flying out to Dubai and I need to go check in on my brothers. If you see Ella, go in with her.

I re-read my text and realize Hart may not know who the hell Ella is. I find a picture of her and Reed hanging all over each other and send that.

I don't get a response. I wait three seconds and send another text.

Or Val. She's solid.

I return to my photo roll, find a picture of Ella, Val, Reed and me out by the pool last summer. I crop out Reed and myself and send Hart the modified image.

Ella's the blonde. Val's the one with the bob and the mole.

Still nothing. I glance at the clock. Do I have time to drive over to Hart's house, pick her up and drop her off? I decide I do if I hurry.

I drop my bowl off on the marble table in the entryway and hurry to the kitchen where I left my backpack. Ella's there eating a yogurt and fruit.

"Where are you going?" she asks.

"Hartley's, Astor, and then the hospital."

"Hartley? Is that a good idea, Easton? Shouldn't you wait until you see if Seb wakes up?"

I swing around to confront Ella. "What are you talking about? The accident wasn't her fault."

"I know that, but Sawyer is hating on her right now. I don't think it's good for him to know that you're hanging around with her."

"Then don't tell him," I say, irked by Ella's position.

"But—"

I ignore her complaints and jog to the door. I don't need to hear that stuff, especially not after I told Hartley to walk in with Ella and Val. All the more reason to drop Hartley off and make sure she gets inside the school okay.

After that...fuck, I don't know what to do after that. Maybe I can convince Hartley to skip and come to the hospital with me. But then where do I put her? Sawyer will blow up if he sees her.

This is a fucking mess and I don't have a good solution. I'll figure it out when I get to her house.

I'm coming to pick you up, I shoot off. Tossing the phone on the passenger seat, I power up the truck and head for Hartley's. I check for a response when I reach the gate at the end of my lane and then again at the stoplight a mile down and then again at the intersection near her house, but I see zero replies.

When I reach her house, I debate whether I should go in. Her father hates my guts. There's a fifty/fifty chance he's at work. I've gambled on way worse odds, I decide. I hop out of the truck and hurry up the front walk. At this rate, Hart's going to be late for school.

I take the stairs in two leaps and press the doorbell. It rings and a few seconds later, I see a figure through one of the glass panes. The door swings open to reveal Mrs. Wright. Shit.

Her mouth drops open. "Easton Royal?"

I give her my brightest, winningest smile that makes nuns want to pinch my cheeks and mothers want to fuck me. "Yup. I'm here to pick Hartley up."

The door slams in my face.

"Go away and don't ever show your face here again," I hear through the heavy wooden door.

I've never been good with orders. I pound on the door. "I told Hart that I'd pick her up."

"She's already at school. It started ten minutes ago. Now leave or I'll call the police!" Hartley's mom yells. "My husband is an assistant district attorney. He will put you in jail!"

I swallow a sigh and drag a hand through my hair. This day is a clusterfuck and it's not even eight a.m.

CHAPTER ELEVEN

Hartley

I STICK MY THUMBS UNDER the straps of my backpack and smile and nod to everyone. I feel like I've been thrown back to kindergarten, stumbling off the bus without my mother's hand in mine and wading past the legs of the teachers and older students, searching for a friendly face—any friendly face. Easton said to wait for him, but I've been standing on the curb for what feels like forever.

A bright blonde swath of hair catches my eye. Felicity's about ten steps ahead of me. There are three equally blonde girls huddled around her. Part of me wants to run up and hide in that group of girls. The other part of me knows Felicity would bite my head off and then step on my bloody, exposed neck. So I trail behind.

I'm not sure why she hates me, but she does. I'm positive it has something to do with Easton, possibly something to do with Easton and me. Were they dating at the time that I slept with him? Of all the things that bother me about my loss of memory, the sex one is the worst. I can't remember who saw me naked. Who laid their hands on me. Who I touched in return. I can't remember any of it. But they do. Some of the boys that walk by have seen me—my bare chest, my stomach, the private place between my legs.

And it makes me feel sick and violated even though I must've given them all consent. So, yeah, of all the things I despise about my amnesia, this is at the very top of my list. It keeps me awake at night, makes my stomach churn and my head ache. I scan the passing boys, straining to find some kind of recognition, some kind of familiarity, but there's nothing.

My gaze swings back to Felicity. She didn't even try to hide her glee last night as Kyle and she took turns detailing Easton's sins. Easton's a pill-addicted drunk who will stick his dick into any available hole. The only reason he's popular, swore the two of them, is because his father owns this town. I'd wager it's because he's wickedly attractive and has a smile powerful enough to knock a statue off its copper base.

As for me, I'm a cheat and a liar. I cheated on Kyle. I cheated in math. Felicity even implied I cheated to get into Astor. I don't really understand that one.

I'm not convinced everything they've told me is the truth. They both have an ulterior motive, one that I don't fully understand at this point. I'm guessing, based on the not-very-well-subdued violence in Kyle's voice, that his beef with Easton has to do with an ex-girlfriend—the one that Easton screwed in the pool. The reason for Felicity's hatred may also stem from an Easton-related incident, but her happiness at my circumstances makes me believe that her anger is related to me in some way.

One thing I feel must be true is that I did hook up with Easton, which seems the most improbable of all the things Felicity has laid at my feet. God created a billion men, developed the perfect face, and stuck it on Easton Royal. It's unfair the way his dark hair droops slightly over his right eye, making your fingers itch to brush it back. It's criminal how blue his eyes are. Dark-haired boys should have unthreatening and bland eyes, not piercing blue ones that make you think of oceans and seas and skies on the sunniest, prettiest days. His chest is broad and his arms are defined, but not bulging in a gross way. He's the vision that you conjure up in your dreams at night.

It's hard to comprehend that a specimen of male beauty like Easton would ever be interested in me. It's not that I'm a dog in the looks area, but there are leagues that a person plays in. My league is not the same as the Royals'. The Royals date girls in college, the ones who are the head of the cheer squad or president of their sorority. The Royals date girls with money, girls who are listed in the Daughters of the Revolution directory, girls who are beauty queens or television personalities or Instagram models. They do not date dumpy, round-faced girls who live with foulmouthed sisters, DA dads, and social-climbing mothers.

Me dating Easton Royal is about as likely as me hooking up with one of the members of BTS—in other words, not likely at all.

But he showed up at the French Twist last night. He gave me his jacket when I shivered, not from the cold, but from anxiety. He looked at me in a way that's too tender and too familiar for people who are only acquaintances. The cold that seemed to have set into my bones began to thaw under that intense blue gaze. I wanted to crawl into his embrace and ask him to hold me until this nightmare was all over.

But when we talked about his partying and the things I'd heard him being accused of, his words all sounded like half-truths and it seemed like he was dodging a bit. I think he was lying to me about stuff. And withholding stuff. But telling the truth about other stuff. It was so confusing. Felicity's and Kyle's words swam around in my head until it ached and all I wanted to do was go home and hide. Since I don't remember anything, I don't have any way to counter their accusations.

And he's not here this morning. Did I really expect him to keep his promise? I rub my hands together and give myself a short pep talk.

Rely on yourself. You can do this. It's just school. This won't last. You can do this.

Maybe not everyone is staring at me, but it feels like it. It's as if I'm standing on stage giving a big speech with no clothes on and everyone in the audience is pointing and laughing.

Is she the one who lost her memory? Is she the one who put Sebastian Royal in a coma? Is she the one? Is she the one? Is she the one?

Yes, I want to scream. I'm the one. I'm the one who caused you to trip on the flat sidewalk, the one who copied your geography notes, the one who stole your boyfriend. *It's me!* I want to scream, because I just don't fucking know.

Mentally exhausted, I pin my chin to my chest and make my way up the stairs of the massive three-story structure that appears to house most of Astor Park Prep. Long wings stretch past either side of the main building. The sidewalk leading up to the front doors is wide enough to drive two semis down. Surrounding the buildings are acres of pristine, carefully cut grass that is still green despite the late November cold. The benefits of living in the South, I suppose.

I long for a narrower sidewalk, a smaller entryway, and crowded halls where I could be just one of the hundreds of students hurrying to class. Instead, it feels like there are more lockers than students. Using the school map from my notebook, I find my way to my own locker and then stare at the lock in dismay. I don't remember the code. I try my birthday. Nothing happens.

I enter my zip code and the year. The lock holds. I squeeze my eyes shut and strain to recall more numbers. Dylan's birthday pops into my head. When that fails, I enter Parker's. A phone number floats to the top. Still nothing. I chew on the corner of my mouth in vexation. Why didn't I think of this beforehand? I didn't remember I went to Astor, the stupid uniform feels like it's made for someone other than me, so why would I know my locker code?

"Problems, Hart-*lay*?"

I glance to my right to see Kyle smirking at me. I wish he'd go away. There's no way I dated this guy. Even if I was a liar and a cheat, I had to have *some* standards. Standing next to him makes my skin crawl. And frankly, if we did date and we did sleep together, those are things I'm happy to forget.

"Nope."

"You ready for your first class?" There's a malicious note underlying his words, but I've had enough of Kyle and his not-so-helpful pieces of information. Instead of responding, I merely turn and walk away.

"Hey, I was talking to you," he yells at my back.

I keep moving, ignoring the questioning faces and the way my cheeks are turning bright red in embarrassment.

"Bitch," he yells.

At least he's not acting like we're dating anymore.

I keep my head down and try to draw as little attention to myself as possible. At lunch, everyone's attention is diverted by a fight. A blonde with hair the color of honey launches herself at a dark-haired girl with tight curls. I hear one of them yell about trees and houses and wonder what kind of circus Astor Park Prep really is.

By the end of the day, I'm worn out—emotionally and physically. I drag myself to calc, the class I supposedly cheated in. The room is nearly empty when I arrive.

The teacher, a very pretty woman who doesn't look old enough to have graduated from college, is standing at the front. Her red lips turn down at the corners when she spots me. Someone's memory still works even if mine is gone. The schedule has the teacher listed as C. Mann.

"Ms. Wright, how nice to see you back in class."

If awards were given for snideness, Ms. Mann would get a big trophy. I dip my head and survey the desks. Which one did I sit in? The few students who are already in their seats avoid my gaze. They don't want me to sit by them. I opt for one in the far corner. I've had enough eyes on my back to last a year.

"That's not your seat," a curly-haired brunette informs me when I start to slide behind my chosen desk.

Ass half onto the chair, I blink dumbly. "We have assigned seats? Where's mine?"

This wasn't a problem in any of the other classes today.

"No, dumbass. That's Landon's seat. He's sat there the entire class."

This is frustrating. "Okay, then where should I sit?"

Instead of answering me, the brunette raises her hand. "Ms. Mann, Hartley can't go back to sitting in her old seat. It wouldn't be fair to the Royals."

The Royals...plural? Easton's in this class? Maybe he meant wait for him in class. He might've thought I would remember.

"I know, right?" a boy pipes up. "They've got enough on their plate."

I twist around to stare at the boy whose spindly arms look about as frail as my pencil. "I was in a car accident and landed on my head. I don't have rabies."

He makes a face.

"Sit there." Ms. Mann points to a desk in the front right, near the door.

"Fine." I stomp up to the desk and throw myself down in the seat. I make a big deal out of unzipping my backpack and slamming my notebook onto the desk, because I'm tired of trying to hide.

I'm here. Deal with me. I cross my arms and glare at every student who comes in. Some are taken aback. Some don't look at me, and others shoot daggers in return. None of them are Easton. One pretty blonde pauses as she enters, looks at me under her eyelashes, and then takes her seat after another student enters behind her and gives her a small shove.

Curious, I track her to her desk. As the students trickle in, a steady buzz of conversation starts humming. There's a lot of discussion about a dance that took place and who came with whom. There's debate about whether it's institutional misogyny that props up attendance for the terrible boys' basketball team as opposed to the small crowd that watches the really good girls' team. And there's talk about a party at Felicity's house. She's bringing in a band—a band so big that even these rich kids are semi-awed.

"I heard she paid half a million."

"For what?"

"New Year's Eve. We're seniors so we might as well go out with a splash."

"Easton, are you going? Oh, he's not here." The student hadn't realized. She moves on. "Ella, what about you?"

"It depends on how Sebastian is doing," the pretty blonde who eyed me earlier says.

Ella. She's the foster sister. The one that Kyle and Felicity said Easton wanted but couldn't have. I can't remember why. It had something to do with one of his brothers, but maybe I'm mixing that up with another girl.

"Oh sure, of course. I'm sorry," the student stammers and quickly changes the subject. "Anyway, man, it's cold, isn't it? I hope the party is inside."

The hum of whispers doesn't stop when the lecture starts, and Ms. Mann makes no attempt to quiet anyone. She writes a few notes on the board about the limits at infinity and orders us to solve problems in section 3.5. There are fourteen of them, which makes the entire class groan in dismay.

She ignores the pleas to cut the assignment in half and takes a seat behind her desk, where she proceeds to glare at me every five minutes or so. Felicity says that I cheated, which would explain those pointed stares, but I don't feel like a cheat—however a cheat feels.

Ms. Mann starts talking and I fix my eyes forward, trying to concentrate on the topics at hand. The equations aren't easy, but I understand the base principles, and the new concepts simply build on those. I catch on quick. When we're given free time to solve a set of problems, I finish before anyone else and without errors. While waiting for the rest of the class to complete the in-room homework, I flip to the earlier sections of the textbook looking for the areas where I must've struggled.

But I don't come across any. Derivatives, the extrema values, the open and closed intervals and the critical numbers all make sense. I take a sample problem finding the extrema of $f(x) = 2 \sin x - \cos 2x$ and solve it, checking my work in the back.

There isn't a past section that stumps me. What's confusing is why I would've cheated in this class at all. I *know* this stuff.

Baffled, I decide I'm going to confront this head on. After class is over, I loiter in my chair until only Ms. Mann and I are left in the room.

"What is it?" Ms. Mann asks impatiently.

"You probably heard, but I lost my memory."

"I have heard. It seems very convenient." She eyes me dismissively.

"Not for me," I mutter to myself. To her, I say, "I heard I was accused of cheating in this class, but I feel like I understand the material."

"Then don't cheat next time."

"How was it that I cheated before?"

She huffs out a noise—half laugh, half grunt of disgust. "Are you asking me for advice on how to cheat?"

"No. I'm trying to fill in the blanks—"

"You better leave before I start suspecting that you cheated on your homework today. The best advice I have for you, Ms. Wright, is to keep your head down and make as little noise as possible. Now if you'll excuse me, I'm going to prepare for tomorrow's lessons."

In other words, *get out and don't talk to me again.* A little stunned, I gather up my pencil and notebook. I didn't expect my first day back at school to be a picnic, but I didn't think it'd be a nightmare like this, either. At the door, I turn back. "I'm sorry. For whatever I did, I'm sorry."

She doesn't even look my way.

After the last bell rings, I hurry to the bus line. I find a small group of students toward the end of the wide boulevard in front of Astor Park and join it, standing behind a girl wearing cute white boots with her Astor Park uniform. The boy in front of her pokes the girl's shoulder. She peeks behind her and meets my eyes.

I smile. She frowns and scuttles forward.

Being an outcast is not fun, I decide. I wonder what bus I take home. I know that the girl in front of me doesn't want to talk, but if I get on the wrong bus, that'll be worse than being bitched out here on the sidewalk where only a couple of people are watching.

"Excuse me, can you tell me which bus goes to West and Eighty-Sixth Street?" I ask, naming an intersection near my house.

"What are you talking about?"

I repeat myself. "I'm not sure which bus I should take."

The girl rolls her eyes. "What are you, dumb? There are no

buses at Astor."

"She's not dumb; she's pretending she can't remember nearly killing Sebastian Royal," supplies her male friend.

"Why did they even allow her to come back here? What if she gets into a car? She could kill us all." The girl shudders.

"That's why she has to take public transportation. The cops took her license away." The boy declares these lies without hesitation. I gape at him.

"Thank God," the girl says. "Let's go. I don't want to stand here anymore. The air pollution is making me sick."

The boy grabs her hand and the two jog toward the parking lot. Shame, deserved or not, paints the tops of my ears red. At this rate, someone's going to smear a scarlet letter across my chest and I'll have to start answering to the name Hester. Tears prick at the back of my eyes.

Whatever I'd done in the past must have been terrible to have to endure this. I'm blinking back the tears when a car honks, and I look over to see a good-looking face peering out from the driver's window.

"Hartley? I guess you don't remember me, but I'm Bran. We were friends. I can drive you home."

On a different day, I probably would've said no. I don't know this guy. I've already got a shit reputation and climbing into a car driven by a strange boy isn't going to help, but I've reached the end of my rope. I grab the door handle and climb in.

CHAPTER TWELVE

Easton

I ARRIVE AT THE HOSPITAL a little after eight, but Seb's not in his room. "In testing," is the hurried response one nurse throws at me. His twin is slumped over the end of the bed, drooling onto his arm. I lever the two-hundred-pound kid onto the mattress and try texting Hartley again.

> *Classes going ok? We still talking about the gender equity in Feminist Theory? My fave class, u know.*

She must think that's a bad joke.

> *How abt calc? Anything new and exciting?*

I read over my texts. Man, these are dumb as hell. I shove the phone in my pocket and go lie down on the uncomfortable sofa. I don't know how much Dad donated to get this wing of the hospital built, but I don't think any of it was spent on this furniture. The sofa's as hard as granite.

I rifle through my backpack and pull out the *Sports*

Illustrated I brought from home. We're supposed to be reading to Seb these days. Apparently while you're in a coma, sometimes you can still be aware of your surroundings. Comas sound like one of those night terrors where you're half asleep but feel awake, and someone is standing at the end of your bed but you can't move. I play music for Seb, tell him some shitty jokes, read some memes off the Internet, and quote *The Godfather* to him.

After a while, I push to my feet and find something to eat. Halfway through my club sandwich, my phone pings. It almost flies across the room in my haste to pull it out of my pocket. But it's not Hartley. Instead, it's a video from Pash, and features two of our friends having a hair-pulling contest in the middle of the lunchroom.

He captions it with: *Where's the mud pit when you really need one?*

I zoom in and out, trying to locate Hartley, but I don't see her. I text Pash the fist-bump emoji and ask where Hart is.

Where's Hart?

Dunno.

Take a pic of the lunchroom. Send to me.

I'm not there anymore. It's 5th period now.

I get a picture of his feet and the tile floor. Pash has no classes with Hartley, so this isn't helpful. I send him thanks anyway and tuck my phone back into my jeans. I'll go see her tonight when Ella comes to sit with Sawyer.

When I return to the recovery wing, I check in at the nurses' station.

"Is Seb back yet?" I lean over the counter and scan to see if his chart is lying out—not that I'd be able to understand it.

The nurse on duty spreads her arms over the confidential records. "We finished testing twenty minutes ago."

"Any update?" I ask hopefully.

"I'm sorry, but there is no change."

That fucking sucks. I make my way down to Seb's room, but before I go in, I take a couple calming breaths. Seeing Seb lying motionless in his hospital bed is fucking awful. Each time I go in I'm torn between wanting to shake him until his eyes pop open or throw shit around the room until the sick feeling in my gut dissolves. But Sawyer's upset enough for the entire family. He doesn't need to see me losing my cool. I'm here to bring a little levity to the situation, otherwise we're all going to drown.

I crack my jaw, paste on a grin, and push the door open.

"We missed a fire school day. Pash texted me a video of Margot Dunlop and Dian Foster getting into it over Treehouse. He's been doing both of them at the same time and neither of them knew it."

Sawyer doesn't look up from the hospital bed where Seb is now lying. I toss my backpack in the corner and drop into one of the empty chairs.

"Go shower and then eat," I tell my brother. "You look like you're two steps away from trading places with Seb."

Sawyer still doesn't move. I push out of the chair and walk over to him. He doesn't acknowledge me. I snap my fingers in front of his face a couple of times until he blinks.

"What?" he asks sourly.

"You smell like ass."

"So?"

"So go use the shower. Seb's probably in his coma because every time he wakes up it smells like a garbage can and he figures he'd rather be in his perfect dream world where everything is sunshine and fucking roses."

"Fuck you." Sawyer folds his arms across his chest and digs his butt into the chair.

"I'm not into incest, kid."

"Oh, and I am?" Sawyer explodes. "Is that what you're saying? That this is some kind of punishment because of that?" He points a shaky finger at the bed.

I back up with my hands up in the air. What in the hell is he ranting about? "No. It was a joke."

Sawyer and Seb have been dating the same girl for over a year now. There's always been a lot of commentary on it because, well, it's weird and different and, probably, in some eyes, wrong. I couldn't care less.

"Did someone say anything?" I look around for a target. What my brothers do with their dicks is no one's business.

Sawyer's hand falls to his lap. He leans forward, scrubbing his face with the heels of his palms. The kid looks exhausted. There are huge bags under his eyes. His skin has taken on a pale, ashy complexion. Even the muscles in his biceps look smaller. I wasn't kidding when I said that he looked like he needed to be in a hospital bed.

"I went to confession," he mumbles into his hands.

"What?" I'm confused. "Why? We aren't Catholic." Mom used to attend the Bayview United Baptist church, but Dad hasn't gone since her death. He still gives a lot of money because good businessmen do that sort of shit. People down here are big on church, as if showing up in a pew on Sunday can wash away all the bad deeds you did during the week.

"I know, but I thought it might help."

Sawyer's at the end of his rope if he's going down to the chapel to list out his sins in hopes that some greater being is going to bring Seb back to us. I crouch down and put an arm across the back of his chair. "So you went to confession, told the man wearing a paper collar that you were into kinky shit, and he told you that's why Seb is laid out in the hospital bed."

Sawyer holds still and then nods slowly, his hands still covering his face.

"I don't think God works that way. There are plenty of churchgoing people who die all the time."

"I know." He rubs his eyes with his palms, still shielding himself from my view. It's obvious he's upset about more than whatever that priest said to him.

"Hey." I touch his shoulder, but he still doesn't look up. "What's going on?"

He mumbles something I can't make out.

I lean in closer. "What?"

Sawyer finally raises his head. His eyes are flat, his tone even more so. "Lauren broke up with me—us," he amends ruefully.

"Fuck." But I'm not surprised. She hasn't been here at all as far as I've seen. "Did she call you?"

He snorts. "Text. 'I can't see you anymore. This is too hard.'"

Class act, that girl. I was never crazy about her, but always treated her with respect for the twins' sakes. Out loud, I say, "I'm sorry, man."

"Yeah, well, at first, I was worried about how I was going to tell Seb, but now I don't know if I'll get a chance."

"He's going to wake up," I say with more confidence than I feel. "And then the two of you will find an even hotter chick to flaunt in Lauren's face and she'll kick herself for being stupid enough to dump you guys. And you know what else? You leaving for five minutes to shower and eat isn't going to be the difference between Seb waking up now and Seb waking up in a half hour. Besides, you know if the places were switched, you wouldn't want him sitting here all day either."

He searches my face as if I have some answer to the universe there. Whatever he sees must satisfy him because he gives a small nod and stands. He sways a little—unsteady like Bambi. I have a sudden flashback to when the twins were five and running down the beach, tripping every other yard because their feet were too big for their bodies. And you couldn't offer them a hand because, even then, these two only wanted to rely on each other.

"Go on." I give him a gentle but firm shove on the shoulder. "I got this. Let your older brother do something useful for once."

"If he wakes up—"

"I'm going to smother him with the pillow. What the fuck? Of course I'm going to come get you." I give him another push and then another until he's moving of his own accord.

I wait until he disappears into the bathroom before taking a seat. Then I get up immediately. Sawyer's sat so long in this one chair that the cushion is permanently indented to the shape of my brother's ass. Shaking my head, I grab another chair and drag it next to Seb's bed.

"You should wake up. You're worrying your brother. He's

making himself sick sitting next to your bed all day."

Seb remains motionless.

"Ah, hell, maybe it's better where you are." I run a hand through my hair and lean back. "You're probably driving fast cars, sleeping with gorgeous girls, eating good food without anyone nagging you. Remember how we used to have fun as a family?"

There used to be picnics on the beach, trips on a moment's notice, Mom coming home from Paris with her hands full of orange and black boxes. We'd have movie night in the media room with popcorn and homemade milkshakes. Mom did a lot of the cooking, so Sandy, our housekeeper, wasn't around as much. I strain to reach those memories, but I can't pull up any solid images—only fleeting feelings. These days the only time I can recreate that atmosphere is after a drink or five.

I shift uncomfortably in my seat. I really need a drink. I glance at the clock. Sawyer's been in the shower for five minutes. The water's still running. Can I sneak out, find the gift shop, and get back before he notices?

I'm halfway out of my seat when the shower turns off. Fuck. I sit back down.

"Seb, as soon as Sawyer's gone, I'm going to make a booze run. That way when you wake up, we'll have something on hand to celebrate with." I knock my fist against the bed, but Seb doesn't move. I get up and grab my backpack. "I brought some porn for you today." I pull out the flight catalog. "They put the AAV 510 into production. The twin engine goes a sweet 285 miles per hour and can travel 8500 nautical miles before refueling, which is enough to get from New York to Tokyo without the stop in Anchorage. The interior kits are

Napa leather and mahogany—matte not gloss because that shit is out."

Sawyer strolls out of the bathroom wearing a set of hospital scrubs and toweling his hair. "What the hell are you reading to him?"

"Plane porn." I wave the spec sheets for the new small-engine luxury plane Atlantic Aviation is finally producing after ten years of design and testing. I wish I could get into the pilot's seat of this baby. It's the most powerful personal jet with the longest fuel range of any small plane out there. It's going to revolutionize international travel for a certain segment of the population—the people who can't afford the quarter of a million it costs to rent a private jet internationally yet who don't want to fly commercial. The waiting list is already about five years long at this point. This is the deal that Dad's in the process of closing now.

"Borrrrrrring." Sawyer wrinkles his nose in disgust. It's the one interest Seb shared with me that he didn't share with his twin.

Doesn't share, I quickly remind myself. He's not dead, damn it. He still loves planes. Present fucking tense.

"The hospital gear looks good on you." I feel like I'm seeing future Sawyer here. A doctor in the Royal family? I could see it.

"You should get him some real porn."

"I dunno. What if he gets a chub while I'm telling him about how Sarah and Sasha are getting it on? The guy can't whack his own meat and I'm not going to do it for him."

Sawyer broods for a minute before saying, "What else are you going to read to him?"

I give my younger brother a shove. "What are you? The

hall monitor?"

"He's my brother," Sawyer says, crossing his arms obstinately. The pose makes him look about ten years old, pouting lower lip and furrowed brows.

"Mine, too," I remind him.

"He's my twin."

"And you don't ever let us forget it. Go and eat or I'll sit on you until you cry for mercy."

"You can't do that anymore."

"Wanna bet?" I arch an eyebrow. I spend more time lifting and fighting than any of my brothers these days. "You've been wasting away in here. I could hold you down with one hand tied behind my back."

Sawyer must be feeling vulnerable because he doesn't argue. Instead, he gives me the finger and then walks out.

I take my seat again. "You need to wake up and save us all from Sawyer. He's turning into an old man. Okay, where were we? Oh yeah. I'm going through the options. So this baby seats twenty peeps and has a full shower and lav setup. Where we're really making the dough is in the finishes. Also, I heard Dad talking about a military stealth plane that they're putting into testing. Goes Mach 6. Obviously not as fast as the North American X-15, but at least it doesn't have to be carried like a baby plane and dropped like a bomb before it can actually fly." I flip over the page.

I don't even get an eyelid flicker.

"You're as bad as Hartley. I've texted her a dozen times and she's leaving me on read. You're getting the latest news about the coolest toy Dad has ever made and you're pretty much ignoring me. Can you at least squeeze my finger?" I grab Seb's hand. *Can she at least read my damned texts?*

I drop my head into my free hand as a wave of helplessness washes over me. I could really use a drink. Really, really. *This is all going to turn out okay,* I tell myself. I suck in a deep breath, sit up, and start reading again.

CHAPTER THIRTEEN

Hartley

MY SECOND DAY BACK AT school isn't much better than the first.

"Felicity says you can't remember a thing," one girl says to me as I'm washing my hands in the bathroom before lunch.

"Come on, Bridgette. You know it's an act," another girl retorts. She puckers her lips and dabs on a red gloss. "I'd want to pretend nothing happened, too, if I nearly killed Sebastian Royal."

"Did you hear that Lauren didn't visit once?"

"I heard they broke up. I stopped by the hospital after school yesterday and Sawyer looked so down." Another girl, this one with dark hair and perfect skin, joins us at the sink. "I hope the Royals show up at the party because I know exactly how to cheer him up."

"With your tongue?" laughs the lipstick girl.

"You know it."

The two exchange high-fives.

I feel crowded between the four girls—all so pretty in their modified uniforms. Their skirts are shorter than mine.

Two of them have black shirts that are hanging open with graphic tees underneath, while the dark-haired girl wears a white one, untucked and unbuttoned to reveal a stunning lace tank beneath.

I look at my own plain white shirt and long plaid skirt and wonder how I can feel so dowdy when I'm wearing practically the same thing.

"Don't bother coming, Wright. No one wants you there," says the one who wants Sawyer.

"I wasn't planning on it," I mumble.

"Why? You think you're above it all because Easton Royal fucked you?" She places her hands on her hips. "Please. You're nothing but a cheap slut. Your daddy bought your way into school and now you're trying to sleep your way into our group, but that's not how it works with us. We want nothing to do with you."

For all I know, Bridgette is right—that I used Easton to be part of the "in" crowd here at Astor. That act seems consistent with a girl who cheats, blackmails, and is banished from her home for three years, so while I want to argue, I don't know if I have the right to do so. One thing I'm certain of is that post-accident Hartley does not want to hang around with toxic people.

"I'm not interested in being part of your group." I tug a paper towel out of the holder and dry my hands as Bridgette and her crew stare in disbelief.

Out in the hall, I find that my hands are shaking. I ball them into fists and stuff them into my blazer pockets. Before I can push away from the wall, three guys stroll past. One stops and backs up until he's standing in front of me.

"Hartley, isn't it?" The boy's taller than me by a couple of inches and broad in the shoulders, with a thick neck and big lips.

"Yes." I search his face for a sign of recognition, but my mind is blank.

He reaches down and lifts the hem of my skirt with his phone. "What you got under there?"

I slap my skirt down and jerk out of reach. "None of your damn business."

"Oh, do I have to pay before I look?" He tosses a smirk over his shoulder to his waiting crew, who appear highly amused at this dildo's antics. "What's the going rate for a peek at the puss? Fifty? A hundie? Don't worry. I'm good for it, aren't I, guys?"

It's impossible for me not to turn red, but I'm only one part embarrassed to about three parts enraged.

"If you're so good, then you wouldn't have to fork out any cash to get in a girl's pants, would you?" I sweep past him, my heart pounding so hard that it's going to break through my ribcage at any moment.

I tense, ready for the moment he grabs my wrist, but he only mutters that he's "better than anyone you've had."

My tolerance for abuse and bullshit has reached its max meter, so I avoid the lunchroom, opting for a health bar from a vending machine near the library. This day has sucked and it's only half over. My head's pounding, my ribs hurt, and my hands are still shaking from my encounter with the boy in the hallway. I wonder what I have to do to get expelled from Astor Park. Cheating only gets you a suspension. I would know, right?

I let myself wallow in self-pity until the health bar is gone. I toss the wrapper in the trash and push open the library door. What I need is answers.

I find an unoccupied computer and open a Word doc. On the blank page, I start listing all the "facts" that I've picked up, assigning each a number based on a scale of believability. Five means I'm convinced it actually happened. One means hell frickin' no.

Dated Kyle – 1: I only have his word for it.

Slept around – 2: More than one person has mentioned that I'm kind of, well, free with my charms.

Hooked up with Easton – 5: Okay, maybe not hooked up, but there's something there. A guy doesn't show up at a pastry shop at ten at night, give you his jacket, and drive you home without having some connection.

Bran drove you home, my little voice reminds me. He said we were friends, didn't know if I dated Kyle, but confirmed I had been suspended.

Cheated – 5.

I look at the bare list. I know four things about myself? What about the food I like to eat? Or the music I like to listen to? Why don't I have any friends? I stare at the cursor, blinking blinking blinking…

The light bulb turns on. This is the twenty-first century. There's no one alive that doesn't have a digital history. I must've taken pictures of myself. I must've have memorialized what I ate and the cute outfits I wore and the fun places I hung out at.

Once I find my accounts, I can piece together my memories—no matter how shitty they are.

I start opening browser windows, typing in the addresses for every social media site that I can recall. I run search after search, using my name, my birthday, my address.

There are many Hartley Wrights on the Internet but none of them are me. There's a Hartley Wright in Oregon who is a nurse, and another one in Georgia who knits. There's a Hartley Wright three years older who attends UCLA and looks like she's living the best life, what with her squad of friends, extensive closet, and super-hot boyfriend (although not remotely as hot as Easton Royal). But there are no accounts for me.

How in the world is this possible? It's like someone deleted everything associated with me.

I'm able to locate my cousin, Jeanette, but her profile is private. Quickly, I make an email account and sign up for Facebook so I can send her a friend request. She doesn't immediately reply. I slump in my chair. Like me, she's in school. Unlike me, she's not skipping classes.

I drum my fingers on the desk. The lack of information seems so odd. Maybe I just don't know how to do an online search. It's not like I've ever looked myself up before, and I can't remember searching others, either. I think...I think I've always been a head-down, keep-to-myself person. It's possible that there aren't any pictures out there because I didn't have a lot of friends in that school up north. I sense that I'm not someone who takes many selfies, probably because I'm not in love with my chubby face.

Maybe I didn't hang out and party, but instead stayed in and read books. That would explain why I'm in some advanced classes here at Astor even though I don't feel particularly smart.

Sighing, I close all the browser windows and think of my next course of action. I still need a phone. I'm going to have to ask my parents for one. I wonder if I had a job at the boarding school. Do I have any money? There wasn't a wallet in my desk and my purse is missing.

Since the Internet is giving me nothing, I guess my clues are in my house and with my family. I spend the rest of the afternoon creating new social media accounts in case anyone from my past wants to contact me.

Against my better judgment, I look up Easton Royal. He has an Instagram account that has about fifteen pictures—mostly of planes, his truck and his brothers. While he's not much of a selfie taker, there are plenty of pictures of Easton out there. In them, he's almost always smiling, looking impossibly gorgeous and almost always with his arm around a girl. There's several of him kissing different girls. I find a couple of him with Felicity. She looks at him as if she's already booked their wedding venue.

He doesn't take a bad picture. Not when he's sweaty and disheveled after football practice, not when he's arriving to school half asleep, not when he's standing at the pier in front of the Ferris wheel—*wait a second.*

That's the picture Felicity shoved in my face at the hospital. I didn't get a close look at it before. The picture on the screen is so pretty it looks fake. The lights of the pier are like brush strokes against a black canvas. There's an ethereal glow in the center, highlighting a tall boy bent over a shorter girl. His hand is in her hair. She's clutching his waist. Her cute cropped hoodie is riding up, exposing a sliver of skin. Their lips are fused together. My heart rate picks up and butterflies flutter in my stomach. I trace the outline of his back and then press my thumb against my lips.

What had it felt like to have been kissed by *him* like *that?*

I scroll through the Easton Royal hashtag (because, of course, he has his own hashtag). I pause on one that was taken a year ago. It's dark, but I can make out the two individuals in the picture. It's Easton and his stepsister/foster sister/ whatever, Ella. She looks hot in a black bandage dress with cutouts. His hands are plastered to the places where her bare skin is exposed. Her arms are wrapped around his neck. Their lips are fused together. His eyes are closed. It's an intimate, tender moment beautifully captured and it makes me want to vomit.

Easton screws around a lot – 5.
Easton likes his foster sister – 5.
Felicity's right about a lot of shit – 4.

Unfortunately.

The bell rings. I force myself to turn off the computer. The chair at the end of the table scrapes against the floor, catching my attention. I look up and meet some girl's eyes. She gives me a quick onceover and then flounces off without a word.

The urge to run after her and apologize is strong despite the fact that I don't know her and don't know why she's mad at me. It's possible I did her wrong before and can't remember. Who knows how many boyfriends I've slept with, how many classes I cheated in, how many times I hurt people?

The accident is the world's slap in my face. Wake up. Wake

up and do better. I straighten my shoulders. I don't know who I was before, but from now on, I'm going to be a decent person.

I head directly for the bus stop in front of the French Twist, only a quarter of a mile away from Astor. The route takes me to the shopping center and from there I can grab the No. 3 line, which will drop me off close to home. It's a hassle, but it's doable.

As I'm walking along the sidewalk, I hear a honk. For the second day in a row, I look up to see Bran Mathis waving at me. From what I got during our conversation yesterday, he's the new quarterback of Astor Park's football team, isn't filthy rich like everyone else at this school, and he seems like a really nice guy.

He pulls over and brakes. "I was going to get some ice cream for my mom. Want some?"

CHAPTER FOURTEEN

Easton

"Do you want anything?" I ask Sawyer. We've been working on assignments for our missed classes for the past two hours and I, for one, am ready for a break.

My brother looks better. There's more pink in his cheeks. The bags under his eyes are more the carry-on size than the fifty-pound luxury steamers that were parked there for the last few days. Between Ella nagging him and me threatening him, he had two meals yesterday and got in at least six hours of sleep. Today, we're aiming for three meals and ten hours of sleep. We've already had breakfast and lunch, played some *Call of Duty* on the PlayStation, and this homework.

What would really be good for Sawyer is to get out of the hospital. Even better if he went back to school. If he needed to watch over someone, he could keep an eye on Hartley for me.

I asked Ella how Hartley was doing. Her "I don't know" was snippy, but I chalk that up to her anxiety over meeting with the lawyer today. Anything that reminds her of her bio dad, Steve, sends her mood into the shitter.

Sawyer shoves his chem book away and casts a guilty glance toward Seb's bed, as if Sawyer isn't allowed to enjoy anything while Seb's comatose.

I jump up and grab my wallet. "I'm getting a double fudge shake from IC's."

Sawyer licks his lips. That's his favorite.

"Um..."

"Yeah, I'll get you a large," I say, not giving him the option.

The drive over to IC is fairly short. It's halfway between the hospital and school. A ton of the Astor Park kids hang out here and I'm not surprised to see the small ice cream shop full when I arrive.

Dom, one of my football teammates, is leaning against the counter along the window feeding his girlfriend, Tamika, from their shared banana split. "Yo, Royal," he yells. "What's up? You drop out?"

"Been at the hospital."

Dom's face becomes comically contorted as he tries to find the right expression. His girlfriend bops him hard in the chest. "Dom. Act civilized for once."

Not that he feels it. Dom's two-hundred-fifty pounds of solid muscle. He'll be at Alabama next year, throwing fear into the hearts of college quarterbacks. "Yeah, sorry," he mumbles, and I don't really know if that apology's directed to me or his girl.

"He's sorry," she clarifies. "His momma would be so embarrassed."

"Don't tell her," he says, looking horrified. "I was just making a joke!"

"It's fine," I reassure him. "It's crowded today." I glance toward the line, not registering anyone in particular.

"Yeah. Willoughby did a pop quiz in Government on Constitutional Amendments." Dom looks ready to cry. And I get it. His mom is scary.

"Sounds like I picked a good time to skip." I pat him on the shoulder. "I'll see you later. I need to get back to the hospital."

I turn to get in line when a five-foot-three-inch body slams into me, spilling an ice cream cone down the front of my BAPE sweatshirt.

"Oh my God, I'm so so sorry." Hartley swipes her hand down my chest, leaving a smear of vanilla ice cream in her wake.

Tamika pushes Hart out of the way and slaps some napkins into my hand. "Girl, you just ruined a fifteen-hundred-dollar sweatshirt with your messy self."

"Fifteen hundred?" Her jaw drops open.

"It's fine," I assure both of them.

Hart's head pops up and her eyes grow saucer-big.

"Is something wrong?" A new voice enters the fray. I look up to see Bran Mathis, a transfer student and the quarterback of my team, peering over Hart's shoulder.

"Yeah," the girls chorus.

"No," I say at the same time.

His eyes dart from the front of my sweatshirt to Hartley and then back to me, lingering on the stylized ape on the front. Unlike Hart, he recognizes the brand. It doesn't matter, though, and I tell them that.

"It's no big deal." I smile down at Hartley. "You look good. Taking care of yourself?" I check her over to see if there are any signs she's still suffering—physically—from her accident or, God forbid, her dad hurt her again.

I don't see anything out of the ordinary. No bruises or cuts or scrapes. No winces of pain or stiffness in the way she moves. A section of her hair falls forward to cover her eyes. I reach out to sweep it back, but a hand comes down on her shoulder and moves her out of the way.

Dom sucks in a breath. Tamika squeaks.

I blink in confusion, following the male hand from my girl's shoulder all the way up to Bran's face. It doesn't register at first—Bran's hand on Hartley's shoulder. Bran's hand where my hand should be.

Hart looks confused, too, like she's not sure why Bran's touching her. I reach out and shove his hand away.

"Not cool, dude."

"Really? You're telling me what's cool? Come on, Hartley. You can have my cone." He pushes his cone—one that's already been in his mouth—toward her face.

I'm not processing what's going on here. Bran Mathis is all over my girl—touching her and telling her to put her mouth where his was? Hell no.

"Thanks, but I'll buy her a new one."

"I don't need—" she starts to say.

"We're actually leaving," Bran cuts in. "I've got to get home."

Hart nods. She actually fucking nods. "Okay. I'm sorry about the sweatshirt. I can clean it for you."

"You can clean it for me?" I repeat like a dumb fuck.

"Yes, if you want. I have your jacket, too."

The room tilts and everything's off kilter. While I'm texting her nonstop, worrying about her every night, sleeping on the floor of her old apartment, trying to convince my baby brother to leave the hospital and go to school so someone can protect Hartley while I'm unable to, she's getting busy with Bran-fucking-Mathis?

Furious, confused and hurt, but refusing to show it, I slap my mask back on—the one I always wore before Hartley came along. "Bro, when I said we were on the same team, I meant football, not doing the same chick."

Hart says something, but the rage storm is thundering too loud in my head to hear. I don't go to school for two days and she's hooked up with the Astor Park quarterback? It's like I'm the one that hit my head a week ago. I'm suffering hallucinations and my current timeline is some grotesque parody of what's going on in the right-side-up world.

"You're just determined to fuck your head up even more, aren't you?" I say to Hartley.

She furrows her brow in confusion. "W-what?"

"The doc said you're not supposed to rely on other people's memories." I wave an angry hand at Bran. "You're not supposed to listen to stories they tell you about yourself, your past—"

Bran interjects. "Hey, I'm not telling her any stories—"

I silence him with a glare, then turn to Hartley. "What you're doing is dangerous," I mutter, and then I leave, because if I stay one second longer, all of the chairs lining the plate-glass storefront are going to be through the window and lying on the curb. The urge to hit something, to drive my fist into something and hear a sickening crunch when the impact lands, is too strong. I jerk open my truck door, nearly ripping it off the hinges.

"Why do you care what she thinks?"

Hanging on to the side of the door, I spin to see Felicity standing a few feet away. She's traded her Astor Park gear for some high-end athleisure. Silk Prada track pants and a cashmere bomber jacket. It's an outfit that would look good on Hartley. I could buy it for her—I shove the thought away.

"It's none of your business."

"She's not worth your time," Felicity continues as if I haven't said a word. "You're richer than Bran. You're better looking. You have better social status. It's natural for the two of them to gravitate together. They operate on the same low sphere." She waves her hand from side to side close to her waist. "You and I, Easton, we belong up here." The hand moves above her head. "Together."

"I'd rather stick my dick in the exhaust pipe of my truck than in you," I reply, and climb into my truck. Felicity doesn't move and I end up having to drive up on the curb to avoid hitting her.

That girl is operating on her last few brain cells if she thinks I'm ever going to get together with her. If she were the last woman on earth and I had to screw her in order to live, I'd throw myself into the nearest volcano.

But she's right about one thing. I do think I'm better for Hartley. It's not that I have more money than Bran, although that's true, too. It's that I'll fight for her. Bran showed some interest in Hartley when she first showed up at Astor Park but after one talk with me, he gave up. He doesn't deserve a second chance. I'm not done with Hart. I'm never—I slam on the brakes, having missed my turn to the hospital. I jerk the truck into reverse and whip it around in the middle of the road, ignoring the honking horns and angry shouts of nearby motorists.

I give them the one finger wave and shoot into the hospital driveway, leaving the truck in the valet lane. I toss the keys to the waiting attendant. "Easton Royal," I say through clenched teeth and then whip through the front door without waiting.

I'm still hot when I reach Seb's room.

"That didn't take long," Sawyer chirps when I storm in.

I throw myself onto the rock-hard sofa and flip on the television.

"Did you bring me a shake?"

"You said you didn't want one," I growl.

"I never said a thing. You told me you'd bring me a large."

"If you want one so bad, get it your own damn self." I jab the channel button and flip through the options—none of them are good. ESPN? Who wants to watch bowling? USA? Is that *Baywatch* again? How old are these fucks? MTV? Teen pregnancy? Thanks but no.

"What crawled up your ass and died?"

Hart, I want to scream, but I don't because I'm not a baby. I'm a man and I don't get torn up about shit like this. About girls moving on to other guys. About people who you care about giving up on you. Those emotions are for the weak and stupid.

I gave all that up when my mom killed herself. Her promise to love me forever lasted until I was fourteen. And Hartley never said those words to me. There are no oaths broken, no lies stated. She can't even remember me. I'm that unimportant.

"This fucking room did." I fling the remote aside. "We don't need milkshakes, Sawyer. We're not ten. We need booze. That's the only way we're going to make it through this shit."

"Yeah?" He sounds intrigued. "But does the hospital allow that?"

He whispers the last part as if talking about it is as illegal as drinking it.

"How will they know?"

"Where are you going to get it?"

I grab my backpack and rip it open. Inside, at the bottom, are the two bottles of Smirnoff that have been clinking around in there since the last football game of the season. There's only about a third left. I twist open the cap and offer the bottle to him.

"You carry around a bottle of vodka?" Sawyer says in surprise, taking the booze and tipping it to his mouth.

I feel a twinge of guilt, but I shove it aside. Is it that abnormal to carry around a little liquor? It's not like I've drank anything in weeks—not since the accident. And I don't plan to drive right now. I'm here until Ella shows up, and by that time I'll be sober. A few ounces of Smirnoff won't be getting me tanked. I might not even get a buzz.

"There's not much here." Sawyer swipes a hand across his mouth.

"There's more in my truck," I promise, because it's true—I always stash a few extra bottles in the trunk compartment where I keep the car jack. Grinning at Sawyer, I tip my head back to pour the vodka straight down my throat.

CHAPTER FIFTEEN

Hartley

IT ALL HAPPENS SO SUDDENLY. The ice cream falling off the cone. Bran's hand resting on my shoulder. Easton storming out. Every eye in the joint seems to be stuck on me. I don't think I was ever the center of attention before my accident, because it doesn't feel comfortable. I glance down to double check that my zipper is up, only to see I'm still in my Astor Park plaid skirt.

I'm all put together—at least on the outside. On the inside, I'm confused and shaky and want to sink into the floor. But in the two days that I've been back at school, I've learned quickly that a show of weakness is an invitation to be targeted.

I straighten my shoulders, tip my chin up, and walk out. The afternoon sun hits my face and momentarily blinds me. I trip on my own two clumsy feet and nearly face-plant into the concrete. Chagrined, I slink over to Bran's car and wait for him to join me.

He does about five minutes later, carting a new cone for me.

"Here. I didn't want you to go home empty-handed." He holds it out, but I don't take it, because I'm at the point where I'm concerned that taking an ice cream treat is a substitution for an agreement to go down a path I don't want to travel.

"What was that all about?" I ask.

"What was what all about?" He blinks innocently while taking a bite of his own cone.

I don't appreciate him playing dumb and I give him a look that says exactly that. Since he's not completely clueless, he rubs his lips together and glances away.

"I thought you said we were friends," I say. He's lucky it's cold outside or that ice cream would be dripping down his fingers.

"We were. We are," he says to the parking meter.

"Then why are you acting like there's something more between us?" I mean, it's possible, but I doubt it. I'm not conceited enough to think that I've somehow managed to land the most popular kid in my bed, as well as the high school quarterback. All of this attention—the venom from Felicity, the treatment at school, this boy with the sunny smile carting me around town for the last two days—all of it stems from something that's only loosely related to me. The center of the storm is Easton Royal. I'm just getting kickback from floating in the jet stream behind him. "What do you have against Easton?"

My question flusters Bran so much he doesn't answer right away, taking refuge behind his cone. I wait until he finishes it, which doesn't take him long.

"I like Easton," he says. "He was a scary defensive end and I'm glad that I didn't have to face him on the field for a game. He's fun to hang around with, but…"

There's always a but. I'm starting to get riled up on Easton's behalf. "If he's a good guy, then maybe you shouldn't be doing stuff that intentionally pisses him off. I'm not a game piece that you can move around to score points off of other people."

Bran scowls. "That's not what I'm doing."

"Then explain."

"Fine." He folds his arms across his chest. "He's a player, all right? I don't want to see you taken advantage of in your condition."

Bran sees me as weak and vulnerable. A damsel needing saving. I might not be in top form at the moment, but I can fight my own battles.

"I don't know much about what happened to me in the last few years, but I plan to figure it out, and that's probably something I should do alone. Thanks for the snack and the ride." I start to leave.

Bran's hand snakes out and grabs my wrist. "Hartley, wait. I'm sorry. It was a kneejerk reaction. My sister got dicked over by a guy like Easton, and I didn't want to see it happen to you. That's all."

Gently, I peel his fingers off my wrist. "I believe you, and I appreciate your concern, but I'm still taking the bus."

I leave him on the curb and walk off toward the bus stop. Taking those rides with Bran didn't feel right before but I couldn't figure out why. He was nice and nonthreatening. He didn't make any moves on me. He answered my questions to the best of his ability, even the awkward ones about my cheating. But I never felt fully comfortable with him. It wasn't until I ran into Easton that I realized why.

Guilt had spiraled through me when I looked up into

those ocean-blue eyes. I felt like I'd done something wrong. When Bran's hand came down on my shoulder, a moment of shock and hurt flashed across Easton's face before the shutters slammed down and he tried laughing his way out of the situation. I felt as bad as if Easton had walked in on me and Bran naked.

And Easton's totally right. I've been doing everything that the doctor advised me against. Every night I strain to remember who I was for the last three years, and every day someone inserts some version of their truth into my head. Or I absorb it. Either way, it's all mixed up like my head's full of M&M's and Skittles. I can't tell the chocolate from the candy and when I try to, I get an awful taste.

So maybe I don't look back. Missing those three years is awful, but isn't it worse trying to remember and failing? Or trying to remember and coming up with only really bad things? Maybe this is a gift? How many people get a very real opportunity to shed themselves of the guilt over their past sins and move forward unfettered?

Why don't I take this restart and form new relationships—with my parents, my sister, my teachers and my Astor Park classmates. I should count my blessings. It's not everyone who gets a diploma from Astor Park Prep. I'll be able to get into nearly any college I want based on the strength of my high school degree. Astor Park is *that* prestigious.

What good is it to try to build a past with fragments of other people's memories? They aren't even memories, then, only stories—fictionalized events. If I had to create a film reel of my past, I'd be the heroine. Someone who read to the lonely elderly at retirement villages or who saved animals or dug trenches in villages. I wouldn't be this spineless social climber who used anyone within her grasp to move ahead.

Straining to remember or trying to make up for things I did in the past is only doing more harm than good. From now on, I'm going to own my memory loss. If someone seems to not like me, I won't ask what I did, but instead ask for forgiveness. I'm going to stop entertaining stories from people like Kyle and Felicity, because even though some of the things they've told me are true, they aren't helpful.

So what if I can't remember the giddy sweetness when I first held a boy's hand or the triumph of getting a good grade on a project I slaved over? Or the warmth during the holidays sitting around a tree, singing carols and beaming with joy as people I love open gifts I carefully chose for them? It doesn't matter, I tell myself. I can create new memories. And these ones won't be tainted by whatever horrible moral code I had before my fall.

I climb onto the bus, drop my change into the coin slot, and take a seat in the back.

I'll experience all those firsts again. The first love. The first kiss. The first time. I swipe the tears away from my face. It's a miracle, really. A salty rivulet seeps into the corner of my mouth. The tears are coming faster than I can brush them off.

A true blessing.

I repeat this to myself all the way home, hoping that by the time I step into my house, I'll believe it.

CHAPTER SIXTEEN

Easton

"It smells like a distillery in here," Ella's voice says from above. It sounds like she's speaking through a tube, a long one.

I gesture for her to come closer. "What'd you say?"

"You stink."

Something wet and heavy lands on my face. "The hell!"

"Can you stop slurring your words?"

I'm not slurring them. I'm speaking perfect English. Something must be wrong with her hearing. "What's wrong?"

"Ugh. Sawyer. Sawyer! Oh, hell. You're drunk, too. Just perfect. I'm sorry, Callum. But neither of your sons can come to the phone right now. They finished off a bottle of vodka."

I raise my fingers. It was three. How insulting she thinks we gave up after one nearly empty bottle.

"Pour water in their faces? I threw a washcloth on Easton and he barely moved. Yeah, I'll try again."

A washcloth! That's what this thing is. I shove it off my face. It takes two tries before I can dislodge it enough to be able to breathe. "Give me the pho—"

Splash!

A deluge of water drowns out the rest of my words. I shoot straight up from the sofa and blink angrily at Ella through the fluid dripping into my eyes. "What the hell?"

"That did it," she says into her phone, surprise in her voice. She listens to whomever is on the other end of the line—did she say Callum?—and throws me a towel.

I catch it and wipe my face, not taking my eyes off her in case she decides to dump another gallon of water over my head. My brain sluggishly churns into gear. She's talking to my dad.

"I have no idea if he's capable of carrying on a conversation. He's got a towel in his fist and he's probably imagining squeezing my neck with the same force."

I'm not gonna do that, but I am mad. Ella and I have always been tight. I didn't think she'd rat out my drinking to my dad.

I shove off the sofa and pluck the phone out of her hands. "How's Dubai?"

See, I remember what's going on. My personal triumph lasts all of a second because the room starts spinning. Dad says something I can't make out because it's hard to concentrate on what he's saying when I'm busy focusing on not tossing my metaphorical cookies all over the marble table. "Can you repeat that?" I ask.

"I asked you to take care of everyone while I was gone. You promised that you could handle it."

There's a pause. I guess he's waiting for my input. "I'm handling it."

"By getting your underage brother drunk in the hospital room where his twin is lying comatose?"

This time the churning sensation in my stomach has nothing to do with my liquor intake. "Well, when you put it like that, it does sound bad," I say, cracking a shitty joke.

There's a prolonged silence on the other end of the phone as Dad is probably fantasizing about throwing me off his hundred-and-fifth-floor hotel room balcony.

"I'm waiting for you to grow up, Easton. You're eighteen. God help the people beyond Bayview, because I'm going to have to unleash you on them."

He makes me sound like an ecological disaster...although, didn't I once tell Ella we Royals were like a Category 4 hurricane? Maybe he's not so off. Still, it's not awesome to hear your father run you down like this. Another shot of vodka could make this lecture so much more tolerable. I search the room, trying to locate my backpack. Did we drink it all or is there at least one bottle left?

"Until you can prove you're a functioning adult, I'm going to treat you like a child. That means in addition to no flying, there will be no car."

"I don't drive a car. I'm a truck guy."

"I swear to Christ, Easton Royal!" he explodes. "This is not a joke. Life is not a joke. Your behavior is very dangerous. Straighten up or you'll spend the next semester at The Citadel. From this point on, you have no wheels, you have no money. If you want something, you'll have to get permission from me and I'll want the request in written form. Do you hear me?"

"I think the whole floor hears you," I reply. I run my tongue around my dry mouth. I'm feeling super dehydrated. Where is that damn bottle?

"I only care to get through to one person, but I don't think it's working. I'll be back in twenty-four hours. Try not to fuck up too much until then," he booms and then he hangs up.

I stare at the phone. "He hung up on me."

Ella reaches over and plucks the device from my hand. "Are you surprised? You're drunk in a hospital, Easton. Your little brother is passed out—the one whose heart is aching because his best friend and twin is in a coma. You're cracking jokes about it because, for some reason, it's too hard for you to apologize. I love you, East, but your wheels are coming off."

A dark, mean feeling rises in my chest. She's not even family. Her last name isn't Royal. It's O'Halloran. She shouldn't even be here. The only reason she's even living at our house is because my dad felt sorry for an orphan who he found stripping in some dirt-hole club. She keeps her place in this family by sleeping with my brother. She—

"Durand's here to stay with the twins. I'll drive you home."

My dad's driver steps into the room, a magazine rolled up in his large fist.

I swallow my angry words.

"Super." I stalk over to my backpack and throw it over my shoulder, pretending that the clinking noise it makes is the result of two soda bottles rubbing together rather than the empty Smirnoff containers. Shame prickles through me, and I find it hard to look at Ella. If she knew what I was thinking, she'd be hurt.

When did I become this asshole? That's my brother Reed's role. Mine has always been the fun-loving Royal. The guy who knows how to have a good time. Is Ella right? Are my wheels coming off?

It's the hospital. Between Hart showing up with Bran, and Seb still in his coma, I'm losing it. I rein in my temper, remind myself that Ella's on my side even if she isn't acting like it, and exit behind her. Neither of us says a word as we walk down the hall or when we step into the elevator to the first floor. The silence feels heavy and awkward as if she knew what I was thinking.

I try to break the ice. "The hospital is actually the number one place to have a bender. If you're in any danger, there's a nurse to hook you up to an IV."

She sighs. "And I'm sure that was your first thought when you refilled your underage brother's glass, wasn't it?"

"The twins drink all the time, Ella. You think this is the first time Sawyer's gotten wasted?"

"That's not the point. He shouldn't be drinking when he's this upset over Seb—"

"Did you become Sheriff since I last saw you or what?" I snap. I'm having a real tough time keeping the big ammo back. Does she want me to bring up her damn past?

"Excuse me for caring," she snipes back.

The pressure in my chest grows again. "Listen, Ella, I already have a dad, so why don't you back the fuck off," I growl.

"Fine." She throws up her hands and stomps out. "I'm worried about you, okay? I love you. I don't want you to end up in a body bag!"

"Yeah, well, I will if I don't let off steam now and then," I shout back.

"Is there a problem here?"

We both jerk around to see a cop staring at us with an anxious expression. My dad will have a coronary if he gets a call in Dubai that Ella and I got hauled into the city jail for fighting. I don't know how much more trauma my family can take.

"No," I say.

"No," Ella choruses at the same time. "We were just leaving," she adds and grabs my hand. I let her drag me along behind her until we reach her car.

I shake her off and climb in, moving the car seat back as far as it goes. Deciding it's best if I keep my mouth shut, I close my eyes and pretend to rest.

Unfortunately, Ella's not done with me. "Val saw you with Felicity at the IC. What did she want?"

Shit, there are spies everywhere.

"To suck my dick." I prop my knee up because there's no room in Ella's tiny car for my legs. How does Reed even fit in here? I swear my old man bought this matchbox of a car so that Ella and Reed wouldn't have any space to mess around in it—not that it's stopped them. The two can't keep their hands off each other, and their bedrooms are about ten feet apart. The only thing that keeps them from screwing like bunny rabbits is Reed's absence. He's up at State during the week so Ella spends most of her nights alone.

I suspect they do some kinky shit using their computers, but I'm not real interested in their sex life, particularly since I've been in a serious dry spell. Hartley and I never made it that far—not for lack of effort on my part. She wasn't ready, so I had to tuck my dick away. That wasn't easy. Beating the meat is never as good as being inside a girl.

"What's the sigh for?" Ella asks. "Felicity?"

"Fuck no. I'm thinking about how many times I've had to jerk off because Hartley wasn't ready for sex."

Ella groans. "Really, East? You could've kept that information to yourself."

"Babe, you asked what the sigh was for. I answered. If you don't like the answers, don't ask the questions."

"Fine. Fine." She sinks into her seat.

I refuse to feel bad for snapping at her. Or sharing some lewd thoughts with her. Ella ratted me out. If she's not interested in my business, she should learn to keep her damn nose out of it.

"Where's your spare set of keys?" I ask.

"What for?"

"What do you think?" I frown at her obtuseness.

"I can't lend you my car, Easton. Callum said we're not allowed to help you."

For a girl who used to strip for a living to pay for her bills, her straight edges are sharper than flint.

"Ella, now is not the time to remember obedience. We don't answer to Callum. We Royal kids are our own country. The only people in charge are us and if we stick together, then we're strong. It's once we start eating our own that the walls all fall down."

"Is that what you think?"

"It's not what I think. It's the truth." Has she forgotten her own past? The one where we stood by her, held her up under the Royal name, served as her fucking shields? I'm starting to lose it.

"I don't know, East. Remember what you said before? About how all you know is tearing stuff down and not building it up? I feel like we're on the verge of ruin. Like we're standing on the Cliffs of Insanity and one wrong decision and the cliff will drop away."

I try to joke because if I don't, I might bite her head off. "You're thinking this way because you're not getting enough dick. I'd offer you mine, but I don't think Hartley would like it." If she ever remembers she's dating me.

"God, Easton, it's not all about sex, okay? It's about us as a family. Sebastian's in a coma. Sawyer's unraveling each minute that Seb is not awake. Gideon is wrapped up in Savannah and can't see past her tits, while Reed is busy with college. You and me"—she waves a finger between us—"we have to be the adults."

"Here's the problem with you, Ella. You don't get what it means to truly be a Royal. Adulting is for people who don't have trust funds or five-figure weekly allowances. In order for our great economy to roll along, you and I have to spend that money—that means we go out and pursue fun in all its glorious forms."

"And how do you propose to do that while Seb is in a coma? Because Callum has thrown all his money at the problem and Seb still isn't awake. Have you looked at your other brother? He's like a zombie. A walking coma victim."

I blow out a long, frustrated stream of air. "You're a real buzz kill." My old man took away my pilot's license last year after a hard bout of drinking. I figured I'd just wait him out. Eventually, he'd cave. He always has in the past. Not this time, though. It's just gotten worse. "I can't believe Dad took my truck away."

I mean, yeah, if I wasn't drunk, I wouldn't have confronted Hart's dad, which means she wouldn't have driven away upset and Seb's speeding would've been another day on the road. Still, it's one thing for me to feel guilty and a whole other thing for my dad to be placing the blame on me.

Ella shoots me a sad look. "And the motorcycle. You're fully grounded now, not just from flying but all forms of motor vehicles. He said Durand will drive you from now on."

"I'm not even the one who got in the accident. It was Seb." But I don't say it with much conviction, because I feel pretty damn guilty.

"And he's paying for it, isn't he? Callum doesn't want to lose another one of his sons."

"Come on, Ella. You know this is bullshit. I'll just buy another car. I can easily do that with the money in my bank account." I've got more than one account. There's a checking account, a savings account, a money market account, a brokerage account, and, obviously, my trust fund. So Dad cut me off from my trust. Big whoop.

Her gaze shifts to stare out the window. Suspicious at her evasion, I pull out my phone and navigate to the bank app. Sure enough, it's zeroed out. I open my stock app, but I can't even get into it. The password's been changed. I check the other apps and those too are locked.

"Motherfucker!" I heave my phone against the dashboard. There's a sickening crack as it falls to the floor. I pick it up and run my finger over the broken screen. "How'd you find out about this?" I demand, with barely leashed fury.

She still can't look me in the eye. "Callum texted and asked me to drive you home. He called you a dozen times. He was worried."

"That asshole lets me drink all the time when I'm at home."

"*Home* being the operative word," she cries. "When you were home, he could monitor you. But, East, sometimes you take it too far. Sawyer shouldn't be drinking right now, not in the state of mind he's in. He's already messed up as it is."

"Yeah? So why can't he have a fucking moment's peace in his head after everything he's going through?" I shout back. "That's all we want! For the voices in our heads to shut the fuck up!"

"Reed says—"

My rage hits an incandescent level. "I don't want to hear what motherfucking Reed has to say."

My brother and arguably my closest friend are conspiring against me. In my family, I've always been the odd kid out. Reed and Gid were the oldest. They were super fucked up but stuck together, keeping their secrets that nearly got Ella killed and Reed thrown in prison. The twins were nearly one unit. They spoke their own silent language, took all the same classes, swapped clothes, played the same sports, slept with the same girl.

Mom gave me extra attention because of it. This is why I'm getting shafted now. Reed is jealous because he always wanted more of Mommy's time and didn't get it. Now he's turning Ella against me.

"Don't be mad," she says.

I nearly bite my tongue off in an effort to not respond. The minute she hits the brakes in front of our house, I shoot out the door. She shouts something behind me, but I don't care enough to decipher it. If they want to push me out of the family, they're doing a damn good job.

I haul ass upstairs to my closet. I press a button under the center shelf and wait the long ten seconds for the false panel at the back to rise. Once the safe is revealed, I punch in the code and grab my cash. It's not a lot—only five grand, but I should be able to find a poker game in town to win a little more. I stuff my LV cabin bag with some underwear, a change of clothes, my stupid fucking Astor Park uniform, and toiletries.

Once that's done, I make a call to Pash, one of the few decent people I know. Day or night, the guy is always on his phone. Predictably, he answers after the second ring.

"What's going on, man? I'm in the middle of something." He sounds strained.

"I need a ride."

"What happened to your truck?"

"It's getting serviced."

"Don't you have a fleet of cars there? Oh shit—right there, baby."

I roll my eyes. Of course, Pash is still answering his phone in the middle of a lay. "My old man is piss-his-pants scared another kid is going to end up in the hospital. None of us are allowed to drive except Ella."

This time Pash's groan is nonsexual. Ella's reputation for driving no faster than thirty-five miles per hour is a well-known phenomenon at Astor Park.

"Dude, I'm so sorry. Can you give me… Hold on, babe." He pauses, apparently trying to calculate how long it's going to take to finish.

"Forget it." I'm not so hard up that I'm going to interrupt a friend's happy time. "I'll call for a car."

"Thank God," he says in relief. "I'll call you later."

"Don't worry about it."

"No. This won't last long. Ouch. Damn. No, I'm going down on you. I told you I would. Shit," he says into the phone. "I gotta go."

I swallow a laugh, feeling a little more normal. My world is screwed up, but everyone else's is operating as usual.

I step outside so that Ella and I don't piss each other off even more. I walk down the long drive to the entrance gate. While I wait for the car, I pull up my texts to Hart. She still hasn't read them. That makes me mad and sad and frustrated. Why in the hell is she hanging out with Bran? Does she remember him but not me? That thought makes me want to chuck my already broken phone on the asphalt until it's nothing but a pile of tiny metal pieces. Of course, if my phone is destroyed and Hart tries to text me, I'll miss it.

What is Bran doing? Is he fucking with her head like Felicity? Is he trying to get in her pants now that she's vulnerable? What kind of sketchy asshole behavior is that? I scroll through my contacts. I have him in here. I'm sure of it.

"Gotcha," I say when I come across his entry. I shoot him a text.

Don't fuck with my girl.

He responds immediately. *I'm looking out for her.*

Me: That's not your job.
Bran: You're not around.

The hell I'm not, I type in, but before I press send, the accuracy of his accusation sets in. He's right, that fucker. I'm not at school. He is. As long as I'm playing watchdog for Seb at the hospital, Hartley is on her own over there at Astor Park.

I shove my phone back in my pocket without responding

to Bran. I'm letting this go for now, because as pissed as I am that he's treading on my territory, Mathis is a good guy. He'll—I clench my teeth and my fists—he'll look out for Hartley at school. She needs that.

But he better stay the fuck out of her pants.

"You're going to the east end? Is that right?" my driver asks ten minutes later, after I slide into the backseat. He's a thin male with a nose two sizes too big for his face. He taps his screen as if he's sure that it's malfunctioning.

"Yup."

"You work here?" he asks, jerking his head toward the house.

"Something like that." I slip a pair of headphones over my head, and the driver takes the hint by shutting up. The place I'm going is a far cry from the one I'm leaving, but it's the only place I can think to go.

She's not there, but it's her home. And mine now, too.

CHAPTER SEVENTEEN

Hartley

I'm not so sure that I was sent away so much as I ran away, I decide later that evening. The Wright household is a nightmare. My dad is glued to his phone twenty-four/seven. My little sister, who I remember being moody, has turned into a full-fledged demon seed who's likely to kill me off in my sleep some night. My oldest sister hasn't been to the house since my first day home. My mom talks constantly about what a certain Mrs. Carrington is doing. This week Mrs. Carrington is doing a soup cleanse.

"We should try it," she suggests to Dad as he devours his pot roast and sweet potatoes.

He doesn't look up from his phone.

"It's very nourishing. We could do plant-based or bone-based broths. Mrs. Carrington read this article to us about a company out of Los Angeles that sells a month-long program. It's very reasonable, but if you don't think we should pay for the food I'm sure I could come up with a few recipes of my own."

"Can you believe this shit?" Dad answers, shaking his phone at us. "Callum Royal is getting nominated for another philanthropic award. Can't anyone in Bayview see through his carpetbaggin' nonsense? He's just buying everyone off so they can't see what a corrupt son of a bitch he is."

"Callum Royal's family has been here for about five generations," Mom chirps. "I wouldn't call him a carpetbagger."

Dad slams his hand on the table. We all jump. "You'd stick up for Jack the Ripper if he had enough money."

Mom pales and Dylan looks like she wants to slide under the table.

"That's not true, John. You know I don't like the Royals either." She pushes the potato dish into my hand and gestures with her chin to give Dad another helping. He's already had two. Maybe she thinks he can be put into a carb coma and he'll stop being mad at her.

In the short time I've been home from the hospital, I've learned we all give my dad a wide berth. He has a temper and a sharp tongue, which, I suppose, serves him well in the courtroom. His phone rings and he takes the call right there at the dinner table.

No one is surprised, so I act like it's normal, too, even though I think this is weird. Why not get up and go to his office? Why not wait until we're done eating?

"How was school today?" Mom asks to distract me.

It works. I swing my attention away from my father.

"It was good," I lie. Or maybe it's not a lie but rather hope. I'm speaking the future I want into existence.

Across from me, Dylan snorts. She hasn't been in a good mood since I returned from the hospital.

I set my spoon down and gather up my patience. "What is it now?" I ask. "Am I eating wrong again?"

Last night, my baby sister told me the way I chewed my food made her want to hurl. She made gagging sounds at the table until Dad yelled at her to go to her room.

"Everything about you is wrong. You shouldn't be here."

"I know. You've told me that a million times since I got back from the *hospital*." I emphasize the last word, but the little shit doesn't care. In fact, if she could get away with it, I think she'd put me back there.

"You're gross."

"Thank you for your unasked opinion."

"I wish you'd stayed in New York."

"I heard you the first dozen times you said it."

"You're gross."

"You already said that, too."

"But you're still sitting here, exposing me to your grossness." Dylan turns to Mom. "Why is she back? I thought Dad said he never wanted to see her again."

"Hush," Mom chastises and flicks a guilty look in my direction.

Dad never wanted to see me again? I twist to stare at him, but he's still occupied with his phone call. "There's going to be a lot of press involved," he's saying. He sounds excited about this.

"You said she was going to ruin everything and that she had to be punished for that," my sister presses.

"You need to hush up, Dylan. Now finish your dinner." Mom's lips thin. "And you, Hartley, go put your uniform in the dryer so it smells nice for tomorrow."

"Yes, ma'am." I rise ungracefully and knock the table with my hips, sending Dylan's nearly full milk glass spilling over.

"God, you are such a clumsy bitch," she snarls.

"That's enough!" bellows Dad.

The three of us jump in surprise. I hadn't realized he'd hung up the phone. By Dylan's shocked face, she didn't either or she never would've cursed.

"That's enough," he repeats with a sneer. "I'm tired of your garbage mouth. Are you taking your medication?" His hand is curled into a fist.

I shrink back. Across from me, a shaft of fear skips across Dylan's face.

"Y-y-yes," she stutters, but the lie is so obvious that I wince in sympathy.

"Why isn't she taking her goddamned medicine?" Dad bellows at Mom.

She wrings the napkin between her fingers. "I give them to her every morning."

"If you did, she wouldn't be acting like a little bitch, would she?" He abruptly pushes away from the table, sending everything tottering.

Dylan's eyes well up. "I'll take it," she mumbles. "I missed it just today."

Dad's not listening. He's in the kitchen, jerking open a drawer and pulling out a pill bottle. With the amber container clutched in his hand, he marches back and slams it down on the table. "Take it," he orders.

My sister stares at the medicine as if it's poison. Slowly, her arm rises from her lap, but she doesn't move fast enough for Dad.

"I'm tired of your bullshit." He sweeps the bottle out of her reach, wrenches it open and pours what seems like half the pills into his palm. "You're a moody little shit who cusses like the only thing she has in her mouth is trash. I'm not going to stand for this. Do you hear me?" He squeezes her mouth in his hands until it opens.

"Stop! I'll take it!" Dylan cries. Tears are running down her face.

"Dad, please," I say, reaching across the table as if I can somehow stop this. This is crazy. He's using too much pressure. The skin of Dylan's jaw is turning white where his fingers are pressing into her face.

"You sit down. I told you she was a bad influence on Dylan. She should've never been allowed back in this house." He shoves two pills into Dylan's mouth, seemingly oblivious to the tears that are dripping onto his hand. "Swallow it, girl. Do you hear me? You swallow it right now." He pushes her mouth shut, covers her nose and lips with his big hand until she swallows.

I glance to Mom for help, but she's not even looking at us. Her gaze is pinned on the back wall as if by pretending she can't see this insanity, it doesn't exist.

"You done?" he demands.

Dylan nods miserably, but Dad still doesn't let her go. He forcibly opens her jaw again and runs his finger inside her mouth, even to the back of her throat until she gags. Finally, when he's satisfied, he releases her and sits down, calmly wiping his hands on the napkin, and then picks up his phone.

"May I be excused?" Dylan says stiffly.

"Of course, dear," Mom answers as if nothing out of the ordinary just took place.

Dylan flees from the table. I stare after her.

"I…" How do you tell your parents that you disagree with their parenting? That this is all wrong. That they shouldn't be treating their children like this.

"I can see you're upset, Hartley," Mom adds, "but your sister really needs this medication and sometimes when she doesn't take them, she hurts herself. Your father is simply trying to protect her."

"It doesn't seem like that." Without another word, I flee the dining room, running after Dylan.

She's locked herself in her bedroom. I can hear the muffled cries. My own jaw aches in sympathy. "Hey, it's me."

"Go away," she snarls. "I was fine until you came along."

"Please, I just want to help."

"Then go away!" she screams. "I wish you died in that accident. Go away and never come back."

I back away. She's upset. Super upset and who wouldn't be? If Dad grabbed my face and poured pills down my throat, I'd be crying in my room, too. But Dylan's words feel personal— as if she's angry at something I did. My vow to forget about the past is idiotic. I can't move forward, not while everyone else's reaction to me is based on their memories. I wish I could remember this. If I'm only allowed to recover one thing, let it be why my relationship with Dylan is so screwed up.

I drop my forehead against her door. "I'm sorry," I tell her. "I'm sorry I hurt you. I don't remember, but I'm sorry."

She responds with silence, which is a thousand times worse than her insults.

"I'm sorry," I say again. "I'm sorry." I slide down until my ass hits the floor. "I'm sorry." I repeat the words on loop until my throat grows sore and my butt is numb. And still there's no sound in return.

"Hartley, come away from your sister's door," Mom's voice urges from above.

I twist around to see her climbing the stairs. She stops halfway up and motions for me to meet her. I shake my head because I don't have the energy.

"Your sister has issues, don't you remember?"

I shake my head. My last memories of Dylan are of her as a child—a moody one, but a child nonetheless. This young thirteen-year-old girl going on twenty-five is new to me.

"She gets in these moods because she doesn't take her medication." Mom twists her fingers. "And then your father gets angry." She waves her hand in agitation. "It's a vicious cycle. Don't take it personally."

I nod, welcoming the absolution even if I don't deserve it.

"Come away from there now." She waves again, this time for me to come to her.

I move slowly toward the stairs, sliding my butt down one step at a time like I did when I was a baby.

Mom presses money into my hand. "Take the car and go see your friends. There must be a place that you can hang out at for a while. Just until your father calms down."

I don't want to leave. I want to crawl into my bed and pull the covers way up over my head and sleep long enough for this nightmare to be over.

"Where would I go?" I ask hoarsely.

A flash of annoyance skips over her face. "Go and meet with your friends. It's barely eight. They must be out doing things."

"I don't think—"

"Don't think. Just go."

And somehow that's how I find myself sitting behind the wheel of my mom's Acura staring at the lights at the intersection of West and 86th Street, not sure what direction to go. Not sure where I belong in this world. Not sure if I can take another day of this without completely falling apart.

CHAPTER EIGHTEEN

Easton

"Pash, you are the man," I crow as I dump the contents of the paper bag I ripped out of his hands five seconds ago. "Was your girl too mad?"

"I promised to buy her a Birkin, so I could run over her dog and she'd still keep my place warm. This is…interesting," he comments, looking around the apartment. "Are you doing some kind of social experiment for Ethics like Barnaby Pome did last year?"

"What? No." I kiss the two bottles of Ciroc and line them up on the counter next to two glasses and the bag of ice I discovered at the convenience store on the corner. Who knew ice came in bags? "Pome's an idiot. Didn't he get worms or something fucked up like that? I don't even take Ethics."

Ethical Lifestyles is a whacked-out class at Astor Park. The intentions may have been good when the class was conceived, but we Astor kids know how to fuck up anything. One guy almost burned down the school trying to smoke his classmate's hemp-only clothes. Another girl got sent to the hospital after trying to live in a tree for a month. The worst was Barnaby Pome who decided to be a fruitarian and would only eat fruit. As the semester progressed, he said he would only eat fruit that was grown on its own roots, which is apparently super hard in this day and age of biologically cultivated foods. He took to scavenging on the Bayview shore and in the woods over on the golf course. It was only a matter of time before he was going to get sick. Rumor has it they found a foot-long tapeworm in his stomach from something he'd eaten off the forest floor.

"Then what's all this?"

I glance up from sorting through the goodies Pash brought me to see him standing in the middle of the apartment, turning in a slow circle. "It's an apartment."

"I know that, dumbass, but what are you doing here?"

"It's Hart's apartment," I say simply. That should explain everything.

But Pash doesn't get it because he keeps asking questions. "Then where's Hartley?"

"At her parents' house."

"There isn't anything here."

"Gold star for you, Captain Obvious." I stare at the pile I sorted. There's a vape, e-juice, a couple bags of chips, a small baggie of weed and some papers. Where's the good stuff?

"Are you sleeping on the floor of this hellhole because you're hoping that Hartley remembers where you guys had sex and comes running back here?"

I stiffen and shoot Pash a glare. "First, you don't talk about Hart like that. Ever." I stare steadily at him until his eyes drop to the floor. "Second, there's nothing wrong with this place. It's cozy."

"Fine, but you do realize you're looking like a nutless wonder waiting for the headcase to remember she's in love with you."

Pash's bravery stems from a friendship that started when we were young enough to think that eating dirt was the bomb, but I warned him once. I cross the distance in two strides and have his collar in my fist in the next one, driving him straight into the wall.

"I told you not to talk about her like that."

His eyes widen in alarm. "S-s-sorry, man," he stutters, clawing at my grip.

"It's not happening again, is it?" It's not really a question.

Pash gets that. He nods furiously. "Never again. Never," he vows.

I release him and stomp back to the stash of goods on the counter.

"Dude, this was a Prada limited runway edition from the upcoming Paris show," Pash complains. "I just got it two days ago straight from Milan."

"I feel real bad for you. Where's the coke I asked you to pick up? Or Molly?"

He clears his throat. I eye him suspiciously.

"Yeah, the thing is, I'm worried about you, E-man. You're acting all weird since the accident."

"Because I don't want to hear you talk shit about my girlfriend?"

"No. Because you're ignoring your friends, you nearly ran over a kid in the school zone earlier today, and you look like you've already been on a twenty-four-hour bender. I care about you and that's why I didn't bring you any hardcore drugs. You want them, get them your own damn self." Pash jerks his collar into place and stalks toward the door. The flimsy wooden piece nearly falls off the hinges as he slams the door behind him.

The echo of his footsteps is the only sound I hear for a long while. Even the voices in my head—the ones I try to drown out with the pills, the booze, and the fighting—that are always there are silenced. In the quiet, I feel it. The intense loneliness that I try to keep away. The gaping hole in my heart that I've tried to fill with girls, girls, and more girls becomes a canyon that has no bottom, no end. I'm no longer on the edge, staring into the abyss. I'm in it. I'm freefalling in this endless darkness.

I grab the first bottle and rip it open, foregoing the glass and the ice and guzzling it down. If I could inject the alcohol into my veins I would.

I take the bottle over to my carry-on and sit on the floor. When I close my eyes, I trade the canyon for a different dark. One where the clouds are closer to the sky. The black night is broken up with streaks of red and green and white. Hartley's hand is in mine. She's laughing. Her face is close enough to raise my blood pressure—among other things.

It's been more than two weeks. Her perfume still lingers in the truck. I can still feel her silky black hair sliding over my fingers. Her mint lip gloss tingles on my tongue. I pretend that she's here and her slight weight is bearing me into the tacky linoleum. That her fingers are unbuttoning and unzipping and that my fingers are tugging and unwrapping her delectable body. I let my hand drift down to my pants, but the sensation of my hand on my own dick only accentuates my loneliness.

Why can't we go back to that point two weeks ago, when my brother was conscious and Hartley remembered me? I gulp down another big swig and then another until the sharp edges of the day are whittled soft and the blackness becomes a swirl of color.

CHAPTER NINETEEN

Hartley

I DECIDE TO GO TO the library. It's busy despite the late hour.

"We close in thirty minutes," a gangly teen says in a snippy tone. I nod and hug my jacket closer around my shoulders.

Actually, it's not my jacket. It's Easton Royal's. He gave it to me the other night after Felicity and Kyle ambushed me at the French Twist. I haven't returned it. I don't have a phone, but this is Bayview. Everyone knows the Royals and it would be easy enough to find out where he lives. I could drive there right now and lay the jacket on the front porch.

I run a finger over the zipper and sniff the collar for the hundredth time. The scent is growing fainter with each time I pull it on, but I can't stop wearing it. I'll return it. I will. Just not tonight.

I tug the leather close around my chin and type in the name of the medication Dylan was forced to take. The web results say it's to treat bipolar disorder and migraines, and that if she takes too much she can die. I try not to be concerned, because on the Internet every symptom eventually leads to death. Medical websites are the grim reaper decision trees. Did you take a pill? If yes, you'll die. Did you not take a pill? If yes, you'll die.

Still, I'm worried, so I dig deeper, trying to absorb as much as I can in the short time I'm here. I can feel the hostile eyes of the library worker lingering on my shoulders.

As I read the description of bipolar disorder, a lot of Dylan's actions begin to make sense to me. She probably does need the medication and if she hadn't taken any today then the number of pills she swallowed isn't dangerous. Still, Dad scared the shit out of me. I think the solution here is to make sure Dylan takes her meds. That way Dad doesn't have to lose his temper and Dylan doesn't suffer the intense and debilitating mood swings.

The information makes me feel marginally better.

"We'll be closing in five minutes." The announcement comes over the loudspeaker.

I tap my fingers restlessly on the keyboard. Do I check the messenger app and see if my cousin Jeanette has responded? I wonder— No, I've made up my mind not to wonder any longer. Besides, I don't want to piss off the library worker. I wrap that excuse around me like Easton's leather coat and scurry out to my car.

When I start the engine, I realize the thought of going home makes my skin crawl. But nothing in Bayview feels familiar to me. Maybe that's partly due to my lack of memory, or maybe it has to do with the fact that I haven't lived here in three years. There's no place where I put my roots down, no place that has my stamp on it, no place to hide, or vent, or celebrate.

The image of the pier flickers in the back of my head, but it's not a memory of the past, just a memory of the picture I saw. Of Easton holding me so tenderly—his big frame bent over my body as if he could shield me from the rocks that life pelts at you. I run my tongue across my lips wondering what it felt like to be kissed by Easton Royal, to have his hand wrapped around the back of my neck as he held me steady for the press of his mouth. Was that our first kiss or our last?

A strange, hollow ache develops in my chest and despite the distress that invades the empty spaces in my mind, I welcome it. It's *something*.

I start the car, turn off my brain, and just drive. I drive down Shoreview, the frontage road that runs parallel to the shore. There are endless white fences and magnolia trees interspersed by the occasional gate or long drive. None of them strike any chord with me. I drive on until the streets get narrower and the lawns grow smaller and smaller until there aren't lawns at all—just concrete and dirt and gravel.

On the east side of town, the buildings are short. Some of the windows are boarded up. The cars on the street are old and the fresh ocean scent is replaced by gas, frying oil, and garbage.

I end up in front of a small two-story house with an outside staircase that looks like it's about to fall away from the frame of the home. The place is lit up from top to bottom. The odor from the alley beside the house is strong enough to penetrate the car's windows. A balding man is sitting on the porch wearing a barn coat and rubber boots, and smoking a cigarette. I don't know why, but I get out.

"Hey there, girl," the man greets me between puffs. "Thought you weren't coming back."

It takes a second for his words to register, but when they do, I nearly trip over my feet in an effort to reach him.

"I got in an accident," I tell him. "I got in an accident and—" I stop right before admitting that I had lost my memory. What if he's dangerous? Why would I know him? Is he my...? I can't even think of the right noun to put at the end of that sentence.

"Yeah, I know all about that, girl." He takes another long drag, then blows out a cloud of smoke. "Got your apology cash, 'member?"

I frown. "My apology cash?"

He lifts a brow. "For wrecking my car? Your friend dropped off the fat envelope you asked him to deliver. Don't know where you got that kind of cash, not gonna ask, either." He winks. "That Volvo wasn't worth half what you gave me for it. And if you're here to see him, go on up. He's home."

Wrecking his car? An envelope full of cash that I asked my "friend" to drop off? Here to see who? Who's here? My confusion levels hit an all-time high.

"Um..." I take a breath. "Yes, I'm here to see him," I lie, and my gaze drifts toward the upstairs apartment. "He lives up there?"

"Stays here once in a while, from what I can tell. When your parents cleaned out the place, I rented it out to him." He drops the cigarette on the floor and grinds out the butt with the heel of his boot. "But if you're aiming to move back in, you can work it out yourself, since you two know each other. Don't really care who stays up there. I'll consider your rent paid through until February." And with that, he disappears inside his house, leaving me shell-shocked.

I remind myself to breathe, and start processing everything he just revealed. I lived in this place. I had access to money because I paid rent here—probably on a monthly basis. Given that it's the end of November, I'd paid through December. My parents not only knew about this apartment, but also came and took all my *belongings* from it. Where is my stuff? Everything in my bedroom is new except for a few pieces of clothing. Did they throw it away? Are they hiding it? What would be the point in that?

All the promises I made to myself about forging beyond the past are forgotten with these small glimpses of my past. I charge up the stairs, nurturing the idea that there's a living, breathing individual upstairs who knows me. No one from Astor would live here. They drive cars that cost more than this whole house. The person is someone who knows me outside of Astor, outside of my family, and therefore someone who can be real with me.

At the top landing, I throw myself at the door, pounding on it fiercely until I hear footsteps. Clasping my hands together, I hold my breath as the door is whipped open.

"What the hell are you doing here?"

"Easton?" I gasp.

If I was forced at gunpoint to list all the people who could possibly be living in this apartment, Easton Royal would've been the last on the list. In his bare feet, jeans, and a tank top so thin that I can make out every ridge in his defined abdomen, he still looks too expensive for this shabby environment.

"Nice jacket," he drawls, reaching out to flick the tab collar.

Self-consciously, I tug on the jacket's hem. I'd forgotten I was wearing it. I clutch the hem tightly. "Um, I meant to give it back to you but I didn't know how to get in touch."

"A phone call would've worked. A text, even." He leans his long frame against the doorway, effectively blocking out the view.

"That man downstairs…" I trail off. "He's the landlord?"

"Jose?" Easton nods. "Yeah, he owns this place. Good man."

"He said something about me wrecking his car." I rub my temples. "And then paying for it, and my friend dropping off the money, and…" My head is beginning to hurt again.

Easton's blue eyes take on a serious glint. "You borrowed his car the night of the accident."

"Oh." A horrible jolt of guilt brings the sting of tears. "And then I crashed it?" I moan. "That's awful. He must hate me."

That gets me a shrug and a faint smile. "Nah. I took care of it. Paid him more than the insurance ever would've. Trust me, he's thrilled."

I gape at him. "You took care of it? Why?"

He gives another shrug, not answering the question. "Want to come in?"

"Yes." I don't wait for him to move aside. I don't wait for another invitation. I charge forward and then come to a sudden halt in the middle of the empty room. I guess it's not entirely empty. There's a black bag in the center of the room crunched together in the middle. I also spot a crumpled Astor Park blazer, a pair of tennis shoes, and two towels. A bottle of vodka, a baggy of some dried green stuff, and a case of beer sit on the counter.

My eyes widen at the weed and booze. Is this some kind of Astor Park crack house where I provided alcohol, drugs, and…me? Is that how I paid for this place? The urge to vomit all over the floor seizes me. Did I earn money by selling my body to Astor Park boys? Is that why my parents got rid of everything? Why they're so cryptic? Maybe it's why I got sent away in the first place.

The insults Kyle hurled at me about being easy ring in my ears. I wanted to write that off as him being an asshole who made up things to make me feel bad, but as I turn in a slow circle, seeing nothing in the room but a few personal items that I assume belong to Easton, I can't help but wonder.

"Is this… Did we… What is this place?"

Easton closes the door quietly and crosses over to the counter. He uncaps the bottle of vodka, pours two glasses and then holds one out to me. "Your old apartment. What did you think it was?"

I take the drink and roll it between my sweaty palms. Do I tell him that I fear I'm a teenage prostitute and he's one of my marks, or will the fact that *that's* where my head went to reveal some deviancy I'd rather keep hidden? I mean, I could just go with the response that I'm surprised that I wasn't living with my parents and in a part of Bayview I don't think any respectable girl frequents. Those are as truthful as the worry about turning tricks.

I open my mouth to go with the parental thing but end up blurting out, "Did we have sex here?"

Easton nearly chokes on a mouthful of vodka. "Is that what you remember?" He coughs.

I know I'm bright red, but now that I've started down this road, I might as well finish. I can always throw myself off the edge when I reach the end. "No, but there's nothing here except this stuff"—I jerk my thumb over my shoulder at the bag and clothes—"and that stuff." I point my index finger toward the weed and liquor.

"You're pretty good at calculus, Hart, but your simple math skills are questionable. You can't add up a weekend bag and a miniscule amount of weed and get sex shack." He finishes his glass and refills it.

"Then what does it add up to?" And how many glasses of vodka is he going to drink? I shift uncomfortably and my foot knocks into something. I look down to see an empty vodka bottle near my toe.

Easton strides over and picks it up, acting as if this is completely normal. But as he bends over to toss the bottle in the trash, I see the tops of his ears turn red.

"When you lived here, you slept on a sofa. I figured I'd sleep there too when I rented the place. I didn't realize it was empty." He straightens and tilts his head, studying me for a long moment. He comes to some conclusion—one he doesn't share immediately—and walks over to pluck the still full glass out of my hand. He pours mine and his down the drain, picks up his wallet, and throws his blazer over his shoulder. "Come on. If we're not going to drink, let's get something to eat. You're going to need something in your stomach."

Those are somewhat ominous words, but as Easton places his warm hand under my elbow, I realize that out of everyone, I trust him the most.

CHAPTER TWENTY

Easton

I DRANK TOO MUCH. THAT was my first thought when I opened the door to see Hartley standing on the rickety landing wearing my Saint Laurent jacket that I gave her the night she had that god-awful meeting with Kyle whatshisface and Felicity Worthington.

When she walked into the empty apartment with not one of her personal belongings there to jog her memory and all the hope drained into her shoes, I felt that I hadn't drunk enough.

I want to wrap her up in my coat and take her some place where memories have no meaning—a place where only the present is important. Where the lost and confused look that haunts her eyes is chased away with wonder and joy. The problem is I don't know where that would be.

I wanted to take her skiing on the Swiss Alps or swimming in the Mediterranean, but instead, I'm walking her to the corner store where they sell beer, bags of ice, and stale potato chips. Who knows, maybe something here will jog her memory.

"What are you hungry for?" I ask.

She stops in front of the hotdog roaster. "I'm not sure. It's weird because I don't even know if I like hotdogs," she says, peering into the contraption that rolls the hotdogs over a few heated coils. She tilts her head toward me. "Do you know if I like hotdogs?"

"You ate corndogs and funnel cake at the pier and didn't seem unhappy."

She rubs her lips together as she stores this tiny little tidbit into her empty memory slots. I wonder what it's like, knowing nothing of the past. If you asked me two weeks ago, I'd have said that memory loss is a blessing. You wouldn't have the feelings of grief or hurt or even jealousy. You'd wake up and life would be this glorious blank slate. After seeing Hart's anguish, I know that's not the case. Since regaining consciousness after her fall, she hasn't had a moment's peace.

You can see it in the way she's always looking around, her eyes darting from person to person and object to object, searching for *the* thing that will jolt her memory and break through the barriers that prevent her from seeing into the past.

Unless what her doctor suggested was true and there are memories she will never retain—that they were literally knocked out of her.

I feel guilty getting mad over seeing her and Bran together at the ice cream shop. Hartley doesn't know that she's supposed to be by my side. That thought sends a spear of pain through me, which answers the dilemma from earlier. I haven't drank enough, because if I had, the alcohol's lead blanket would've prevented that shard from piercing the skin.

"Do you want a hotdog?"

"Sure," I answer even though I don't. I'd prefer the forty ounces of beer staring at me from behind the glass.

"Anything on it?"

"Mustard."

She carefully applies a thin zigzag of the condiment, wraps the hotdog carefully as if she's done this a million times before, and hands it to me. "This seems familiar. Did I work at this place?"

"I don't know. You waited tables at a diner. They could have had hotdogs there, but I can't remember." I paid more attention to eavesdropping on the frantic and disturbing conversation between Hartley and her older sister than the menu.

"I worked at a diner?" Her eyes grow wide and her voice gets a little high. "Which one?"

She has that same panicked look she had earlier when she first looked around the apartment. I have no idea what she's thinking.

"The Hungry Spoon. It's about a mile or two that way." I jerk my thumb over my shoulder.

"I had no idea." She rubs her head wearily as if this whole ordeal is exhausting for her. Her scar flashes into view, reminding me that she lives with a man who broke her wrist.

She always said her wrist injury was an accident, and since she didn't seem concerned about it, I tried not to be as well. I guess I'd pushed that out of my head along with everything else to make room for the elephant-sized worry over her injuries and Seb's that planted itself in my brain. Now that I'm with Hart, and her head injury isn't my main focus, part of the anxiety has receded and I'm starting to remember details about her past. I'm beginning to see how trauma could cause you to forget shit. I haven't hit my head and I'm already losing it from fear alone.

"Are you okay? Are you hurt anywhere?" I blurt out.

She blinks at me, bewildered again. "Yeah, I'm fine. My ribs are still a tiny bit sore, but overall, I'm good. My body's good, at least."

"Okay." I breathe a little easier. She seems entirely sincere. "Let's get our stuff and go home." *Home.* The word slips before I realize what I'm saying. I glance in her direction to see if she caught it, but she's preoccupied with loading up her hotdog with every condiment known to man. There's no sense in putting a bigger burden on her than there was before. Maybe her old man changed. I want to believe that.

I force a smile on my lips. "That's a crime," I tell her.

"What is?" Her head pops up, jerking to the right and left as if trying to see if there's a cop ready to arrest her for abuse of relish.

"You're not supposed to put ketchup on the dog and there's a specific order you apply the condiments in."

The corner of her mouth lifts. "The hotdog police haven't appeared yet, so I'm going to risk it. After all, isn't the fault really with the store? They put the ketchup out. This is obviously entrapment."

"They're waiting outside. They don't want to cause a scene in here. Plus, if others see them arresting you the word will get out that this is a honey trap," I inform her with a grin. I haven't seen her smile in so long I forgot what it looked like.

"If I'm arrested, everyone's going to hear about it," she jokes. When both dogs are wrapped, she carries them toward the counter. Over her shoulder, she calls, "Can you grab me a Diet Coke?"

I walk over to the fridges and pull out the bottle of soda. My eyes drift toward the booze. The conversation coming up isn't going to be a fun one. It'd be loads easier if I had a few forties in my belly. Or maybe one in hers.

"Coming, East?"

Her using my nickname drags my attention away from the booze. Man, I'm so whipped. I snatch another bottle of Diet Coke and amble toward her.

She's leaning over the counter holding up a prepaid cell phone. "I can get the phone for sixty bucks, but how much per month for the service?"

"Another thirty."

Hart fingers a hundred-dollar bill.

"Did you lose your phone?"

She nods. "Yeah, Mom said it must've gotten wrecked in the accident. That or the towing company lost it."

That answers why none of my texts were answered. I feel marginally better. I gently nudge her aside and lay down the sodas and a few bills to pay for the food and the phone. This one can make do until I buy her another.

"Wait, I have money," she protests.

I ignore her and so does the clerk.

As we wait for him to make change, she thrums her fingers against the counter, clearly debating something.

Finally, she stops and asks, "Do you remember me?"

The clerk looks up from the register. "Um, no, should I?"

"I didn't shop here before?"

"No clue." His eyes dart in my direction, seeking help.

"She's got amnesia."

"Wow, that's a thing?"

"Yeah, a real thing," Hart replies. "I must not have shopped here often, huh?"

"I guess not. You ate food from the diner at times. Sometimes you let me feed you."

"Oh." Her shoulders drop.

"I'll take you to the diner if you want. You can ask them stuff."

"What's the point?" She sounds so discouraged.

"If it makes you feel better," the clerk chirps, "I'll remember you now."

"No. That doesn't make me feel better," she retorts, grabbing her phone and rushing out.

"Eh, sorry, man. My bad," the clerk says.

"It's fine." I gather up the rest of the stuff and join Hart outside.

"Sorry," she says.

"For what? Being upset? Why do you have to apologize for that?"

"For being rude inside."

"You weren't rude. He made a bad joke." I fling an arm around her shoulders and steer her toward the apartment. "You sure you don't want me to take you to the diner? We can go right now. It's open twenty-four hours."

"I don't know. If you'd asked me a few days ago, I would've said yes immediately, but now…I'm afraid."

"Of what?" I slow my stride to match her shorter one.

"Of what they'd say. What if I was a terrible co-worker and they hated me? I think I've reached my limit of how much I can handle being told I'm awful."

"You were never awful. You worked other people's shifts when you could. I don't know how much you actually worked there. You told me once that they didn't offer you as many hours as you would've liked."

She falls silent, thinking about what I told her.

"You seem to know a lot about me. What else do you know?" she asks quietly, burrowing into my jacket as if the leather can soften the blows that she thinks are about to come at her.

"Not enough," I reply, "But I'll tell you anything you want to know." I hesitate then, not for my own self-preservation, but because I don't want to inflict more damage on her than she's already suffered. I railed into her earlier about relying on other people's stories, and now I'm offering to do the same thing and I feel a bit hypocritical. But it's clear she's desperate for answers, and I've never been able to deny this girl anything. I do, however, offer her another out. "Your doctor said we were supposed to let you remember on your own. It hasn't been long, Hart. You sure you don't want to wait it out?"

She takes a deep breath. Under my arm, her shoulders rise and fall with the inhale and exhale. "Earlier today, after seeing you at the ice cream shop, my plan was to move forward. I was going to forget about the past and forge new memories."

"But something happened to change that?" I guess.

She sighs. "Maybe."

"You can tell me anything. I'm not going to judge you." My past is an ugly one and I'm afraid to tell her about it, but I've come to the conclusion that if I'm not completely honest with her, she's not going to ever trust me. She told me the night outside the French Twist that she needed someone to be straight with her. That has to be me, which means I have to confess all the shit things I've done in the past. But that can wait, because if I don't get the hotdog inside of her before the talk, I bet she's going to lose her appetite. I nudge her ass with my knee. "Up. Our food is getting cold and the Coke is getting warm."

She jogs up the stairs without argument. I toss the bag on the floor, grab two glasses, and throw some ice in them. I eye the vodka bottle and decide that Hart may need a stiff drink.

She toes off her shoes and removes my jacket, laying it carefully on the floor. She scoots over to the middle of the room and starts spreading out our grocery snacks. Once she's done, she inspects her prepaid cell phone. It's nothing fancy, but at least I can contact her now.

"Hey, toss that over here," I ask.

She does without hesitation. I punch my number in and then put it on her fave list. "There. Now any time you want a hotdog, you can text me." I hand the phone over and push my bag behind her back so she has something to lean against. "But don't get too used to this fancy treatment," I tease, trying to lighten the mood. Her face is stiff with tension. "I don't buy gas station hotdogs for just any girl."

"I would hope not. It's pretty much the same as asking them to be your girlfriend."

"Nah, this is marriage stuff." I bite off half the dog.

"How do you figure?"

"Girlfriend stuff is the planned-out shit because you're trying to impress someone. Marriage stuff is the laidback things you really enjoy doing and you're comfortable enough with the person that you don't have to impress them."

She thinks about this for a moment while she chews. "Did we do the planned-out shit before I lost my memory?"

"You remember dating?"

She gives me a half smile. "No. It's more wishful thinking. I don't know what happened between you and me." She ducks her head. "In fact, I worried when I first came in that I was a teen hoe, taking money in exchange for sex."

I choke on my food. I choke so hard, Hartley jumps up and pounds me on the back. My eyes water and I gesture for the soda, which she rushes to retrieve. I down half the bottle before my throat clears and I can finally say, "You thought you were a prostitute?"

"I think the preferred term is sex worker," she replies primly. Her hands are folded on her lap and her jean-clad legs are pretzeled into a lotus pose. With her long black hair tucked behind tiny shell ears, it's hard to imagine her as a "sex worker" as she puts it.

"Well, you weren't." My right palm has the calluses to prove it.

"How would you know?" She scowls adorably.

"When we reached puberty, Uncle Steve took each one of us boys to a whorehouse in Reno so we could lose our V-card to a professional," I say flatly.

"Oh."

"Yeah, oh." I don't know why I told her that. Maybe because it's the least offensive part of my past and I'm trying to dribble out the bad parts in small portions so she doesn't run screaming from the apartment. "You really don't remember shit, do you?"

In the back of my mind, I had a kernel of doubt about her

amnesia, but it's real and it's tormenting her. I want to scoop her into my lap and tell her it's all going to be okay. If there was a way to shield her, I'd want to do that. Which is why I can't be drinking anymore. I set the half-empty glass of booze away from me. I need to be *here*, mentally and physically for her.

"Your doc said not to fill your head with stuff, but I'm willing to tell you anything I know and you're ready to hear. Do you need another refill?" I nod toward the vodka in her hand. I shouldn't drink it, but she might need it.

"No. I need a clear head for this. Lay it on me."

"What do you want to hear?"

"Everything. I don't know a thing about my past. My phone, my purse, and all my social media accounts are gone—if I ever had them in the first place. The stuff is my room is so new you can see the cardboard creases in the curtains. But here's the weird thing, Easton. I can remember things like stores and directions and a few events from when I was younger. Like when Felicity first came to my room, I thought she was Kayleen O'Grady. We met in kindergarten. I remember having a music teacher by the name of Dennis Hayes. Felicity told me Kayleen moved away three years ago and Mr. Hayes got run out of town a year after because he turned out to be a pedophile."

I stiffen. "Are you saying you think you were one of Mr. Hayes' victims?"

"No." She waves a hand. "I looked that up online at the library. He was having an affair with a seventeen-year-old student, which is wrong, obviously."

I relax at that news and sort through the other stuff. "Do you remember your family?"

She runs a finger along the scar on the underside of her wrist. "Some. I remember going to Parker's wedding. I remember doing small things with Dylan like braiding her hair or playing with her Legos. I read to her sometimes…" She trails off, still rubbing the scar. "Sometimes we'd fight. I can't remember what we fought about, but I recall yelling at each other."

Hart had said that her sister had extreme moods, which reminded me a little of myself. I'd been diagnosed with ADHD and for a while my mom made me take meds, but then the voices in her own head took up too much of her time and attention. I used booze and other pills to compensate. I guess I still do.

"But nothing in the last three years," I guess.

"Definitely nothing in the last three years. I don't even remember what happened here." She holds up her wrist.

"I do." My eyes drift to my vodka. What I wouldn't give to down half a bottle, pass out and not have to tell Hart that her dad hurt her. But that's a coward's way out, and, for all my faults, I like to think I've never been a coward.

"I saw a picture of you on Instagram," she says.

Her change in topic surprises me, but I recover quick enough. "Searching me up, are you?"

She doesn't bother denying it. "Yes. You. Me. Felicity. My cousin Jeanette. I messaged her and she responded, but I decided not to read it."

"Why's that?"

"Because after running into you today, I decided I didn't want to remember. My brain decided that I should forget about certain things and so that's what I was going to do."

"Was?"

"Yeah, was. Because forgetting about the past only works if we all have the same memory loss. You remember things. My sister remembers things. My parents remember things and all of your memories impact how you react with me today. Even Felicity and Kyle are motivated by something I did to them before."

This makes sad sense to me. "Yes and no. I don't know what Kyle's deal is. If I had to bet, it's because he's getting something from Felicity. You and Kyle don't know each other. You have zero classes together and you never hung out. You were busy. When you weren't at school, you were working your ass off. Hell, sometimes you even skipped school to go work."

"Really?"

"Really." My gut is churning. The lies I told before, the sins I've tried to hide, they need to come out now. "Come here." I crook my fingers.

"Why?" she asks, but she scoots close enough that our feet are touching.

"I'm gonna need to hold your hand to make it through this." I'm not even joking, but I smile as much as I can so she doesn't freak out.

I lay out my hands, palm up, and wait. She looks down at my hands and then up at my face, pondering what I'm about to share. When she slides her palms on mine, I feel a tremor in them. I close my fingers tight around hers, wishing it was more than her fingers that I was holding.

"I'm not a very good person," I begin, trying to keep my gaze steady, trying to keep my eyes on hers, trying not to look away like a spineless candy-ass. It's hard, especially because right now her eyes are soft and pretty and warm and at any minute they could turn cold with disgust. "I'm not a very good person," I repeat. My hands are growing sweaty. Holding hers was a dumb idea. Why do I care so much? Why does it matter what she thinks of me? I let go, but she catches me and tugs me forward.

"Don't."

"Why not?" I say hoarsely.

"Because I'm gonna need to hold your hand to make it through this." Her lips tilt up at the corner. She scoots closer until our legs are pressed from knee to ankle and our combined hands are in her lap. "I don't want to know about the past if it hurts you. Don't tell me if it hurts you. I think we've both been hurt enough to last a lifetime."

I'd like for that to be true, but we're not moving a step forward without me being straight with her. I gather my courage and start talking. About how I did Felicity dirty, agreeing to be her boyfriend and then treating her like a piece of trash the next day. About how I slept with my brothers' girlfriends because they were the ultimate forbidden fruit. About how I had liked Ella because she reminded me so much of my mother and when she kissed me at the club, I knew it was to make Reed jealous and I played along because hurting people was fun for me. About how my mother killed herself and it was my fault.

My throat is sore and my eyes are red when I finally shut up. My hands are no longer in Hart's. Instead, I'm lying down, using her knee as my pillow. I don't know how I got into this position, only that I don't want to leave it—ever. She keeps rubbing a finger across the top of my forehead and it should be soothing, but instead my dick is waking up and reminding me that we haven't had any kind of touching in a long damn while.

Which is why when she bends down and her hair falls like a curtain around my face, blocking out the world, I don't move away. Which is why when her lips touch mine, I don't push her aside immediately. Which is why I kiss her back. Why I grab her head, twist around until she's underneath me. Why I gather that long spill of hair and tug until her mouth falls open.

When she shoves her fingers into my hair and licks to the roof of my mouth, a trail of heat burns a line from my tongue to my dick. It's like we're at the top of the Ferris wheel again, only this time we don't go around in circles. Our car is sent flying out into the dark night, spotlights provided by the carnival lights.

But the kiss isn't enough for me. She's been lonely? Me fucking too. I've been lonely since my mom died. I've been aching since my family divided itself into tribes that didn't include me. I've been dying inside while trying to keep a smile on my face because I'm scared if I let that dark cold spread beyond the box I'm trying to keep it in, I'll end up doing the same thing my mom did.

I roll over onto my back, grab Hart's knee and tug it down next to my hip. She does the rest of the work, repositioning herself until she's fully straddling me—a leg on either side. Her lips taste salty and sweet and her mouth is so soft and wet. The blood pounds in my head and my dick screams for some closer, softer, better contact. My fingers dig into that juicy ass of hers and jerk her forward until we're fused together.

The heat of her body eats away at the fuzzy edges created by all the alcohol until everything in the room is sharp and clear. Her eyelashes are spiked with unshed tears that look like crystal-dotted lace against her soft cheek. The individual threads of her jeans rub against the pads of my fingers. When I take a breath, my lungs fill with her scent—a warm honey spiced with citrus. And when she moves, rocking her pelvis against mine, I can hear the swish of her clothes against mine.

She moans against my mouth and I nearly nut in my jeans from the sound alone. Me, Easton Royal, who has screwed more girls—and women—than fifty-year-old porn stars, is rock hard and close to the big O just from a kiss and a little rub.

I've got it bad. So fucking bad for her, and I haven't even told her the worst of it yet.

CHAPTER TWENTY-ONE

Hartley

I DON'T NEED ANY MEMORIES to know this is the best kiss I've ever had, and if this is to be remembered as my first kiss, I'm a lucky, lucky girl. Easton's body is hard as a rock slab, but his mouth is beautifully tender. The way he clasps me to his chest, as if he never wants to let go, makes my heart sing.

This is why I drove here. I wasn't seeking a place, but a person. I'd come home.

I don't know how it happened, but he'd etched himself into my DNA. Can something like this ever be explained? Doesn't it simply exist? Felicity had been right about one thing. I'd fallen for someone immediately. My heart knew. Just as my heart reached out to Dylan, it yearned for Easton, too.

He gasps against my mouth. The way he moves against me makes me bold.

My hands slide down to touch his furnace-hot skin under his T-shirt.

"Hart," he whispers against my lips. I'm not sure if he's pleading for me to stop or go on, so I push my hands up higher, marking each ridge of his abdomen and the valley between. I feel the hot, smooth skin, the hard, wide planes of his chest, and the solid, sturdy shoulders. His hips move beneath me, urgent and seeking.

I don't know how long we would've gone. How many pieces of clothing would've come off, how many parts of his body I would've touched, how many of mine he would've kissed, because he pulls away from my mouth to bury his head in my neck.

Reluctantly, I hold him there, knowing full well that having sex at this moment would be wrong. We're both an emotional mess. The recitation of his past misdeeds brought tears to my eyes, not because I was horrified by what he'd done but because of how much self-loathing I'd heard in them. And I suspect that there are more tales that Easton is holding back that are going to wreck me. But the blood pounding in my ears urges me to wriggle down and find out how the hard length that's pushing into my stomach would feel in my hands.

As if he can sense my dilemma, he gently slides me off his body and scoots a couple hand spans away as if he wouldn't be able to contain himself if he were closer.

"Your first time shouldn't be on a cheap floor," he says.

A gust of relief blows through me. "I haven't had sex before?"

He hesitates. "I don't know. We never talked about it. It wasn't important to me. I mean, I'm no virgin. Why would I expect you to be one? You didn't sleep with anyone at Astor, if that makes you feel better."

"It does, actually." The thought of walking the halls next to guys who have seen me naked was more awful than I could put into words. But the other horror I live with has to do with Easton's brother. I swallow hard and force myself to ask, "Was the accident my fault?"

"Fuck no," he insists. Rolling onto his side, he tucks a hand under his head and scowls. "Have you been thinking that the whole time?"

"I didn't know what to think," I admit. "No one told me anything. I asked the doctor and the nursing staff, but they wouldn't give me a straight answer."

Easton sighs and drops his chin to his chest. "I don't want to tell you, because it's bound to make you hate me and that's the last thing I want."

Fear tightens my throat, but I push out the words of encouragement anyway. "I don't think I could ever hate you."

It's true. All of the things he said before were painful to hear, but only because they came from such a deep well of hurt.

He lifts his head as if an anvil's hanging from it. I catch his eyes and hold them, silently encouraging him to continue.

"It was my fault. I was drunk and mad. Your parents were threatening to send your sister to boarding school like you had been and I thought, because I'm a shithead, that I could solve it by going to see your father. We fought."

An unholy pressure is developing on the nerve right behind my left eye. I blink. "We fought?" I say hoarsely.

"We all fought. You, me, your dad." His eyes fall to my wrist.

I hide the scar against my thigh, instinctively knowing that the truth behind the scar is the secret to all of this.

"You were upset," he continues. His words are slowing down. The crease in his forehead becomes deeper. The muscles in his neck work as he swallows his guilt and remorse. "You drove off. The curve near your house is a blind spot and the twins drive it way too damn fast. They almost hit us once before. We had gone to your house before because you were worried about your sister. Your parents wouldn't let you see her. They were against you coming back to Bayview."

My head feels like it's ready to split open. Acid is climbing up my throat. I can taste it on the back of my tongue. I want him to stop. I roll on my back and throw my palm up. I've had enough. "I don't need to know any more," I announce.

But the silence is worse than his words, because I have to know. I have to know what I did or I won't be able to live with myself.

"Tell me," I choke out.

"Your father broke your wrist."

I break down then. A mix of anger and sadness fills me up and pushes the tears out. I wanted to ignore the evidence in front of me and pretend what my dad had done to Dylan was an aberration, but I knew, deep down, just like I knew how to get here, that there was something wrong at home.

"How did it happen?" I wipe at the tears, but they keep flowing.

"I wasn't there. I didn't know you then, but you told me you were having trouble sleeping. That you went downstairs and saw your father with a woman, and that woman paid your dad to screw up a drug case against her son."

"He took bribes?"

East nods grimly.

"Did I confront him?"

"No. You went to your sister, Parker, who told you to go home and pretend like nothing happened."

"But I didn't." My heart is racing. There's a certainty pulsing inside me. I can't remember the things that East is telling me, but they all feel true. There's no reason for him to lie to me about these awful things.

"No. You caught him getting another buyout. You tried to run back to your house and he caught you. You said he was angry but that the broken wrist was an accident. He packed you up and shipped you off to boarding school. You didn't get your wrist looked at for three weeks. That's why you have such a gnarly scar. They had to break it and then go in and reset it."

I cover my eyes with my scarred wrist and let the waterworks come. I couldn't stop them if I wanted to. This is what my brain thought I shouldn't remember. That my father hurt me and that my family abandoned me. My chest aches worse now than it did after I woke up in the hospital room. It's like someone has reached inside me and snapped each one of my ribs individually and then stabbed me in the heart with one of the jagged ends.

"I wish I could stop crying," I sob.

"Oh fuck, baby. Cry all you want." There's a swishing sound and then a long, heated frame presses against me. He presses my wet face into his shirt and rubs a hand over my back. "Cry all the fuck you want."

I blubber into his chest for what seems like an eternity. When my seemingly endless well finally runs dry and my wails turn to hiccups, East asks, "Are you afraid at home?"

"No. Not for me. For Dylan. Tonight was scary. Dylan needs medication and I guess she didn't take it. We were arguing at the table about how mad Dylan is that I'm home. She cursed and Dad blew up. He grabbed her meds and then forced her to swallow them. It was…ugly." I stop, choking up at this recollection. "He held her face so hard."

"You need to get out of that house. Both of you."

I nod, but I'm not sure what I can do. It sounds like Parker is of no help. She didn't believe me before, so she won't now. Mom? She might be the wildcard, although why did I go to Parker instead of my mom in the first place?

"We can live here. Or I can find a bigger place."

I blink. "We?"

"I'm not letting you go through this by yourself."

His outrage brings out a reluctant smile. "Sorry. I wasn't thinking."

"Clearly not."

My moment of levity doesn't last long. Dylan's in a house with a monster and I've been bumbling around worrying about school and my reputation and all that stupid stuff when I should've been concentrating on her. "My sister hates me. She's been so mean to me since I got back from the hospital and tonight I tried to comfort her, but she refused to let me into her bedroom. She must be so mad that I left her alone to be tormented by Dad."

"You didn't leave her. You were fourteen when you were sent away, which is almost the same age as Dylan is now. Do you expect her to fight your dad? No. You came back to save her."

"I'm doing a shitty job of it."

"Your dad's a lawyer. I don't think you can just run off with your sister. And from the sounds of it, you'd have to kidnap her since she is being kind of a turd at home."

A turd. I stifle a giggle. I'm tired, drained, and hysterical, so anything sounds funny.

"I love that sound," Easton says, a broad smile on his face.

"What sound?"

"Your laugh. It's the best sound in the world."

I roll my eyes. "I'm pretty sure there are way better sounds. Like…um…" I struggle to find an example.

Easton pounces. "Ha! See! Even you agree—Hartley Wright's laughter. Best sound ever."

This just makes me laugh again, which makes his smile widen even more, and then we're both sitting there smiling like idiots, with an occasional giggle flying out of my mouth. I can't believe the power he has. Like, five minutes ago, I was bawling my eyes out, devastated. I'm *still* devastated. And somehow Easton has this magical ability to make me smile even when I'm at my darkest point.

That both thrills and scares me.

"I need to go," I say awkwardly, because our smiling fest suddenly feels too…I don't know. Too *something*.

His arm shoots out and he grabs my hand.

"Stay," he says

I swallow, hesitant.

"For a little bit longer," he adds.

His husky voice and another sweet smile are all the encouragement I need. I let my eyes drift close, using East as my pillow, personal heater, and exclusive source of comfort. I'll rest my eyes…just for a minute. Then I'll go home.

I WAKE UP TO SOMEONE rapping that he's here for his music, real for his music. I sit up and look around to see who's talking, but there's no one here but me sprawled out on East's chest. His head is lying on the balled-up Astor Park jacket.

Beside him, the screen of his phone is lit up. I shake his shoulder.

"I'm up," he mumbles.

I smile a little at his obvious lie and shake him harder. This time he rolls over and shoots me a sleepy smile.

"Hey, babe. You have a sexy dream and want to work out some of the details in real life?"

He's so gorgeous just waking up that I wish I could take him up on the offer. "Your phone is ringing."

He groans and throws an arm across his face. "What time is it?"

"Three." I get up and look around for my shoes. I need to get home. I want to check on Dylan. My movements are sluggish, probably because of dehydration. I cried out my entire water supply.

"In the afternoon?"

His phone stops ringing. I locate my sneakers by the door. "In the morning." I look at his jacket with longing. I don't want to leave it, but it's his. I can't keep stealing his clothes.

"In the morning?" He groans in disbelief. The phone starts ringing again.

Trepidation creeps over me. "I think you should answer it. No one calls this late unless it's an emergency."

He doesn't answer right away and it occurs to me that maybe Easton does entertain random calls in the middle of the night from Astor Park girls. Jealousy prompts me to bend over and swipe the jacket off the floor. He gave it to me, I tell myself.

"Hello?" East finally answers. He listens for about two seconds before shooting straight into the air. "You better not be fucking with me," he half shouts, but he's not angry. A smile is spreading across his gorgeous face. "I'll be there." His hand drops to his side and he turns to me with a blindingly wide grin. "He woke up."

"Who? Sebastian?"

"Yes." East nods eagerly. "He woke up!"

"Ahhhhh!" I scream, jumping up and down. Finally, some good news.

Easton does his own little dance, and then we grab each other and hop around the room like fools until there's a banging on the floor. "Shut the fuck up or I'll kick you out," screams our landlord.

We immediately stop and stare at each other in excitement and wonder.

"He's awake," I whisper, as if by speaking louder I'll send Easton's brother back into an enchanted sleep.

"Damn straight he's awake." He looks around. "I need to get dressed."

"Do you need a ride?" I ask. I don't remember seeing a car outside.

"No. Durand is coming to pick me up."

I have no clue who that is. I grab East's shoes and set them by his feet "Do you have socks?"

"In the bag." He blows into his hand and then sniffs. "Shit, my breath smells like an ashtray. Do you have any mints?"

I check my pockets and come up empty-handed.

"Shit. Okay. I'm going to brush my teeth so I don't knock him unconscious when I talk to him. Holler if you see a big black Bentley out front."

I don't know what a Bentley is, but I keep an eye out for something big, black, and expensive. In his bag, I find extra socks, boxer briefs in black with white stitching that says Supreme, and another pair of jeans.

I want to come with and apologize to his brother, but I don't know if I'd be welcome. Easton said his family doesn't hate me, but how could they not? Even if he says it's his fault and the boys were speeding, it was my car that hit theirs. I put their son and brother in a coma.

"Do you think I can see him?" I ask when Easton comes out of the bathroom. I hand him the shoes, socks, and briefs.

He sucks air through his clenched teeth. "Fuck, I don't know. Let me see how rational Sawyer is. He's gonna be protective of Seb and could go off. We all know it's not your fault, but Sawyer feels guilty and wants to blame someone else."

"All right," I agree unhappily. "But I can at least send a gift. What does your brother like?"

A smirk steals over Easton's face. "Girls."

I grab one of his shoes and swing it at his shoulder.

He catches it with a laugh. "Chocolate-covered caramels."

I raise my arm for another strike. "Are you making that up or does he really like them?"

"He really likes them, you she-demon." He leans down for a quick kiss. "Go home to Dylan, but call me if you need anything. I don't care what time it is—morning, noon, night. Call me."

"Okay."

"And answer your damn texts."

"Yessir!" I salute.

We're both smiling as we go our separate ways, and once again I'm struck by the magic that is Easton Royal. The one person in my life who—at my lowest or my highest—never fails to put a smile on my face.

CHAPTER TWENTY-TWO

Easton

"How are you doing tonight?" Durand asks as we speed away from the shabby apartment that I'm starting to identify as home.

"Worn out," I confess.

"It's been an emotional evening," he agrees.

Boy, he has no idea. All the feely shit really drains a person, but despite my tiredness, my shoulders feel lighter than any other time I can remember. I confessed all my sins to Hartley and she didn't push me away. The stuff about her family tore her apart, though, and that kills me. I need to figure out a plan to get Dylan away from Hartley's asshole father.

I scroll through my messages.

Sawyer: Seb woke up

There's a twenty-minute delay. From the other messages, it appears he called Dad in Dubai and Dad rounded up the troops.

Ella: I just heard from Callum. OMG I'm on my way!

Reed: Fuck yeah!

Gideon: Reed & I will drive down tomorrow. Reed's got a test at 1. Hold down the fort.

Reed: I'm skipping that.

Gideon: We'll be down after Reed's test.

"Is Ella at the hospital?" I ask Durand.

"Yes. She arrived there about ten minutes ago."

"Okay, cool."

Durand makes the trip across town in no time. It helps that there's almost no traffic this time of the morning. I bolt out of the car before he stops, bypass the elevators, and race up the one flight of stairs.

"Shhh," some nurse says to me as I whip down the hall. I ignore her and bust into the room.

"You fucker scared the shit out of us!" I holler.

Sebastian responds with the middle finger. Elation fills me. For a while there, I thought the Royals were crashing and burning like Ella said, but nope. You can't keep us down.

"What do you need? You thirsty? Hungry?" I scan the room, stopping at the wardrobe in the corner. There's probably food and water in there. Sawyer had to be existing on something.

"Thirsty," Seb says, his voice like gravel.

"You sound like you've been crawling out in the Sahara," I say over my shoulder as I whip open the cabinet doors. Bingo. On the shelves, I find a row of water bottles. I grab one, twist it open and hurry back to the bed. "Where's the up button on this unit?" I need Seb to be in a sitting position so he doesn't drown as I try to feed him some water. Fumbling around, I find a little remote and after a false start, I have him at a slight incline.

"Here you go."

The water dribbles out the side of his mouth and he curses. "The fuck, East. Can't you be more careful?"

My eyebrows shoot into my forehead. "Sorry, dude. Nursing isn't in my bag of tricks."

He tries to shove my hand aside—*tries* being the operative word. The boy is weak as a kitten. All that happens is more water sloshes onto the sheets.

"Dammit! Stop hovering! Gahhhh!" He clutches his head.

I nearly drop the bottle of water in panic. "What is it? Holy shit. How do I call for a nurse?" I scramble over to the wall behind the bed and slam my finger against the red emergency button.

"Stop! What are you doing?" Seb attempts to swat me away again.

"Getting a professional in here. What do you think?"

"Where's Sawyer?" he demands, looking toward the door as if he could will his twin to appear.

"Ella took him to get some food. The cafeteria is down on the first floor. Food there is terrible, so I expect the food up here is going to be trash, too. Don't worry. I'll sneak stuff in for you."

"Why would you do that? I'm going home." He sweeps the sheets off his legs and slides them over the edge.

"Are you nuts? You're not going home." I whip his legs back onto the bed and pull the sheet up. Or try to. Seb gets his hands under mine and starts shoving. "This is ridiculous. Wait until the nurse comes."

The door bursts open and in runs the on-duty nurse, her dark ponytail flying high behind her. "Move out of the way," she orders.

I back off.

"Where're you going, mister?" she chides to Seb, who is trying to plant his feet on the floor.

"I'm leaving."

"No, you're not. Hand me the chart at the end of the bed." She holds out her hand and I slap the metal clipboard in it.

Seb glares at the both of us as he struggles into a sitting position. "I want to go home."

"Mr. Royal, you have been in a coma for two weeks. You will not be going home today or any day soon." She slaps a blood pressure cuff around his arm and stares at her watch.

"What's taking Sawyer so long?" my brother whines. "What a dick. I just woke up. He should be here."

"Your twin wouldn't leave the room unless we physically carried him out. He needs to eat or he'll be taking your place here." I scan for signs of injury but don't know what I'm looking for. I inject as much casualness into my voice as I can muster so I don't worry Seb. I don't want to shock him back into a coma with bad news. "Everything okay?"

"All his vitals are looking good," the nurse says. She jots a note in the chart.

My knees turn watery with relief. I grab the rail of the hospital bed. "That's good news. Isn't it, Seb?"

But Seb's too busy staring at the nurse's rack. I clear my throat. When he looks up at me, I make a slicing gesture across my neck. He needs to cut that shit out before the nurse jabs him in the nutsack with one of her extra-long needles.

He raises his middle finger and goes right back to undressing the woman with his eyes.

"Can you tell me where we are?" the nurse asks, thankfully oblivious to Seb's behavior.

"I've already answered this before."

"I know," she tries to soothe him. "But we need to check your vitals each day to make sure that we're providing the right treatment."

"Just answer her," I interject impatiently.

"We're in the Maria Royal Recovery Center—you know, the place my dad built with his guilt money after my mommy OD'd on her prescriptions."

The nurse's pen jerks across the chart. Seb doesn't miss her surprise. "Oh, you didn't know that? I figured it was still common gossip."

"Seb," I admonish. "Let the nurse do her job."

"What do you have under there? Thirty-six D? You look juicy."

I groan and cover my face.

The nurse slaps the clipboard shut with a bang. "You must be feeling better, Mr. Royal. The doctor will be right in."

My own nuts turn cold at the frost in her tone.

"You have a nice ass, too," Seb unhelpfully yells after her.

"Would you shut up, man? What is your problem?" I move over to the head of the bed so I can smother him with a pillow if he tries to heckle his nurse again.

He scowls and crosses his arms. "I'm just having fun. Besides, I wanted to see if the equipment downstairs still works."

I glance down and see a slight tent in the sheets. "Congrats. You can generate a woodie. I could've loaded some porn on your phone if you were that curious."

"Don't be so uptight, East. If you were lying here, you'd be doing the same thing."

"Negative. I've seen your nurse's arsenal of tools—the needles, the tubes, the bedpans." I shudder. "I've got mad respect for her. Anyway, you hungry? Because for the last fourteen days, this is all you've been getting." I tap the IV bag and read, "Total Parenteral Nutrition. Real tasty, I bet. Say the word and I'll get you something."

"Why don't you bring me someone to suck my dick?" Seb snaps.

I know my brother has been sick and passed out for the last two weeks, but I did not expect him to wake up a sex-crazed asshole. "I'm gonna step outside and see where Sawyer is."

"Probably fucking Lauren."

Is that what this is about? Sawyer must not have relayed the bad news, which is understandable.

"I doubt it," is all I say.

My brother's mouth curves into a sneer. "A lot of good you are. Since you aren't doing anything worthwhile, give my morphine bag a squeeze. I have a headache and you're making it worse."

"I'll get right on that." Reminding myself that Seb just woke up from a coma, I force myself to walk out without another word. I'm in time to see Sawyer careening down the hall with Ella at his side.

"How's he doing?" Sawyer asks.

"He's in a bad mood."

Ella grimaces. "Still? I thought once he got his bearings, he'd be okay."

Sawyer laughs. His grin is so wide, the ends reach each ear. "So what if he's in a bad mood? He was in a coma for over two weeks."

"He asked about Lauren," I relay.

My brother's grin disappears. "Shit."

"I didn't say anything."

"Don't. I don't want him hearing any bad news."

"I'm not going to tell him."

Sawyer swings a glare toward Ella. She holds up her hands. "Me either, but the longer you wait, the worse it will be."

"He's going to notice something's off when she doesn't show up," I point out.

"Just keep it to yourself," Sawyer snaps. "I'll decide when he finds out." He pushes past us into the room.

Ella hangs back, and as soon as the door is closed, she turns to me. "Something is wrong with Sebastian."

"You mean because our sweet, docile brother woke up a rude sex fiend?"

"Yes," she nods emphatically, "exactly that. I walked in and he asked me if I was there to give him a blowjob. He said it was my sisterly obligation. And when I reminded him that I was his brother's girlfriend, because I thought maybe he had some kind of amnesia like Hartley, he replied that since we weren't actually related I could climb up on the bed but that he preferred the reverse cowgirl so he didn't have to look at my face!" She ends with a shriek.

The few staff in the hallway turn in our direction. I grab Ella's arm and drag her down the hall, away from curious eyes.

"Like Sawyer said, Seb's been in a coma for two weeks. It's normal to wake up with a boner, and maybe he's not processing his feelings appropriately, but he's probably loopy on drugs. Why don't you go home? Sawyer and I have got this."

Ella casts a guilty look over her shoulder toward the hospital room. "I really shouldn't."

But she really wants to. "Go. We'll be fine," I assure her.

She doesn't need to be told twice. She squeezes my arm, mumbles some platitude, and scurries off. Seb must've really freaked her out.

When I get near the room, I hear a bunch of shouting. I hurry up and push open the door. Inside, it's a flurry of motion.

"What's going on?"

"We're doing tests," one of the staff members informs me.

More people shuttle in, and soon Seb is being wheeled away to get his head examined—literally. All the while, he alternates between cursing the staff out "Fucking get your fucking hands off me, you fuckers!" and harassing them, "On a scale of one to wet, what's the condition of your panties now that you've stared at my dick for five minutes?"

"What was that all about?" I ask quietly when Sawyer joins me in the hall. "Did something set him off?"

Sawyer slumps against the wall, all his smiles replaced with a weary, exasperated expression. "The nurse made him piss in a bedpan."

"Ah, so that's what the shouting was about."

"It took two orderlies and me to hold him back from throwing the pan at the nurse's head. I don't know what's wrong with him." Sawyer looks baffled.

I pat my brother on the back. "He woke up on the wrong side of the bed, obviously."

Sawyer cracks a small smile at this bad joke. "I guess it

doesn't matter. He's awake and that's what's important."

"Yup. Now you can go home."

"What?"

"Go home, Sawyer. You're exhausted. You haven't slept a full night in the last fourteen days. There are finals coming up and you need to take care of yourself."

"Since when did you become Dad?" Sawyer jokes, but I can see the relief in his eyes.

"Since our real one flew to Dubai to get some rich Arabs to buy planes from us. Now that we gotta share part of our inheritance with Ella, the real one has to start making more money."

To my surprise, Sawyer agrees. He must be exhausted. "All right. But if Seb is mad, I'm blaming it on you."

"I can take it."

"Remember—no Lauren."

"Trust me. I'm not bringing it up." If Seb's throwing around bedpans because he can't piss standing up, he's going to do a lot more damage when he finds out his girlfriend couldn't keep her shit together for two measly weeks.

It's nearly three hours later when Seb is rolled back to the room, completely out of it. I follow the staff inside and wait for an explanation.

"We had to sedate him to do the CT," the nurse says when I ask what's wrong. "But everything is fine. You should go home, too. He probably won't wake up anytime soon."

"Someone's got to be here when he does."

"We've really been lax about our rules, but now that Mr. Royal has turned the corner, we need to impose some order for his own health. You want him to get better, don't you?"

What kind of dumb question is that? I seethe. "Of course."

"Then we'll see you tomorrow." She shuts the door firmly behind her.

I shoot off a quick text in the family group chat informing them I'm getting kicked out, expecting Sawyer, at least, to tell me to stay put, but instead I get a single message from Ella.

Sawyer's passed out. Let Seb sleep, too. They both need it. You too.

I think of Seb and his wild antics. He's doing this because he's scared and the last thing that should happen is for him to wake up to an empty room.

Nah. I'm gonna stay.

*Why Easton Royal. That's so adult of you. *winky face**

A strange, unfamiliar warmth spreads through me. I tuck my phone away. Maybe I am growing up. It doesn't feel so bad, after all.

CHAPTER TWENTY-THREE

Hartley

"I'm sorry I came home so late," I tell my mother as I dump brown sugar on my oatmeal.

"You did? I didn't realize. Dylan, where is your helmet?" Mom yells.

"In the mudroom," comes a disembodied reply.

"I looked there already," Mom mutters, tossing a towel onto the counter and disappearing into the nearby mudroom.

Helmet? I wonder what that is for. Dylan comes rushing into the kitchen. I study her closely for signs of injury. Has she accidentally broken anything in the past three years? Were Dad's actions an aberration or is he abusing my sister on a regular basis?

"Hey, Dylan, you doing okay this morning?"

She sticks her head in the fridge and ignores me. She's been avoiding me all morning. When I woke up, I knocked on her door, but she didn't respond. I waited in my room, listening for any sounds in the hall. When I heard her, I leaped out only to be too late. She'd already escaped into the bathroom.

I go over and tap her on the shoulder. "Dylan, are you okay this morning?"

She jerks away from my touch and slams the fridge door shut. "I heard you the first time. I'm fine. Can you go back to leaving me alone like you have the last three years?" Milk in hand, she stomps over to the pantry and pulls out a box of Cheerios.

Guilt lodges in my throat and I have to clear the lump before I can speak. "I'm sorry I was gone for so long. I didn't mean to be. That's why I came home, you know, to be close to you."

"Whatever," she mutters. Her phone is out and she's scrolling through her messages.

I'm sure I sent her some while I was gone. I wonder what I said. Maybe I was really mean to her or she told me things and I didn't listen well, caught up in my own drama.

"I'm sorry," I say quietly. "I'm sorry for hurting you."

She glances at me above the top of her phone. "I'd have to care to be hurt."

"Ouch." I rub my chest and try to laugh off the blow she just dealt. "Okay, I hope you know I love you."

Dylan's response is to pick up her bowl, carry it to the sink and yell, "Mom, did you find my helmet?"

"Still looking."

I rub a hand across my mouth. It's as if they wish I didn't live here.

"It's almost time to go. Can't you just bring it later?"

"Yes, fine. Put your shoes on and we'll go."

I grab my Astor Park blazer and tug it on. The back door opens.

"What about Hartley?" Dylan says.

"Oh, I forgot about her." In a raised voice, Mom hollers, "Hartley, it's time for school."

"God, do we have to wait for her?"

"I'm right here," I respond.

Dylan looks over her shoulder in surprise and then scampers to the car, ducking into the backseat. Mom hurries around to the driver's seat.

"Get in," she says to me. Over her shoulder, she addresses Dylan. "Do you have all your homework?"

"Yeah."

"Don't forget to change before I pick you up."

"Yeah, Mom. I get it."

"Well, last week you didn't remember, did you?"

Dylan falls silent. I flip down my visor and pretend to check my non-existent makeup but really use the mirror to spy on my sister. She tucks her headphones into her ears and stares at her phone.

I really need to know that she's unharmed.

"Mom, about last night. Maybe I can help remind Dylan to take her meds?"

Mom brakes at a stoplight and turns with a surprised look, as if she forgot I was even in the car. "Oh, Hartley. You should get a ride home from a friend. Dylan has horseback riding lessons this afternoon," she says, completely ignoring my suggestion. Maybe she didn't hear me.

"Last night was scary."

"Your father has a temper." She waves it off. "And everything is all right because Dylan will take her meds or she won't be going to the horse show this weekend."

Mom checks the rearview mirror and waits for a response, but we get nothing. Dylan's music is turned up so high we can hear it through her earbuds.

"Dylan," Mom repeats.

My own blood pressure is rising because of Dylan's lack of response. I reach in the back and snap my fingers. She doesn't flinch.

"Dylan, turn that down," Mom shouts as she brakes hard in front of Astor Park. "It's so loud I can hear the music. You're going to lose your hearing."

"Get out. You're making me late," Dylan snaps.

I remind myself that my baby sister is traumatized from last night and God knows how many other nights, and calmly get out of the car.

I'm glad I'm not being yelled at, but there's a kernel of discontent brewing at the fact that it seems like I'm an afterthought to my own mother. It's not as if I want, or need, sympathy, but I was in a bad accident not too long ago, I'm still suffering the repercussions of hitting my head at the hospital, and I'm back after three long years of absence. Shouldn't she be yelling at me for coming home at three in the morning?

I step onto the Astor Park sidewalk, feeling bitchy. Maybe Felicity will get in my face today and I can curse her out. That'd make me feel better. Sadly, I don't get Felicity, but Kyle decides to talk to me in the library during study hall.

He scoots his chair over and lays his hairy arms on my table. "It's all over school that you're screwing Bran Mathis."

"That's what's interesting these days?" I arch an eyebrow. "Why aren't they talking about how I'm joining the circus over Christmas break? My group could really use the publicity boost."

"Circus?" He blinks.

"It's a joke," a student nearby breaks in. It's the first time I've had anyone stick up for me at school, and it's a miracle that I don't jump out of my chair and hug her. I settle for a small smile.

The blonde shrugs.

"A joke?" Kyle repeats. His face grows red like a cartoon character with steam blowing out of his ears. "You making fun of me?"

"No. I'm trying to get my homework done." I reach for my poetry when a sweaty palm slaps on top of mine.

A yelp escapes me. A really loud yelp.

Mrs. Chen's head shoots up from her desk. "Mr. Hudson," the study hall monitor snaps, "we do not touch other students here at Astor Park. Unless you want to have a point docked from your account, you should remove your hand immediately."

Kyle's hand tightens around my wrist. I grit my teeth because this shit hurts. Mrs. Chen opens her laptop. Kyle, recognizing the teacher is going to follow through, releases me immediately, but Mrs. Chen is busy typing.

"Wait, you said if I released her I wouldn't get any points taken off," he protests.

She doesn't even look at him when she responds. "I told you to remove your hand immediately and you didn't. I won't tolerate that kind of behavior."

"Bitch," he mutters. A bell dings. Kyle flips his phone over and shoots to his feet, waving his phone in the air. "That's two points. You took off two points!" he shouts.

"And you called me a bitch. That's insubordination and a violation of rule 4-13 of the Honor Code regarding acceptable conduct. Shall we go for three points or are you going to sit down, Mr. Hudson?"

Kyle sits down with a bang.

"And the rest of you should know that because you are seniors, I expect you to act like adults instead of a pack of wild animals, trying to tear up another student because they're some kind of perceived competition."

"We're not kindergarteners," Felicity complains from another table in the library.

"Then act your age, Ms. Worthington. You all have ten minutes left to study—use them wisely."

I think I have hearts in my eyes as I gaze at Mrs. Chen. She's officially my favorite teacher.

"Thank you," I tell her when study hall is over.

She gives me a terse nod, which isn't exactly welcoming, but I still love her. Outside the library, Kyle is waiting with fury in his eyes.

"Don't think you've won, bitch."

"We're not in a competition so there's no winner or loser," I reply. I check my schedule and see I have music next, which means I should be able to rifle through my locker.

"You're a loser in life."

"Okay." I smile and wave as I run off. Kyle stands dumbfounded behind me. What did he want? For me to argue with him? He weighs twice as much as me and I know that if he wanted to, he could physically destroy me, so I'm not going to get in a fight with him. Besides, it sounds like he's skating on the edge of trouble and needs to be careful himself.

"Are you okay?"

I shove my books into my locker and turn to Ella who has stopped near me.

"How's Sebastian?" I ask immediately.

She wrinkles her nose. "He's…different."

"How so?"

"He just is. He used to be understanding and sweet and now he's like a cranky old man."

The sick feeling I get anytime I remember the accident bubbles in my stomach. "I'm so sorry," I say. The words are inadequate, but I don't know what else to do. I decide to ask, "Is there anything I can do? Like cook his meals or wash his socks? Easton says that chocolate-covered caramels are a good gift."

"That'd be nice, but I might send them. It's not that the accident is your fault or anything, but Seb is just…weird right now." She reaches out and taps her fingers on my arm. "You should concentrate on getting better yourself. Sebastian will come around. Or we will adjust. We're just happy he's still with us."

"Me, too," I say fervently. "But if there's anything I can ever do, let me know."

Her face grows serious. "It wasn't your fault, you know. If it was, Callum would've gotten you charged with something, no matter that your dad is a DA."

The bell rings or I would've replied. Ella gives me a closed-mouth smile and walks off to her next class. Her words provide me with a little comfort, but my next period is Music Study and I use the time to soothe myself, playing Mendelssohn's sonatas all in a major key. The next fifty minutes are the most peaceful ones I've experienced since I woke up.

"Time's up, Ms. Wright," a voice from overhead says through the intercom system. Sadly, I pack the violin away and trudge out to the lunchroom.

The lunchroom isn't so much a lunchroom as a posh restaurant. The ceiling must be at least twenty feet high. The walls are paneled in dark wood and the rectangular tables are draped in white linen. Classical music plays in the background accompanied by the sound of tinkling water from a fountain near the entrance. In one corner, a massive wall of live plants fills the space. The tables in front of the wall are empty.

In the center, I spot Ella with two other girls. One with long reddish hair and the other with a dark bob. Sitting beside them are a couple of other students I'd probably classify as popular. One table over is Felicity and her crowd.

"Wondering where to sit?"

I look over to see Bran at my elbow. "No. I'm going to sit over by the garden."

He makes a face.

"What? What's terrible about there? It looks pretty."

"Bugs," he says and then shudders. I don't know if that's fake or real. "There are a ton of pests over there. Trust me. You don't want to eat there. Come with me." He tips his head toward a table on the far end of the room. It's already half full of very muscular guys.

"It looks like you have a crowd."

"Nah, it's only because Dom's there and he's big enough for two people."

I run my tongue along my lip and consider my options. I don't have many. It's either in the corner with the bugs or with Bran. "Is it really that bad?" I ask.

"I think the question is, am I really that bad that you'd rather sit with the bugs than me?" His eyes twinkle so I know he's not seriously hurt, but his point is made.

"Why are you so nice to me?" I ask as we move through the line. The buffet choices are unreal. I'm never skipping lunch again. Kyle can sit next to me all period and whisper his gross insults and I still won't care because the pumpkin squash ravioli smells good enough to die for.

"Why shouldn't I be?"

"Um, because I was a terrible person?"

"Since when were you a terrible person?"

I tilt my head and study Bran. Is he coming on to me and that's why he's saying I wasn't bad? He's very attractive. He could probably get into a lot of other girls' panties without much effort.

"Did we spend a lot of time together? We don't have many classes together." Come to think of it, I don't think we have one.

He flushes slightly. "Yeah, I'm not in the college ones like you."

Oh shit. Did he take that as an insult? "That's not what I meant. I-I—" I flounder. "I just don't think I'm really popular here, and you're really hot, so shouldn't you be with, like, more popular people?"

He plucks an apple out of a basket and puts it on my tray. "You think I'm hot, huh? Maybe that's why I'm hanging out with you." He winks and picks up my tray, carrying it to the cashier.

She rings him up and swipes his ID card. I hand the cashier mine. She swipes it and then hands it back. "You have any cash?"

"Huh?" I ask. "Why do I need cash?"

She flips the screen around. "Because you don't have any money in your account."

This is embarrassing. The kids behind me snicker and I feel a whole wave of humiliating gossip start to crescendo.

Bran steps forward. "I'll pay."

"Cash only," the lady says. "We're only allowed to swipe the ID once."

He looks frustrated.

"Is there a problem?" Felicity prompts from her table. There's a note of glee in her voice, as if her embarrassment radar has been triggered.

"She doesn't have any money in her account," yells a kid behind me. "And Bran doesn't have any cash on him."

The tips of my savior's ears turn red. I clench the tray between my fingers to keep from flinging the orange pasta all over the loud-mouthed kid.

"You're holding up the line," moans another student. "I've got to get to class."

"Yeah, just let her through so the rest of us can eat."

"We're hungry!"

"This is why normies should never be allowed into Astor."

"It's awful, isn't it."

With each complaint, Felicity's smile grows wider and wider. She's eating this shit up. I'm about to abandon the tray when I remember the money Mom shoved in my hand last night. I dig into my pocket and hand it over to the cashier.

Too bad for you, Felicity, I mutter to myself

"Sorry," I say to Bran. "I forgot I had any money. I guess my short-term memory sucks as much as my long-term one."

"No worries," he says, but his shoulders are stiff. He doesn't like the mocking much.

I want to tell him to relax, but that's something he'll have to learn on his own. As for me, I go to the corner and eat my lunch. I've got more important things to worry about than Kyle, Felicity or Bran. My sister is in danger and since I can't remove her from her home, I'll have to find a way to get rid of the threat.

CHAPTER TWENTY-FOUR

Easton

"I'M HEADING OVER TO THE hospital. You sound like shit. Didn't you get any sleep last night?" I ask Sawyer over the phone. He showed up at the hospital around six this morning, and I went home to catch some shuteye.

"I tried, but I kept worrying. I should've never left."

Translation: Seb's been giving him grief for going home for the last four hours.

"Does Seb want anything?" I throw a leather coat over my shoulder and hustle down the stairs.

"What doesn't he want? I've heard him ask for steak, sushi, a plane, Lauren, his own bed, fewer nurses, prettier nurses, a blowjob, a hand job, to get out of the fucking bed." My baby brother heaves a sigh.

"So you haven't told him about Lauren?"

"No. I called her and told her that Seb woke up. She said that was nice but that we're too much for her."

"What the hell does that mean?"

"I have no idea. Look, I gotta go. Seb's yelling at the nurse again."

Sawyer hangs up before I can respond. An idea pops into my head.

"Straight to the hospital?" Durand asks when I get into the Bentley a few minutes later.

"No. Toy store first and then hospital."

"Which toy store?"

"The one on Kovacs."

Durand doesn't even blink an eye, even though he knows what it is. Hell, everyone above the age of thirteen knows and probably a good half of Bayview's been inside once—ostensibly for gag gifts, but from what the Astor girls say, there's plenty of battery-operated toys that bounce around in the bottom of purses and backpacks.

We make the detour to the sex shop and I pop in, find what I need, and pay. Durand's not much of a talker and I'm worn out, so I close my eyes and doze for the rest of the ride. When we arrive at the hospital, Durand wakes me by turning the volume up on the radio.

"I'll catch a ride home," I tell him as I shut the door. Since Seb is making all the staff wish he would go back into his coma, I put a little extra power into my smile as I say my hellos.

"Rhonda, that's a nice shade on you."

The on-duty nurse, fifty if she's a day, beams. "Thank you, Easton. Blue's always been my color."

"I'm talking about your lipstick. It's a kissing color." I wink, and she blushes like she's twelve and rubs her lips together.

"What about me?" Sarah, her co-worker, chirps.

"I'd have to go to confessional for three days if I spoke out loud the thoughts I'm having about you, Miss Sarah," I tell her.

Sarah pats her blue-rinsed hair and giggles.

On my way to the room, I run into Matthew—one of the orderlies. "Looking extra buff today, my man."

"Did some power lifting this morning," he says, curling his biceps.

I knock my fist against it and look suitably impressed. "Nice, but be careful or the lady patients will fall in love and won't want to leave."

"That's the plan. Full beds, full paycheck."

"I got you." I do the finger gun in his direction and then swing into Seb's room.

"Duck!" I hear, and instinctively I obey.

The wind above my head whistles as something hurtles over my head. I turn around in time to see a food tray smash against the wall and plummet to the ground, leaving a Rorschach blob made up of peas, applesauce, and a mystery meat.

"Food's that bad," I quip.

"This place is a shithole," Seb growls. "When am I going home?" His face is red and I'm a little worried he's going to pop a blood vessel and go back into his coma. Sawyer's in his chair with his head buried in his hands.

"What's your doctor say?" When I reach the bed, I pick up the chart that hangs off the end and flip through, but none of the chicken scratchings have any meaning to me.

"That I can leave when my parent or guardian shows up. You're eighteen. Be my guardian and get me out of here."

"Okay." I go over to him. He's got two IVs in his arm. I begin to tug on one of them.

"What are—" Sawyer lunges for me, but it's unnecessary because his twin has already jerked his arm out of my reach.

"Don't fucking touch my IVs. Are you trying to kill me?"

Seb scowls, covering his wrists protectively with one hand.

"You said you wanted help getting out of here."

He scowls. "You're supposed to get a doctor's release. Not just rip out my IVs. I need my pain meds."

"Then it sounds like you should chill out and shut up until your doc tells you to go home. Trust me, act like a fucking punk a little more and they'll kick you out on the street. Then there'll be no more of this." I flick my finger against one of the IV lines.

"I don't need you to pretend to give a damn. I have a babysitter already," Seb says, sullen as a toddler.

"If you're talking about Sawyer, then no, you don't. He's going home now to shit, shower, and sleep." I squeeze my younger brother's shoulder with my free hand. I can feel him wilt in relief. The kid's been killing himself here. "You've got me to entertain you. Sawyer said you wanted a blowjob? I can't deliver that, but I do have this." I toss the paper bag onto Seb's lap.

He pulls out the sex toy. "Seriously? I don't want this." He chucks it at my head, but he's so weak it falls to the floor in front of me. "Where the hell is Lauren?"

"She's at home." I have no idea, but that's my best guess.

"You shoulda brought me a prostitute."

"I checked with Rhonda and she says bringing prostitutes into the hospital isn't allowed." I pick up the toy and set it on the table.

"Like rules have ever stopped you before."

My temples begin to throb. I jerk my thumb at Sawyer. "Time to go."

He gets up and walks toward the door without another word.

"You're leaving me?" Seb yells. "You're fucking leaving me? I woke up, like, less than twenty-four hours ago and you're skipping out!"

Sawyer freezes.

"Yes, he's leaving, and you get me in his place. Now shut the fuck up and let your brother go in peace," I snap. "Go," I order Sawyer.

He bolts and I don't blame him. I'd run off, too, if I could.

"Who died and made you king?" Seb demands.

"Me." I sit down in one of the empty chairs, tuck my hands behind my neck and stretch my legs out. I've been up for only an hour or so, but my head aches and all I want to do is close my eyes and take a nap.

"What's so tiring about your life? Too many chicks on your junk?" He sounds envious.

I decide to tell him the pathetic truth. "Only one girl and we haven't even gotten to the dry-humping stage."

That silences him. I pop my eyes open to see what he's thinking and find him staring out the window. I remind myself that he was in a bad accident, was in a coma for two weeks, and is probably stir-crazy.

"Did the doctor really say you just need a signature from a parent or guardian?"

"Yes, but Dad's not answering," Seb replies sourly.

"He's coming home. It's a nineteen-hour flight and they have to stop and refuel," I remind him.

"I know." The sheets curl in his fists. He wants to get out of here so bad.

The phone on the nightstand next to the bed buzzes at the same time the device in my pocket vibrates. Dad must be here. Seb's eyes light up as he grabs the phone. Whatever he reads isn't good, though. His bright face turns black as he scans the message. With a curse, he hurls the phone across the room. It strikes right in the middle of the mystery meat mark.

"Good aim," I sigh. Seb is one of the top scorers on the Astor lacrosse team.

"Dad's in London and won't be here until the wee hours of Thursday morning."

"What for?" I pull out my own phone and read the message—bad weather is grounding him.

"East."

"What?"

"You gotta do something."

I make a face. "Like what? We're on the second floor. You want to tie your bedsheets together and climb out?"

A crafty gleam enters his eyes. "There's one person who can help us."

A firehouse full of alarm bells rings in my head. There is someone who has guardianship over us when Dad's out of the country—or at least used to. He could sign off on our grades, permission slips, or anything that a minor couldn't buy without an adult agreement. But that person is persona non grata and Seb knows this.

"No." I shake my head. "No and no. That's a bad idea."

"Why? Because Ella would care? What she doesn't know won't hurt her, and I won't tell if you won't."

"No, because you don't want to owe a guy like that anything. It's like handing your bank account to a drug addict and saying 'Don't take anything.'"

"What's the worst that could happen? He calls us for a favor and we say no."

That doesn't sit right with me either.

"Please, East. I wouldn't ask this if I wasn't desperate, but I swear to you if I have to stay here one more night, I'm going to end up doing something drastic."

I clench my teeth together. I don't think Seb's serious, and it's low of him to throw out that threat when our mom actually did take her own life.

I decide I need to take a break before I do something I'll regret.

"I'm going to get you some water," I say, walking toward the door.

"I have water!" he screams after me.

I take a walk down the hall, stopping when I arrive at Hartley's old room. Head injuries are terrible. Hartley lost her memory and Sebastian lost himself. I run a hand over my own skull. We're all so fragile. One bad fall and the whole world can change. Neither Hart nor Seb asked for this, and I bet if they could go back to the way they were before, they'd do so in a heartbeat. I crack my neck. All I can do is be patient. Of course, I suck at being patient, but what are my other options?

I force myself to turn and walk back to Seb's room. He needs me, even if it's just for me to be a target. He's got to vent and I can take it.

When I return, Seb is dressed and sitting in the lounge area, looking more like a guest than a patient. He's rifling through a *GQ* magazine.

"What's going on?"

He doesn't answer.

"Seb? Why'd you get dressed?"

He finally looks up at me, a smug expression on his face. "I'm getting out of here."

"How?"

As he continues to smile, a flicker of dread snakes through me. "You didn't."

He shrugs. "What's the big deal, anyway? He'll come pick us up and drop us off. No one will care if you don't make a big deal out of it."

"This is wrong." I tug my phone out but realize I can't make the call. I deleted that contact a while back and I don't know the number. I clench my jaw again. "You don't call the devil for help."

"Too late."

"I'm glad you called me." Steve O'Halloran's heavy hand falls on my shoulder, and I do my best not to flinch. It goes to show how dumb the system is that a guy who is charged with murder and attempted murder can walk around free. And don't tell me that his ankle bracelet or million-dollar bail requirement is any kind of deterrent. Steve's got access to a lot of money. He hides it, like a squirrel, all over the place. I started picking up that habit myself. I even got my dad to install the safe in my walk-in closet after Steve showed me a cool one in his bedroom.

I send Seb a killing glare, which he ignores as he climbs into the backseat. He got what he wanted and isn't concerned about any fallout—a sentiment that I recognize and am beginning to realize isn't just selfish and shallow, but actually harmful. The speech I gave Ella about pursuing fun above everything else sounds so idiotic in the face of this.

"Did you forget something?" Steve asks.

"My mind," I mutter under my breath. I wrench open the back door and push Sebastian over.

"Sit in the front," he complains. "I'm sick. I need to lie down."

"Because not sitting in your seat and wearing a seatbelt last time worked so well for you," I say sarcastically.

Seb responds maturely by giving me the finger. I buckle in and ignore the fact that the passenger seat of Steve's new Tesla is pushing my knees into my chest. It's uncomfortable back here, but I'm not sitting next to the man who tried to kill Ella. I already feel about as low as an ant's foot and I'm not going to compound it by treating him like he's a friend of the family.

"How are you two boys?" Steve asks as he motors slowly toward home. The man is a speed demon. We would be home in five minutes if he drove normally. Instead, he's rivaling Ella's pace. At this rate, we'll be lucky to get to our house before the sun rises.

"Great," Seb chirps. "Can we stop somewhere?"

"No," I bark. "We're going home."

I can't effing believe that Seb wants to spend more than two minutes with the dude in the driver's seat. Steve killed a woman, and to cover it up, he tried to kill Ella. Breathing the same air as him is making me sick.

"We can stop anywhere you like," Steve says.

Seb perks up and starts to say something until I place my booted left foot on top of his right foot and press down. At this point, I don't care that he just got out of the hospital. We are going home. My eyes convey a host of very real threats, and Seb knows me well enough to realize these are not empty promises. He might be seventeen, but he's been in the hospital for two weeks and we both know I could put him back there with little effort. He shuts his mouth and leans against the window while I remove my foot and put it back on my side of the car.

"Home is fine," I answer for both of us.

The ride home is mercifully short. As soon as the vehicle stops, I'm ready to leap out. Steve bringing us home won't be a problem if no one knows about it.

"Time to wake up, sleepyhead. You're home." I shake Seb, who fell asleep despite the quickness of the trip. "Come on, let's go," I hiss. The longer we spend in the driveway, the more likely we're going to be discovered.

"Is he all right?" Steve twists around and pats Seb on the knee. "Hey, kiddo. Are you okay?"

"He's fine," I say, but inwardly, I'm worried. Did we bring him home too soon? I shake him harder. Maybe too hard, because he moans with pain and bats me away with a flurry of fists and legs.

"Fuck off," he growls. "Are you trying to send me back into the coma?"

"Sorry." I hurry out of the car and around to his side.

He stumbles to his feet, grabbing on to the car and then me before taking a wobbly step forward.

Steve catches Seb's right side and instructs me with a jerk of his head to take the other. So much for my plan to sneak into the house.

"I can walk." Seb tries to throw us off, but the kid's as weak as a newborn.

Steve and I virtually carry him up the wide steps to the front door. "I can take it from here," I tell Steve.

He smiles. "I wouldn't dream of abandoning you."

I grit my teeth. "Really. We're fine. Aren't we, Seb?"

Seb's head lolls on his shoulders. "Yeah, fine," he says sleepily.

Alarm rises inside me. I narrow my eyes at Steve, feeling suspicious. "Did the doc really sign off on this?"

Steve nods. "Yes. They said his vitals were fine over a forty-eight-hour period and that we should call if there are any signs of degradation of mental ability."

"What in the hell does that mean?"

"It means if I start drooling, you should wheel me back," Seb jokes.

"He sounds good to me." Steve readjusts Seb. "Why don't you get the door, Easton?"

I don't have to, because Ella suddenly appears in the opening, her lips parted and hurt swimming in her eyes.

"What is going on?" she says angrily.

Steve forges forward, dragging Seb behind him. "We're bringing Sebastian home."

"I'm sorry," I mouth to Ella, but she's fixated on Steve, watching him carefully as if he might whip out a gun at any minute and point it at her head.

And why wouldn't she be thinking that? It wasn't so long ago that Steve *did* have a gun in his hand pointed at her.

Shit. I need to get him out of here. ASAP.

I thread my arm under Seb's and hoist him away from Steve. We play a short game of tug-o-Seb until Steve finally gives in.

"Why don't you get Sawyer?" I suggest to Ella.

She nods and backs up, her arms folded across her stomach protectively, her eyes not wavering from Steve. The door stands open behind me, because despite the cavernous size of this house, Ella's feeling trapped and scared.

I lower my brother onto a chair in the marble-floored foyer. He peers at me through heavy lids.

"You okay, bub?" I knock him gently on the shoulder.

"My head hurts." He swipes the back of his hand across his mouth. "And I feel like I gotta throw up."

"Bathroom's that way." I point to the powder room just off the entrance.

He takes a deep breath and then another, clearly trying to battle the nausea, but the sickness wins. He turns gray-green and bolts up, racing to the bathroom. The sounds of his retching fill the big hall.

"You can go now," I inform the man who helped raise me, the one who my mother had an affair with, the one who tried to kill my best friend.

"Since Callum's not home, I think it's best if I—"

"No," I interrupt. "What's best is if you leave." I walk to the door that Ella left open. "Thanks for your help, but Seb shouldn't have called you."

"I'll leave because I don't want to cause you any trouble, son. Ella looked a mite upset." He raises his voice, likely in hopes that Ella will hear him. "I've been wanting to explain, but I haven't had the opportunity. I didn't try to hurt my daughter. I never would. From the moment I learned of her existence, I only wanted to find and protect her. That night…" He pauses and shakes his head in mock sadness. "That night," he continues, "will haunt me forever. I wanted to protect Ella, but instead, I put her in danger."

"Nice performance." I clap my hands together. "I'd give it a C. You're too much of a psychopath to pull off any real emotion, but good try. Time for you to go, though. No one here is interested in any more of your bullshit."

We stare at each other. I tense up, wondering if I'm going to have to fight Steve. I'm young and have a lot of stamina, but Steve's got that old man strength, not to mention his military training. He and my dad were Navy SEALs.

Luckily, I don't have to put it to the test. He drops his gaze and strolls toward the door, stopping when he's even with me.

In a low voice, he says, "You're a chip off the old block, aren't you, son?"

With a wink, he steps out the door, leaving me chilled and unsettled. I hate that he calls me "son." I hate it even more that I suspect it's because I *am* his son. That's what John Wright insisted when I showed up on his doorstep, drunk. He mocked me about DNA tests, about not being a real Royal, about how I'm really an O'Halloran...

I forcibly shove the memory from my head. Fuck Hartley's dad. And fuck Steve. Fuck 'em.

I slam the heavy door shut and turn around to see Ella at the top of the curved staircase. Even from here, I can feel her anger and distress.

"Where's Seb?" There's no background music of vomit anymore.

"Sawyer took him upstairs. Why did you bring him here?" There's no need to ask who she's talking about. "Sebastian wanted out of the hospital and the doctor wouldn't release him to me."

"You're an adult."

"I'm not his guardian."

"Neither is Steve!" she cries.

I squeeze the back of my neck. "After Mom died, Dad gave Steve a backup control over us. A type of"—I have to think of the word—"conservatorship. Every time he's not here, Steve's authorized to make decisions on Callum's behalf. I guess Dad never rescinded it."

Ella turns as pale as a tissue. "What exactly are you saying? That any time Callum's gone, Steve can tell us what to do? He could take me from this house?"

The knot of anxiety that set up camp at the base of my neck is spreading like a disease throughout my entire body. "I don't know," I answer honestly. "Seb—" I break off. I can't put any blame on my sick brother. He needs Ella to help take care of him. "I remembered that Steve had it at one time—he signed authorizations for me to fly when Dad was gone—so I took the chance. It was stupid and I regret it."

"I'm pretty upset you brought him here." She disappears up the stairs but not before I see tears start to fall. She's off to call Reed. I suspect I'm going to get an earful from him tonight, and I probably deserve it. I screwed up bad.

I should've told Seb no. His threat to do something drastic was probably to run down the hall naked, not kill himself. I shouldn't have panicked. There were dozens of other choices I could've made, and while none are coming to me, I know that they had to exist.

Fuck, man. Adulting is hard.

CHAPTER TWENTY-FIVE

Hartley

AFTER SCHOOL ON WEDNESDAY, I find Mom in the kitchen, prepping dinner.

"Dad home?" I ask. It's not five yet, and I'm hoping that he works regular office hours. I need to get into his office. The plan that I cooked up over lunch involved me thoroughly inspecting every piece of paper in his desk in hopes I can find some incriminating information.

"No, dear. Would you please chop these?" She rolls two pieces of fruit in my direction.

"Sure." I wash my hands, rubbing my finger along the scar there. It's a blessing in some ways to not remember how this happened. Then I can live without the burden of those bad memories, but it's only a blessing if I can help my sister and prevent the past from repeating itself. "So Dylan is going to a horse show? Is that a one-day thing?"

"She leaves tomorrow after school and won't be back until Sunday."

Finally, something goes my way. I have a four-day window

to ferret out evidence against my father. I dry my hands, grab a knife and join my mother at the counter. Standing next to her, I realize I'm two inches taller than she is. I hadn't noticed it before, but in the last three years, I've grown. I scan her face. She's grown, too—not taller, but older. Her lips are thinning. There are wrinkles at the corners of her eyes. The skin at her cheeks droops slightly. She looks tired and unhappy.

I don't have any memories where she's laughed from her belly or been completely carefree. Is this adulthood? Or are the lines, etched so deep into her forehead that even Botox can't eradicate them, the result of Dad's behavior?

One question sits at the back of my head, in the core of my heart. It shoots up my throat and slides to the end of my tongue. *Do you love me?*

Desperate to know, I lift my wrist. "Do you know how I broke this?"

Her gaze falls to my scar and then flicks back to my face. Confusion fills her eyes. "Of course. You fell at school."

"Dad broke it."

Mom slams her knife on the counter. "Is that what you're remembering? That's not true. That's the lie your school told you so that they could get out of paying for their wrongdoing. Well, your father fixed that one. They paid all three years of your tuition there." She picks up the blade and returns to chopping onions. "I can't believe that after all we've done for you, that lie is the one you remember."

My mind spins in confusion. Did Easton lie to me? No. He's just repeating what I told him. So was *I* wrong? Had I gotten it completely wrong? And what does she mean by "all we've done for you"? The image of my empty apartment, my missing phone, my completely sterile bedroom combines into a larger, more alarming picture. Had she tried to prevent me from remembering the past because she feared what I knew?

"Where's my phone?" I demand. "And my purse? Where are they? Where is all the stuff you took from my apartment?"

Mom's hand jerks, but she doesn't look up from the cutting board. "The police must've lost them."

Her flat tone gives away the lie. "Like the police lose evidence for Dad's cases when he gets paid off?"

"Get out." Her voice is low and full of menace. "Get out and stay out until you screw your head on straight. I won't tolerate you bad-mouthing your father like this. If you can't stop lying, maybe you'll have to go back to the hospital."

My hand curls around the knife. "You better not be hurting Dylan."

"I told you to go."

I take a shaky breath, lay down my knife, and walk out. I don't go upstairs. I don't think I can spend another minute in this house. I grab Easton's jacket and my backpack and leave. Mom doesn't stop me. She doesn't ask where I'm going. She doesn't want to know.

I pull out my phone and pull up Parker's address. I'm not going to bother calling her. She could hang up on me, but she won't be able to make me leave her house until I'm done talking. There's no bus that stops close to her house. It takes me thirty minutes to arrive.

She answers the doorbell with a frown. "What are you doing here, Hartley?"

"Dad is hurting Dylan," I say without preamble. "You need to come and take her away."

Parker's expression turns angry. "Mom called and said you were spreading these lies again. You almost ruined our family last time. Maybe no one has told you, but you were sent away because you wouldn't shut up about your stories. So for Pete's sake, Hartley, stop lying and we can all be happy. If anyone is hurting Dylan, it's you."

Her accusations rock me back on my heels. "You weren't there the other night," I reply hotly. "Dad had his hand around her face—"

"She wasn't taking her meds. Do you know how dangerous that is? Of course, you don't, because you haven't been around to see Dylan go through this mess. Dad's hand was on her face? Of course, he had his hand on her face. He wanted to make sure she swallowed those pills. You don't know anything. Mom says that all you can remember is your lies, and I see that she's right. Go back to New York, Hartley." Her lips curl. "You're not wanted here."

Then she steps back and slams the door in my face.

I stand there for a long time, staring at the brass doorknob until the swirls on the calligraphic W etched into the center blur in front of my eyes. I don't know what to do. I could go to the police, but report what? I have no proof.

My wrist begins to ache. I rub it. I could get my medical records. Would those tell me anything? I don't even know the name of the school I went to, though. Or where it was. New York is a big state. Who would know?

Jeanette's unread message pops to mind. Hurriedly, I pull out my phone and bring up the messaging app.

Hey! You doing better? Mom said you were in a bad accident and lost your memory?!!! That's so terrible. I don't have much info for you. We lost touch when you went to boarding school in NY. When Nana died, your parents used the money from the education fund to send you there. I can't remember the name of it, but I think it was like Northwind or Northfield Academy. It had North in it. Your old number is 555-7891. I called it but it's disconnected and no longer in service. I wish I could remember more. I hope you feel better!

Shit. I should have contacted her earlier. I need to get home, I decide. I won't go in, but I need to see Dylan and talk to her, let her know if anything happens, I'll be there for her. This time I don't take the bus. My parents' house is only a ten-minute drive from Parker's, so I call for a car. It's a minor miracle, but I arrive at the same time that my sister is being dropped off.

"Dylan!" I rush up to catch her attention. "Did you have a good time?"

She stops, a big smile on her face. "Yup."

She smells of hay and manure and sweat, but her smile is so pretty it doesn't matter. I want to hug her but am afraid she'll reject me. Screw it. I go in anyway, swiftly giving her a two-armed embrace. She barely squeezes me back, but she doesn't push me away, so I call it a win.

I glance over my shoulder, wondering how long I have until Mom comes out and chases me away. "Do you have your phone on you?"

Dylan's brows crash together. "Yeah, why?"

"Because I got a new phone and want to add you. That way we can text during class and stuff." *And at night, in case you need me.*

She slowly pulls out her phone. "I guess. I don't really text much."

"That's fine. I'll try not to bother you." *Come on. Come on,* I silently urge her. "What kind of riding do you do?"

"I'm jumping now." She unlocks her device.

"Wow. That's awesome. Can I come watch?"

"Why would you want to?" she asks, suspicion coloring her face and voice.

"You're my sister and you're doing something cool. Seems like the question is, why wouldn't I want to?"

"You never were interested before." Her fingers hover over the screen.

"I was obviously a shit sister before," I joke, but inside I die a little at this. Dylan's so young and she needed support, but apparently, I was a heartless jerk. "The head injury knocked some sense into me."

"Are you trying to make me feel sorry for you? Because I don't," my sister responds.

"No. That's not my intention at all."

The door creaks open behind me. Ah, shit. "Your number," I say urgently.

She scowls. "Are you leaving me again?"

Again. God, how can one word wreck me so much? She was hurt that I went away to boarding school.

I blink away the tears before nodding. "No. I'm here. I never wanted to leave in the first place, but I can't change the past. I'm here now. That's why I want to exchange numbers. Please. Please, Dylan."

She glances over my shoulder.

"Dylan, it's time to come inside," Mom says coldly. "Your sister won't be joining us tonight."

"I thought you weren't leaving me," Dylan cries.

"I'm not. I promise you. I'm staying in Bayview. Maybe not here in the house, but in Bayview. Okay? Please. Your number."

She hesitates, and I hold my breath.

"Dylan, come inside," Mom says again.

My sister nods and starts walking. I want to die inside, but as she passes me, she mumbles seven digits under her breath. I close my eyes with relief and then hurriedly enter them into my phone. The door shuts behind Dylan, but Mom remains on the step.

"Since you remember you have an apartment, I suggest you go back there. This hasn't been your home for three years. You're not welcome here until you stop with your lies and slander."

Then it looks like I won't ever be coming home. I clutch Easton's jacket in my hand and burn my very last bridge. "I'll be back, but it's going to be to take Dylan away from you."

I turn on my heel and walk off. I don't know how I'm going to do it, but I'm going to make it happen.

I take the bus to the apartment. I hope Easton doesn't mind sharing. When I arrive, the second-floor lights are on. A warm sensation starts to thaw the cold that set in on the ride over. I run up the stairs, noting that the light above the door has been replaced and that the handle is more securely attached. The stairs are still rickety, but I'm beginning to love this shabby home.

I knock lightly but don't wait for an answer before walking in. Easton's at the stove, naked from the waist up. His black knit joggers with the white stripe down the side barely cling to his hips. I lean against the door and allow myself to ogle him for a good thirty seconds. I deserve it, I think. After entertaining about ten different naughty thoughts, I roll my tongue back into my mouth and check the corners of my lips for drool before greeting him.

"What's for dinner?"

"Spaghetti," he says without turning around. "It's the only thing I know how to make. Ella taught me. Want to set the table? There should be a bag full of plates and shit."

I peel my gaze away from his shoulders and land on a small wooden kitchenette set. "Since when do we have a table?"

"Since today. I did some shopping."

That's an understatement. The once empty apartment is now stuffed full. Besides the table and two chairs, there's a new beautiful gray sofa, a white-and-gray-and-black rug, and a mattress set upright against the wall. A number of bags with a familiar red bull's-eye sit on one end of the sofa. I sort through them until I find plates, glasses, and even a box of silverware. There's also a colander, which he's going to need for the noodles.

"Hope those are okay."

Is that nervousness in his voice?

"They're great." I collect two of everything and bring them over to the sink for a quick rinse. There's not much room in the kitchen, so I have to squeeze in next to Easton to get to the sink. He shifts over, but our elbows rub together as we work.

It's so nice after the horror that happened at my house. I don't think I ever want to leave this place.

"I bought them at Target," he tells me as he dumps a bottle of red sauce into a pan with browned beef. My stomach rumbles in appreciation. "That place is the bomb," he continues adorably. "It has everything. I got this table there and the chairs, plus all this kitchen shit. I also picked up the mattress, but I can't figure out how to put the bed together. They had towels and shampoo and everything. Like, that's the only store we need."

I love how he uses the word *we*. I don't feel so alone anymore. I set the strainer in the middle of the sink and take the dishes over to the table.

"Incoming," he says. I turn around to see him carrying a big pot over to the table. "Can you grab the bread? It's in the oven."

I grab a towel—also new—and pull the tinfoil-wrapped garlic bread out of the oven. "How did you know I was coming?"

"Mmm, maybe not knew, but hoped?" He sits after I do, a gentlemanly act I hadn't realized I liked until he did it for me.

If I was told I'd be hungry twenty minutes ago, I'd have called that person a liar, but the smell of the sauce and the buttery bread along with the sweet treatment from Easton makes me ravenous. I scoop about ten servings of noodles and sauce onto my plate and dig in.

"What do you think of my cooking?"

I hold my thumb up. "It's awesome."

He winks at me before attacking his plate. We eat in silence, too busy stuffing our faces to speak. The giant pot of noodles and sauce is almost gone before I call a halt.

I push back from the table and stagger to the sink with my plate in my hands. "I feel like I ate a whole factory of pasta."

"It was good, wasn't it?" He sets his own plate down next to mine. A big smile is stretched across his gorgeous face. He's so pleased with his accomplishment that I want to pinch his cheeks.

But if I touch him, I won't want to stop.

"The best," I agree. "Go sit down while I clean the dishes."

"I can help," he protests.

"Nope. You did the cooking, so I clean. It's the rules."

"What rules are those?"

"Our house rules." I shoo him out of the tiny kitchen area.

He saunters over to the mattress frame and pulls out a baby-pink plastic container. "Do you know what these are?"

"No clue. A hairdryer?"

"This is real man stuff." He flips open the case and displays a set of screwdrivers.

"How do you figure?"

"Because real men put shit together, Hart. How do you not know this?" He unpacks the tools and lays them beside the metal frame.

"Apparently because I have a vagina."

"No. I think it's because you haven't had enough contact with real men." He pauses to flex for me.

I pretend not to be impressed by the obvious muscle definition. "If you say so."

"It's probably because you went to that all-girls' school for so long. Not that I'm complaining. The fewer guys you hang around with, the better for me." He flips the screwdriver in his hand and grins.

I pause, water dripping from my hands. "Did I ever say the name of the school?"

"No. I don't think so. Why?"

"Because I think I need my medical records."

He sets the pink screwdriver on the ground, abandoning his mini construction project. "What happened?"

"I confronted my mom and she said that I broke my wrist at school and that the school tried to place the blame on my family to get out of a lawsuit."

"That's bullshit," he swears. "Why would you lie about this shit to me? I practically forced you to admit what happened. You didn't want to tell me, so it wasn't for attention or sympathy. It was the truth."

"Okay, but how do I prove that? It's been three years. I've been thinking all day about how to get Dylan away from my dad, but that's the only thing I can come up with."

He scratches his head. "All right. We find out where your old school is located. We search the hospitals that were around there and we get your medical records."

"What about the fact that I'm a minor?"

Easton taps his fingers on the ground. "I have an idea. Get your jacket. We're going to see someone."

CHAPTER TWENTY-SIX

Easton

SOMEONE IS LAWRENCE—"CALL ME LARRY"—WATSON, a behemoth of a guy who somehow, for all his size, doesn't look like he has an ounce of fat on him.

"Larry plays on the O-line," I explain to Hartley, but her face registers no understanding. I forgot that football isn't her thing.

Despite Larry's skill on the field, football isn't his thing either. Computers are, though. When he was fifteen, he moved into the apartment above his family's second garage, saying that he needed more space. Never mind that his house is bigger than a couple gymnasiums. His parents let him because they figured it would foster his huge brain.

"This looks like a branch of NASA," Hartley comments as she takes in the five computer screens in the dimly lit room Larry calls an office.

"NASA wishes its setup was as sweet as mine," he brags. "This baby has twenty-four cores of computing power on a dual 3.0 gigahertz Intel Xeon E5-2687W v4 topped off with thirty megs of Smart Cache per processor."

Hartley's eyes glaze over. She's a musician, not a coder. I step in before we lose her. "Here's the deal, Larry. Hartley's lost her memory."

"Oh, that's for real?"

I scowl. "Yeah, of course it is."

He shrugs and swivels around to face his desk. "I was just asking. No need to bite my head off."

"It's fine," Hart assures me, placing her hand on my shoulder.

I take a deep breath and squeeze her fingers. If she's okay with it, I need to be okay with it, too.

"What do you want me to find?"

"Hartley's boarding school. It's in New York and it should have the word *North* and *Academy* in it."

"That's it? You guys should have been able to do this." He types a few things and a screen loads that says Astor Park Prep at the top.

I grit my teeth in frustration. Did Larry not hear me? "We don't need her Astor Park records—"

"Look," Hartley interrupts, pointing to the screen.

Larry's not looking at Hart's transcript, but her entire student file. He flips through the digital pages, stopping on the ones that have Northwood Academy for Girls at the top. "All-girls' school, huh?" He wiggles his eyebrows. "Kinky. Any hot girls there?'

"I assume they were all gorgeous," Hartley says. "We had lesbian orgies every weekend. We rubbed lotion on each other, had tickle contests, and every night ended with a silk pajama pillow party."

Larry's jaw grows slack.

"She's kidding," I insert.

"Man, who cares if she's kidding?" He winds his hand in a circle. "Keep going. I don't care if you're making up these stories or that shit actually happened, just keep going."

"That's it, sorry. Other than the orgies we held every third Sunday as part of our worship to Nyx, the goddess of night. It was quite the ritual. We'd select one freshman from the neighboring boys' school, strip him and then castrate him before feeding his balls to our cats."

Larry sighs. "You just had to ruin it, didn't you?" He turns to his screen again. "I don't see anything interesting here. Good grades. No extracurricular activities. A note that says you don't enjoy participating in group shit. That's it?"

He sounds disappointed.

"No, actually, we're trying to find her hospital records but didn't know where the school was located. Can you figure that out?"

His eyes brighten. "Hospital records? That's a lot more fun. Let's see." He types in the address and retrieves the website of the only hospital in the area. "It'll depend on how much they digitize, but most hospitals scan all their records because they have to send them around. Oh, look, a patient portal," he chortles. "This isn't even going to require hacking."

And it doesn't. Larry is able to enter Hartley's social, date of birth, and mother's maiden name—information he'd gotten from her Astor records—to gain access to her patient portal, which has lab results, x-ray readings, and doctors' notes. It's laughably easy. The world's a scary place, I think.

I lay a comforting hand on Hart's back, but she's too engrossed in reading the details on the screen to notice. I guess the one who's being comforted is me.

"Shit, three weeks undiagnosed break. That had to hurt like a bitch," Larry comments.

"I don't remember." She rubs her wrist.

I don't think she even realizes she's doing it. I bet her body remembers even if her memory is shooting blanks, otherwise she wouldn't always be reaching for that scar.

"I'm a computer scientist, not a doctor, so what are we looking for here?"

"Cause," Hart explains. "How'd it happen? My story changes." She points to the top of the screen. "When I was first admitted, I said I'd hurt it at home, but after the second visit, it says I fell at school."

"And the diagnosis part says that your injury is consistent with a 'direct insult from bracing herself against a fall,'" I read.

Hart and I blow out long, disappointed breaths. There's nothing here that can help us. We can't take this to the police or a lawyer as proof that Hartley's father is a danger. Her shoulders slump and she runs an agitated hand through her hair.

"We'll find something else," I murmur.

She nods, but I'm not convinced she believes me. I wrap my arm around her shoulders and hug her to my side. She's stiff as a board. I wish I could just go over to her house and punch her dad's lights out, but, sadly, this is one of those times when violence isn't the answer. Which sucks, because physical combat is about the only thing I'm good at these days.

I thought I was so brilliant, bringing her to Larry.

"Anything else you want to see?" Larry asks, popping a potato chip in his mouth, seemingly oblivious to the new tension in the air.

Hart's too discouraged to answer.

"What else is there?" I ask for her.

"I could create a profile by combining all of Hartley's social media postings in the past so that you could recreate your memories from there," he offers.

I guess he does pick up on her distress. "You're a good man, Larry," I tell him.

He gives me a tentative smile. "Should I do that?"

Hartley stares blankly at the screen. No doubt she's thinking of Dylan.

"Hart?" I ask softly.

"I tried that before," she finally replies. "And found nothing."

"What'd you search? Your name?"

"Yes."

He grunts. "No one uses their real names on the internet anymore. You have to know your handle."

"I don't know those, though."

"What about before—what IDs did you use before?"

"I didn't have any accounts before thirteen. It was against the rules."

Larry and I turn to stare at her in amazement.

"What?" she exclaims. "That was what all the sites said. You had to verify that you were above the age of thirteen."

"Why didn't you lie?" Larry asks the obvious.

"I…because what if someone found out and then I got in trouble?"

He rolls his eyes and turns his attention back to his computer. I bury my face in her hair to muffle my chuckles.

"What's so funny?" she asks stiffly.

"Everyone lies online," Larry says, his fingers flying across the keyboard.

"Not everyone."

"I can't believe you thought you were a cheater." I tug on a long strand of her hair that hangs down the middle of her back like a stream of ink. "You can't even lie to a machine about your age."

"Whatever." She crosses her arms and glares.

"Can you send me a pic of your face?"

She leans forward to see what he's doing. "What for?"

"I'm going to do an image search."

"You can do that?"

"Sure. It's easy. You've never done that before?"

"No." She looks at me as if I should've thought of it.

I shrug. "I use my phone to text people, look up sports scores, and watch flight vids."

"You people are useless," Larry complains. "Send me a picture."

I fish my phone out of my pocket and zip one over to Larry. He opens it, does a few things and soon we have a page full of girls' faces. I scan the screen, looking for Hartley. As I inspect the first row of pictures, I think this is a stupid idea, but then we come across one where an unsmiling Hartley wearing a god-awful yellow school blazer and black pants is stuffed between a handful of other students, all holding violins.

"Don't tell me," I deadpan, "Your mascot was the bumblebee."

She makes a disgusted sound before leaning forward. "I can see that some things are best forgotten. I'm hideous."

"It's not a good picture," Larry agrees.

I punch him in the shoulder, but way harder.

"Ouch," he cries. "I'm just telling the truth. You're hot now, Hartley."

"Gee thanks, Larry."

He rubs the spot where I hit him and gives us an aggrieved look. "I can't believe I'm getting abused while I'm helping you."

The smile drops off Hart's face at that comment. Abuse is never going to be funny to her.

"Larry, I appreciate this, but this information isn't really what I'm looking for and not just because I look like a reject from the *Bee Movie*." She straightens.

My friend takes the rejection well. "Tell me what you need and I'll see if I can find it."

I can tell she doesn't want to share that she suspects her father is a corrupt man who may or may not be hurting her sister. There's a lot of information I wouldn't want to give out about my family, either, but I don't know how we're going to find the evidence we need unless she's more forthcoming.

"Hart, I know this is hard," I murmur in a low voice, "but could you share something?"

She ponders my suggestion until an idea forms. Her face brightens, and she turns to Larry with suppressed excitement. "You're a good hacker?"

"I don't want to brag but I'm better at getting into computers than East is at getting into a girl's pants."

I bop him across the top of his head. "Dammit, Larry."

"Hey, sorry, it was the only comparison that popped in my head."

"Never mind." Hart waves her hand. "I don't care about that. If I told you my phone number, could you access my past text messages?"

"Oh, yeah, that's not hard, especially if I have your number. I can access your emails, call logs, app downloads, photos, and maybe even voicemails. What is it?"

She reels it off.

"Go sit over there. It'll take me a bit. I have to hack into the SS7. Every text message in the world passes through Signaling System No. 7. Did you know that governments can track your movements anywhere in the world with just your cell phone? They also listen in. You should really install programs on your phones that alert you to an SS7 attack. That two-factor authentication doesn't stop it, either. That's just something the government pushes you to have to make you feel safe. They're always watching. Dummy phones are good, too. I change my phone every three months."

I lead Hart over to a pair of slouchy leather sofas as Larry drones on about the dangers of cell phone communication.

"I hope the FBI agent who's assigned to me isn't too bored, because I stopped watching porn this summer," I joke, pulling Hartley down next to me. I stretch out my legs and try to relax.

Beside me, Hart sits like she's at church, with her hands curled around each kneecap, her shoulders tight, and her face straight forward with her eyes pinned on Larry's back.

I reach up and rub her neck. "What do you think will be on your texts?"

"I don't know, but it must've been important enough for my parents to want to get rid of my phone."

"That's true." I hadn't thought of it that way. I assumed

that her folks wanted to keep her memories blank so she wouldn't remember spying on her father, but maybe it was to hide something specific.

"You think you had pictures or recorded some audio?"

She shakes her head. "I don't know. If I did, why didn't I confront him before? Why did I come back after three years?"

"You were fourteen when you were sent away. What were you going to do at the age of fourteen?" I hate that she feels guilty about this. She's a kid. She shouldn't have to deal with this shit. Just like I shouldn't have had to deal with my mom's suicide, my dad's abandonment, and my idol's betrayal.

Adults should be protecting their kids, not destroying their lives.

"It's not your fault," I say. "You did what you could to survive."

I'm saying it more for myself than anything. I've done drugs, drank too much alcohol, screwed too many girls, but all I was trying to do was survive. I pull her rigid frame against mine and hold her. I hold her until the stiffness drains away, until she stops staring a hole into Larry's back, until she curls onto my lap and clings to me.

Hartley's a small girl. I forget that sometimes when she's fighting with me or smarting off like she did with Larry earlier. But in my arms, I feel her fragility. She tries hard to solve her own problems. Before her accident, she was so closed off—not willing to share even one morsel of information with me. I had to drag everything out of her.

I see why now. Sordid secrets are ones that you try to bury in your basement, not wear like a cape around your shoulders. Now she's finally leaning on my shoulders, but there's a sense of hopelessness in the way she sighs and shifts. I brush a hand down the back of her head, tangling my fingers in the spill of her long, inky dark hair.

"If this doesn't work, then we'll find something that will."

"I know," she mumbles.

She doesn't sound convinced. I tip her chin up so she can see the sincerity in my eyes. "I'm not going to stop here," I promise her. "However long it takes, however hard it is, I'm with you."

She blinks, her silvery eyes flashing in and out from under her black lashes. I keep rubbing her back, riding the bumps of her spine with my fingers. Trying to infuse some warmth into her chilled frame.

She takes one deep breath and then another and then another until the tension finally drains out of her.

"Okay. We're a team." She holds out her hand.

I shake it and then bring it to my mouth. "A team."

She sways toward me, her eyes dropping to my lips. My jeans grow tight and my heartbeat picks up. I tighten my fingers around her and pull—

"And we're in!" Larry crows.

Hartley jumps off my lap and races over to the bank of computers.

I heave a frustrated sigh, pull out my T-shirt and adjust myself. I'm so weak when it comes to Hartley. While my two friends chatter, I try to envision Larry naked, coming out of the locker room showers and scratching his ass. "Want to smell something good," he'd say, holding out his fingers. The team would groan.

My hard-on deflates immediately. I get up and amble over

to join them. They're excited about something. Hart turns a beaming smile toward me.

"I think I know what to do."

CHAPTER TWENTY-SEVEN

Hartley

AFTER SAYING THANK YOU A thousand times to Larry and a promise to keep him supplied with his favorite snack—Doritos—for the foreseeable future, East and I leave and review the treasure trove of information that Larry loaded onto a dummy phone. His magic pulled up my old emails, camera roll, and text messages.

My inbox contains a couple hundred spam interspersed by school assignments. The only other information of interest is a chain of emails between me and Bayview National Trust about an educational trust left by my grandmother that I can access at the age of seventeen. The trustee believed that the money was to be used for college but agreed that the language was ambiguous and said only "educational purposes" and therefore I could use it toward Astor Park.

It is my mom's dream that I attend Astor Park, I had written. *Thank you for making that happen.* So. My parents haven't paid a dime toward my Astor Park tuition. I arranged everything myself, and they couldn't say a damned word about it because Grandma's trust was in my name and I was old enough to access it.

I feel a deep sense of triumph about that, because I was able to outsmart my dad once. That means I can do it again.

The camera roll has nothing of interest. I was disgustingly boring, filling the space with pictures of landscapes, my favorite band members, and the occasional scowling selfie.

It's the text messages that net us a winner. Starting a little after last year's Thanksgiving, I began texting someone named Mrs. Roquet in hopes that she would flip on my dad. At my blank face, Easton quickly explains that Mrs. Roquet is the woman my dad took a bribe from. She gave him money in exchange for getting her son's drug case dismissed. I don't know what set me off at that point to reach out to the woman—my messages only implied I was worried about my sister.

Mrs. Roquet. I'm Hartley Wright. Would you be around to talk sometime?

A day passed without a response. I sent another text.

Hartley Wright again. I'm worried about my sister. I haven't been able to contact her in months. I think you can help me.

After a week of waiting I grew impatient and started spamming her several times a day. I finally got a response back after Christmas.

Stop texting and calling me. I'm blocking your number.

I show these with East with a frown. "After she blocked my number, I must've started calling her from a bunch of different ones," I explain, "because after New Year's she writes, 'If I agree to talk to you, then will you leave me alone?'"

"Do you have any idea when you spoke?"

"It would have to be after April, because I have one message there that says, 'I'm thinking of you and your loss.'"

"April is when Drew Roquet had his overdose," Easton muses.

Larry had found that information for us along with Mrs. Roquet's address. "She must've decided that the punishment for bribing someone was worth speaking the truth." That seems brave to me.

"The last message you have is from this past summer?" East leans over my shoulder to read the screen.

"Right, but nothing else. If I got the statement, why didn't I turn Dad in? I can't imagine that I would've ignored her, right? I wouldn't have gotten this message and let it sit. I did stuff. I got the Bayview Trust to release some of my trust to me. I enrolled in Mom's favorite school, probably to get in her good graces." It hadn't worked. She was hardened against me. I didn't last more than a couple weeks after the accident before she decided I was too dangerous to share the same household as her. She knew I was getting too close to the truth, too close to bringing an end to her perfect life.

But why was the last response I had from Mrs. Roquet from this past summer? And why hadn't I acted on it?

I read the message again.

Sorry it took me so long to get back to you. I had to think about it, but you're right. It's not like my son is around anymore. I should've let him go to prison. Maybe that would've saved him. I paid your father $25K to lose the drugs that Drew had on him, and I'm willing to say that in court if you need it. It's been three years and I think about it every night. I feel better getting it off my chest. Let me know when you want to meet.

"I never told you anything about this?" I ask East.

"No. You said you heard your dad arguing with his boss about dismissing the charges against Drew and you saw him in the car with a different woman, not the Roquet lady. That's when he broke your wrist."

I scratch my scar. "Maybe she changed her mind?"

He folds his fingers over mine. "Let's go to her place. We have nothing to lose by going there, showing her the message and asking for that statement."

"You're right." I still feel awful, like I dropped the ball. Dylan has every right to be angry with me.

Outside, Easton hails a car that takes us five miles over to the north side of Bayview—a true suburbia where the only distinguishing features of the homes are their varying shades of blue and beige. The address Larry found for us is at the end of the cul-de-sac. The house is lit up, so someone must be home.

I suck in a deep breath, screw up my courage, and let myself out of the car. East pays the driver and meets me on the sidewalk.

"Do you want me to come with you or hang back?"

I give the beautiful boy a healthy once-over. "Definitely

come with. One smile from you might make her cave." Plus, I need the moral support.

He grins that devastating half smile, takes my hand and gestures for me to lead the way.

There's a rattan welcome mat on the floor of the stoop and a wreath of ivy and berries hanging over the front door. A peek inside the sidelight reveals that Mrs. Roquet has her Christmas decorations well under way and it's not even Thanksgiving.

"I should've brought flowers or chocolates," I say, rubbing my damp palms against my jeans. "Like what is the appropriate, swear-out-an-affidavit-admitting-you-bribed-an-official gift?"

"Chocolate, definitely. I'll have a box sent to her when we're done."

"Is that considered a bribe? Maybe we better not."

He squeezes my hand. "Just knock, Hart."

A woman comes to the door, holding it open only a couple of inches. "How can I help you?"

She looks us over suspiciously, and I don't blame her. It's evening time, too late for door-to-door sales people, or even Jehovah's Witnesses.

I awkwardly stick my hand out for a handshake. "Hartley Wright, ma'am. You said I should come over to talk. I was in an accident so I wasn't able to come before now." I don't mention that the accident was only two weeks ago. That doesn't seem like helpful information at this point.

Mrs. Roquet frowns. "Hartley Wright? I'm sorry, but can you tell me what it is that we were going to talk about?" She seems genuinely baffled.

"Your son, Drew?"

"Drew? Oh, goodness, do you mean Drew Roquet?" She swings the door open wider. "I remember you now. You came here a couple months ago asking about him."

"I did?"

"She had an accident and hit her head," East pipes up. "She doesn't remember much about her past."

The lady, who I guess must not be Drew's mom, gasps. "Oh my Lord. Come in. Come in." She ushers us inside the house and sits us in the living room. "Can I get you something to drink?"

"No, ma'am," we both say.

"Well, I'm Helen Berger and I bought this house in June from Sarah Roquet."

"Oh." I'm the very picture of a deflated balloon at this moment. "Where is she now?"

"She passed, honey. A couple months after her son went on to his reward, she walked out in the middle of the freeway and got hit by a truck. Terrible thing. Bless her heart. She had lost her son a few months earlier and I guess it was just too much for her." Helen shakes her head sadly. "I shared this with you when you came here in August. You wore that same shell-shocked look. I guess you needed something from Sarah. I'm so sorry you couldn't get it."

"Yeah, me, too," I reply numbly. Ice seeps into my bloodstream. I was too late—both before my memory loss and now. Helplessness weighs me down like an anvil. I drop my chin to my chest because the disappointment makes it too hard to hold my head up.

Easton and Ms. Berger are exchanging pleasantries.

I'm so sorry I couldn't be of more help.

It's nothing at all. Thank you for your time.

Of course. Your friend looks distressed. Can I get you something before you leave?

Nah, we're good. I'll take care of her.

You're a good friend.

Thank you.

East helps me to my feet. "Thank you again, Ms. Berger."

"It's no problem."

With a nudge in my side from East, I manage to scrape together enough brain matter to remember my manners. "Thank you, Ms. Berger."

East hauls me out the door.

"Should I call for a ride or wait?"

I don't answer. I'm too angry—at myself, at my dad, at Mrs. Roquet for dying. I shake off Easton's hand and stomp down the sidewalk.

"I may not have cheated or blackmailed anyone, but I was a coward," I huff out. "I sat on my hands and did nothing. And now I'm out of options. I have three days before Dylan comes back."

"You're not out of options," he soothes.

"The hell I'm not." I swipe my hand across my face, mad that I have tears falling. What good are they going to do me? "Why'd I wait for so long?"

"You didn't wait. You were getting your ducks in order. You knew that at the age of seventeen, you weren't going to be getting your sister away from your family. And you were trying to get into that house to protect her. You got into Astor Park to make your mom happy and you kept your mouth shut about your dad's shenanigans. You were doing what you could."

"It wasn't enough." I press my hands to the side of my skull because I'm afraid the pressure inside is going to make my head explode. "It wasn't enough!"

I repeat it and repeat it, stomping around and kicking rocks, but it doesn't make me feel better. Easton stands to the side, watching me make a fool of myself. Dogs start barking and a few cars in the neighborhood slow to see what kind of maniac is bringing down the property values. One of the passing drivers honks his horn, bringing me to my senses. Red-faced with embarrassment, I drop to the curb and bury my face in my arms.

"Come on." East tugs on my arm.

"Don't wanna," I mumble like I'm five. I guess my tantrum's not over.

"You will." He virtually picks me up and sets me on my feet. He drags me down several blocks until we come to a gas station. "Wait here," he says.

Because I have nothing better to do, I plant my ass on the sidewalk and stare blindly at the stream of cars and customers gassing up their vehicles, washing down their windshields, stopping in for a quick snack. Everybody's life is going on with envious normality while mine is in shambles. The worst of it is that I feel like I had the golden ring—the answer—within reach only to find out that it didn't exist at all.

What ifs and *if onlys* haunt me. What if I'd responded earlier? If only I didn't get sent away in the first place. What if I'd kept my mouth shut? If only I could've convinced my mom that Dylan wasn't safe.

"Let's go," East says.

I look up to see him holding a six-pack and a three-foot-long metal club wrapped in yellow rubber, which my brain helpfully informs me is an anti-theft device. I remember that, but not the shit about Mrs. Roquet. I hate myself.

"I'm not interested in drinking," I respond harshly, irritated that his go-to solution is booze. Getting lit isn't going to solve any of my problems.

"Neither am I." He twists the box around so I can see that it's 7-Up. "There's a park over here. Let's go." He doesn't wait for me.

I watch him walk away for a beat and then drag myself to my feet. He's been so good to me. He's listened to my problems, waited patiently through my tantrums, stuck by me even though I lost all my memories. He's been a real friend. If I didn't have East through this whole mess, I'd be lost. So if he wants to have a drink, then I'm going to sit with him while he has that damned drink.

He's waiting on the black-tarred basketball court for me, the soda at his feet and the club in his hand. He offers it to me when I reach him.

I take it, surprised by its heft. "What am I supposed to do with this?" I ask. "Neither of us have wheels."

"When I get frustrated, I feel better when I hit something. There are always fights down at the docks. Some guys do it for money, but Reed and I would go down there because slamming your fist into a guy's face is real satisfying. I'm guessing that's your style—"

I shudder. "No."

"—so I bought the soda and the club." He waves a hand at the six-pack. "Beat the shit out of this. I promise it will make you feel better."

I'm not convinced, but I take a small swing.

He comes up behind me, wraps his arms around mine and slams the club onto the cans. Fizz sprays up and I jump back, but he holds me steady. "Put some mustard in it, Hart. How do you feel about your dad breaking your wrist?"

Fucking awful. This time I bring it down harder. There's a satisfying crunching sound as the sides of the cans cave in. I don't dodge the spray of carbonated liquid. Instead, I put my shoulder into my next swing. That's for my dad taking bribes. *Whack!* That one's for kicking me out of the house. *Whack!* This one is for Mrs. Roquet dying before I can get her statement. *Whack!* This is for Felicity and Kyle and my stupid fucking memory loss. I slam that rod into the cans until there is nothing but crushed metal and a pool of white fizzy drink bubbling like a dead fish on the pavement.

"How do you feel?" East asks, pulling the club from my hand.

I wipe a sticky wrist across my forehead. "Surprisingly better." Throwing tantrums and beating soda cans into submission might be a temporary fix, but until I get Dylan out of that house, I'm not going to be able to live with myself. I beat back a wave of helplessness. Feeling sorry for myself will solve nothing.

I blow my hair out of my face and try to gather my thoughts. My head's clearer now. I recite the pieces of evidence we do have. "I have a text of a dead woman. My dad would get that thrown out in a second. Anyone can fake a text these days. What we need to do is go to the source."

"Interrogate your dad?" Easton rubs his hands together. "I'm down for that."

"No. We break into his office—his home office."

"Tonight?"

I shrug. "Why not? It's not that late yet, and we're already out and about, Scooby-Doo'ing like pros."

Easton snickers, then goes serious. "You think he keeps anything in his office?"

"It can't hurt to try."

"Are you sure you want to do this? It could really hurt your family."

I settle a hard look at East. "If I don't, he'll hurt Dylan. Best thing I can do is find proof he's taking bribes and then turn him in."

East pulls me against him. "I'm there with you. All the way."

CHAPTER TWENTY-EIGHT

Easton

"I can't believe I'm using a chauffeured Town Car to spy on someone." I didn't want to hire out a car for this spy-capade, so Hartley and I are making do with my dad's driver, who wasted no time picking us up from the gas station. "Can you look a little less conspicuous?" I ask Durand, tapping his shoulder.

He slides down in his seat. "Will this do, Mr. Easton?" He's mocking us, but we deserve it.

This cloak and dagger shit probably looks ridiculous to anyone who doesn't know what's going on inside the Wright household. The idea of casing her dad's study seemed good a half hour ago, but now I'm not so sure. What happens if she gets caught? I'm not going to stand around while her father breaks her other wrist, but I'm not sure how to broach the topic. *Hey, babe, but I might have to beat your dad's face in tonight. Hope that's okay.*

But Hart's tired of doing nothing. She said that she was too passive before. I don't know if that's a fair characterization, but I understand wanting to take action. I'm always in favor of *doing* instead of sitting around.

"No offense, but this car is pretty noticeable." Hart looks worried.

"No offense taken, miss," Durand replies.

"Let's go take a closer look. That's why we're here, right?" I give her a chance to back out.

"Yup," she replies, and hops out.

I guess that's my answer. "We'll be back," I say as I slide out of the car after her.

"I'll be here." Durand's in a cheerful mood. I think he's into this spy shit. It's probably way more interesting than just driving me in a big boring-ass loop from home to school to the hospital and back again.

I flip up my collar against the chilly night air and hustle after Hart, who's stopped in the middle of the sidewalk, staring back down the road.

"The accident happened close to here, didn't it?" she says when I catch up to her.

"Do you remember something?" I search her face for signs of recognition.

"No, but I heard that it took place around the curve." She points to the sharp corner that we passed.

The nightmarish scene flashes in front of my eyes. The back end of her car crumpled. Glass from the twins' windshield strewn on the gravel. Seb's body twenty feet from the Range Rover.

I turn my back on the scene and block her view. If she can't remember, what's the point of dwelling on it? It's not going to undo the accident. "You're both better now," I say. "That's what's important."

She stares past my shoulder and then nods sharply as if trying to come to terms with it. "Right. Okay, let's do this." She looks around, taking in the houses, many of them mansions, lining the street. The Royal property is large enough that we can't see the house next door, but the homes in Hartley's neighborhood aren't as isolated. "Should we pretend we lost our dog and that's why we're running through people's backyards and looking into windows?"

I cough lightly to cover a laugh. "That might attract more attention than you want."

"We don't have a choice. Mrs. Roquet is dead. The only option we have left is to get direct evidence from my dad." She shoves her hands inside the pockets of my navy overcoat, her shoulders hanging so low, they're going to brush the sidewalk soon.

"Let's walk in the back, along the property line," I suggest, because she's right. This is as good as anything.

"What if someone shoots at us because we look like we're going to rob these houses?"

"Your jacket is worth a couple of mortgage payments. I don't think anyone is going to mistake you for a burglar."

"Of course it is." She rolls her eyes. "Do you get an allergy if your clothes cost less than four figures?"

"Yes. Yes, I do. And my dick shrinks, too."

"Only you, Easton, would be confident enough to joke about your dick getting smaller."

"Big dick problems," I solemnly intone. We reach the end of the lot line. No dogs are chasing us yet.

"How can you sleep in that shabby apartment if you like nice things?"

Because it's your place, I want to answer, but I don't think she's ready for that. "Because it's private. I don't have to deal with the twins or Ella." *And you're there.* "Why were you okay with it? Your house isn't a shack."

"Eh. It's not that nice inside. I think my parents bought it because they wanted to look richer than they really are. We don't own designer gear like you do. Mom talks about how expensive things are. Keeping up appearances are important to them. When I asked Parker for help, she told me I was making the family look bad."

"That sucks."

Her shoulders hitch slightly. "It is what it is."

She sounds resigned. Out of all the things that make me angry is how Hart's family abandoned her. My brothers and I may fight, Seb may have woken up a completely different person, but we're always there for each other. And when Ella came into our family, even when we weren't entirely sold on her, the minute someone tried to hurt her, we were ready to defend her. Family stands up for family.

I guess I'm Hartley's family now.

"This is it," she whispers. Hart's backyard is decent-sized but bare, with no real landscaping work done. Mostly grass and a couple trees. Her family's mansion is dark except for a single room on the end of the first floor where a blue light flickers. Someone's watching television.

"The fourth window over on the first floor is my dad's office."

I study the back. The wraparound porch has two sets of French doors, one set leading to the kitchen, the other to the family room. The latter doors are where Hart thinks we can go in. Apparently the security alarm hasn't worked in years, so

I'm not overly concerned that alarm bells will go off once we enter the house.

"What's your plan of attack?" I ask her.

"From what you said, Dad was pretty bold. He met with people in the house, so I bet he has stuff in his office."

"Wouldn't it be in a safe?"

"Maybe? But what's the harm in looking? What's he going to do? Kick me out?"

He might hit you and then I'd have to hit him back. But I keep my reservations to myself.

She creeps over to peek inside the family room. "Mom's on the couch, but I think she's sleeping."

I pop up from my crouched position to take a brief inventory of the scene. Mrs. Wright does look like she's out. Her head is tilted awkwardly to the side and the remote is lying in her slack hand. Mr. Wright isn't around.

"Maybe he's out meeting with a client," Hart says quietly.

We sidle along the house and stop below her dad's office. She peers in the window and gives me the thumbs up sign. The office is empty. She scuttles over to a large metal barbecue and reaches underneath, where she swears there is a key to the patio doors. I hear the scrape of metal against metal and a small exclamation of excitement.

"I was right," she crows, flashing a key in front of my eyes.

"Awesome. Let's go." Her enthusiasm is contagious, and I tell myself to loosen up. There's no real danger here. This is her fucking family house. If she wants to case her father's office, then that's what we're going to do.

She fits the key into the lock and starts to turn the handle when we hear his voice.

We both drop to the ground, lying as flat as we can against the concrete slab.

"I told you I'm taking care of it, but these matters are delicate and need to be dealt with slowly and carefully, otherwise we're both going to get into trouble."

Hartley reaches out and grabs my hand. I squeeze it back. She bats at it. She wants something.

"What?" I mouth.

She holds her hand up to her ear. She wants me to call someone?

No, she's shaking her head. She mimics holding a phone and then points it upward. It finally occurs to me. She wants me to record this.

I pull out my phone and open the voice memo app to start recording. I hope this works.

"I want to be paid in cash. I don't care how difficult it is to get five million in cash. That's how I want to be paid."

Five million? No wonder he can afford to live in this house on a DA's salary. It must be a big case, too, because what else would be worth that? A sick feeling burbles in my gut. There's only one really big case that's going on in Bayview right now— Steve O'Halloran's murder trial.

"I did try to scare the girl into not testifying, but she's stubborn. So I'm going to have to fix the matter by botching some evidence. Your attorneys should be smart enough to get the case dismissed on those grounds."

There's another moment of silence as Mr. Wright listens to the caller.

"If you're so worried about your daughter's testimony, then my suggestion is to make it so she *can't* testify. Do you see me having a problem with my daughter? I know how to keep the little bitch in line."

My veins harden to ice. Make it that Ella can't testify? Is he suggesting Steve *kill* Ella? Rage and fear form a lethal combo in my chest, making my ribs ache. No way. No fucking way is Steve getting his hands on Ella.

Beside me, Hartley is equally stricken. The *little bitch* line hurt her, I can see it in her eyes. Not for the first time, I wish I could strangle her father to death. And if I had any doubts before about what this conversation means, Mr. Wright has now crushed them. Steve is trying to buy his way out of the trial, and Wright is more than happy to help, so long as he gets his payout.

"I want half tomorrow, a deposit of sorts. I won't go near that evidence until I have half the money. Meet me at Winwood Park at ten. And remember, I want cash."

A wave of nausea crashes over me. Hart didn't ask me to back her up hoping to put her dad in prison. She just wants to be able to free her sister. But I can't be quiet about what I've just heard. Ella has to know that her sperm donor, the one that tried to kill her, is trying to weasel his way out of serving any time for killing my dad's former girlfriend. And that he might be coming after her again to stop her from testifying against him.

This is a fucking awful dilemma.

"That asshole," Mr. Wright fumes. He disappears from the door and we hear him yell, "I'm hungry! Make me a sandwich," his voice fading with each word.

Hartley jumps to her feet and gestures for me to follow her. We race back in the direction we came from, and she doesn't stop running until we reach Durand. She opens the door with shaking hands and says, "Go. Please, let's go."

"Where to?" Durand asks, shooting me a worried glance.

"I think we'll need to go to your place." She raises her anguished eyes to mine. "You need to tell your dad when he gets back."

"So you know," I say, my heart thudding loudly.

"It's Ella's case, isn't it?" She sounds miserable.

"Yeah, it is." My throat hurts bad. "If we tell my dad, he won't stop until yours is put away for a very long time."

She swallows and it looks painful for her, too. "So be it."

CHAPTER TWENTY-NINE

Hartley

"They're meeting tomorrow night," I finish, slumping in emotional exhaustion. "Or wait, I guess that would be tonight, since it's technically morning now." It's past two a.m. and I'm ready to keel over.

Callum doesn't look much better than I feel. He's literally been traveling for the past twenty-four hours, and you can see it in the weary lines of his face. We waited up for hours for him to get in from London. I expected it to be even later, but unlike normal people, Callum Royal doesn't have to go through Customs or wait at the baggage carousel. I guess that's the perk of having your own plane.

Easton wraps an arm around my shoulder and hauls me close, daring Ella or his dad to say a word against what I've just told them. Neither of them does. Ella's too angry and Callum is...I think shocked and saddened, as if he can't believe his longtime friend has sunk so low. I think what scared him the most is the implication that Steve might harm Ella to stop her from testifying, and that my dad was actually encouraging it.

Ella had gone pale during that part, but now her face is red with anger. She wants Steve's blood, and I don't blame her one bit.

"Is that it?" Callum asks.

I nod. "That's it. Or at least, that's all I know."

I hand him my phone with Mrs. Roquet's message on it, and he reads it carefully.

"This is the woman you saw," he prompts.

"Yes."

"But she's passed away now?"

"Yeah, we went over there tonight and the neighbor said that after her son died from an overdose last year, Mrs. Roquet lost the will to live. I think that's why it took her so long to respond to me. If you look at the time stamps on the messages, I waited over six months for her to text back."

"It was her that brought you back to Bayview," Easton guesses.

"I think so."

Callum sets both my phone and Easton's on the desk behind him. "I'm going to be straight with you, Hartley. I can't allow this to happen. I have to protect my family at all costs, and that means exposing this corruption and stopping your father."

"Dad—" Easton begins.

I cut him off with a raised hand. "No. I understand. All I want to do is protect my family too. I need to get Dylan out of the house before all of this becomes public. I'm afraid he'll take his anger out on her. Will you please help her?"

"Of course he will. Won't you?" East answers, his chin jutting out determinedly.

"Yes, I will," Callum replies. "I'll call my lawyers and have them demand another meeting with your dad, and I'll have

Durand watch your sister. We'll keep them apart for as long as possible. When this does become public, we'll have your family moved to a safe environment."

It's all that he offers, and while it's not enough, at the same time I feel guilty about accepting any help. This isn't my fault. My dad's actions have nothing to do with me, but we're connected all the same—by blood, by our name.

"We need pictures of them together." Ella speaks for the first time. "We can't rely on just these messages and the audio. Without photographic proof, it'll be too easy for that asshole to get away."

I don't know if she's referring to her dad or mine.

Callum nods. "I'll take care of that, Ella."

I expect her to argue, but she just gives a terse nod and leaves. Easton pulls me to my feet. I feel dead inside. When I get to the apartment, I'm going to collapse on the first soft surface.

"Come on," he says, tugging me along behind him.

"This isn't the way to the front door," I object.

"I know. You're about to fall over, so I'm taking you upstairs. You can sleep in my room and I'll bunk in Reed's." He casts a glance toward Ella, as if to seek her permission, but her eyes are staring in zombie-like concentration ahead of her. She has a lot on her mind, and I again remind myself that none of this is my fault even though it makes me sick inside for what she's going through.

"I think I'll just go home."

"No." Ella's voice rings out clearly in the hallway. She stops at the base of the stairs. "No," she repeats. "Come upstairs. We need to plan."

"Plan?" I mouth to Easton.

He shrugs in confusion but pushes me toward the stairs. Reluctantly, I climb the marble treads, my sneakers squeaking against the tile. We turn right at the top.

"Dad's rooms are down there," Easton explains. Ella's room is the first one down a wide, long hall.

"Come in," she says.

Inside is a Barbie-pink bedroom. Pink walls, pink carpeting, pink upholstery, pink ruffled curtains. It's a princess bedroom if the princess was younger than ten. And never in a hundred years would I guess that the cool blonde girl would have this sort of love for pink.

"Dad decorated it," East tells me, grabbing a pink chair and shoving it under my ass.

"It's horrible, isn't it?" Ella says, climbing on her bed. She pats a space next to her, gesturing for Easton to sit down, but he doesn't go.

He places a hand on my shoulder. He's picking sides and I don't like it. This is his family. He shouldn't have to choose between me and his family.

I stand up. "I don't want to sit," I tell him, and then put a little distance between us. He looks hurt, but it's the right thing to do. I fold my arms and nod my chin toward Ella. "What do you need?"

"I don't want to leave this to Callum. It's not that I don't trust him, but let's say something happens and Callum's guy doesn't get the right picture. No one is going to be invested like you and me"—she flicks a finger between us—"so we should do it."

"Okay."

"No," Easton says at the same time.

"Why not?" I turn a frown on him.

"Oh, I don't know. Because it's fucking dangerous?"

"Winwood Park has a bunch of trees lining the parking lot," Ella says. "We can hide there."

"Sounds good to me. Do you have a camera?"

"Yes—"

"Did you suffer brain damage, too, Ella? And what about you, Hart? I thought you just lost your memory, but it looks like you lost your mind, too," Easton rants. He points to Ella. "Your dad uses guns." He points to me. "And your dad may or may not have killed Mrs. Roquet to keep her quiet. We know he's violent enough to have broken your wrist. Adding two plus two equals staying the hell out of it."

Ella stares at him, then turns to me. "Yes, I have a camera, but no night vision on it. I'll go to the store to get one in the morning."

"Sounds like a plan. I don't have a car, but there's a bus that stops about three blocks away if you don't mind walking a bit."

"Are either of you listening to me?" Easton bellows.

Ella and I both shut up.

"Could you keep it down?" grouses a voice from the door. "I'm trying to fucking sleep. I just got out of the hospital."

We all spin to see Sebastian standing in Ella's doorway, blinking owlishly at us. His dark brown hair is sticking up on one side and he's wearing adorable blue satin pajamas with brown monkeys stitched on them.

"Sorry," Ella says, rising from the bed.

When his gaze swings to me, he rears back in surprise. "What the hell are you doing here?"

"I, ah—" I grimace. I don't know what to say and seek Easton's help. Should I tell him the truth or do Easton and Ella want to keep it on the down low?

"She's here to help us make sure that Steve goes to prison," Easton answers. "And don't swear at Hartley."

"I'll swear at whoever the hell I want," retorts his brother. "Especially this piece of trash who nearly killed me."

"Seb, that's not nice," Ella protests. "You know it was an accident."

"Screw nice. I drove that curve a million times and never had an accident until this bitch came along."

Easton lunges forward. I grab his arm.

Ella runs to get in between the brothers. "That's enough," she scolds. She pushes Sebastian out of the doorway and says over her shoulder, "You two go to bed."

A muscle in Easton's jaw jumps, but he gives a sharp nod. "Come on," he says, and flips our grips so that he's holding my arm instead of me hanging on to his.

He marches out, down the hall, flings a door open and shoves me inside. The door slams shut behind him, but not before I hear Sebastian say, "I can't believe you're letting this bitch sleep in our house."

I don't know what Ella's response is.

"I'm sorry," Easton says, and stomps across to a set of closet doors. He disappears inside.

"Don't be. Your brother has every right to feel the way he does." Anxiousness gnaws at my stomach. How can Easton and I ever be together when his family is so opposed to it? Loneliness is a terrible feeling, and I don't want Easton to experience that. It's awful not being welcomed by your family.

It's a vile mixture of humiliation and abandonment. It's every birthday party that was held that you didn't get invited to, every game you were picked last at, every rejection you received multiplied by a million. It's standing alone in a big vast desert and thirsting for one single drop, not of water, but of affection, attention…love.

"Easton, I don't think I should be here."

He comes out, blankets in his arms. "I'm going to sleep on the couch. You can have the bed."

I don't move. "Did you hear me?"

"Yeah, but I'm not going to let you go, so you might as well get ready for bed. There's an extra toothbrush here." He tosses something at me and I reflexively catch it. "Do you want, like, pajamas? I can lend you a T-shirt or Ella might have real girl ones."

He stands there, his hands on his hips, his feet braced and his body tense as if he thinks I'm going to make a break for the door and he's going to have to tackle me to stop it. As always, whenever I'm with him, all my doubts dissolve and the cold is replaced by a bone-deep warmth. Easton is my sun, I realize.

"Are we going to have to wrestle about this?" he says. "Because if so, let's get naked and on the bed. It's the only wrestling I allow in here."

I glance over my shoulder at the big boat-sized bed. My cheeks heat up at the thought of the two of us rolling around on that bed. Kissing each other…touching each other. I want to kiss him again so badly, but I'm too chickenshit to make the first move. So I respond with sarcasm. "I bet you've had a *ton* of wrestling matches in this room. More than I could count, probably."

He offers an innocent smile. "Nope. I have not had wrestling matches in here before. I'm a virgin."

My jaw drops open. "Really?"

He nods in earnest. "Yes. Since you don't have any memories, yes, I am a virgin. Now go change so we can go to sleep."

I start toward the attached en suite and stop at the door. "Since you're a virgin, I'll remember to be gentle with you our first time."

I take an immense amount of pleasure in closing the door on his shocked face. Nothing about these past few days has been particularly funny, but Easton's expression puts a smile on my own face. I might not be great at flirting, but that parting remark was pretty hot. Go me.

I brush my teeth, wash my face with a bar of soap that smells like cedar and orange spice, and throw Easton's shirt over my head. It goes down almost to my knees.

The lights are off when I open the bathroom door.

"You done?" comes his gravelly voice.

Suddenly shy, I scamper over to the huge bed and climb under the covers. It's large enough that all five Royal brothers could probably fit on here. Hearing the sounds of Easton getting ready is strange. I'm used to silence, I think, which would make sense because I lived by myself in that apartment, and from the lack of social media pictures it appears I didn't have many friends.

It's pleasant. No, *pleasant* is a mild, meaningless word. It's…wonderful and I don't want to go back to the time in my life when there were no sounds but the ones I made. I think that's why, when my very own personal sun steps out of the bathroom rubbing a towel over his hair, I say, "The bed's big enough for a family."

He stills. "It's a king."

I sit up, reach over to the other side and flip the covers down. "Get in."

"Why, Hartley Wright, are you going to deflower me?" he gasps in mock dismay. Or maybe it's mock eagerness. Who knows?

"Not tonight. I know it's your first time, so I want to ease you into this. We'll start by sharing the bed."

East throws the towel behind him, hits the lights, and dives onto the mattress, landing half on top of me and half on top of the bed. "I don't trust you," he teases.

"I can tell," I say dryly as I push one of his heavy limbs off me. "You're the very picture of a scared virgin."

"I know, right?"

I throw a pillow at his head. "Get under the covers."

He takes the pillow, bunches it under his head and repositions himself so that he's lying next to me.

"Aren't you cold?" I ask, trying not to stare at his bare chest. Easton Royal doesn't wear pajamas and I'm pretty sure that if he were alone, he wouldn't be wearing anything to bed, not even his black boxer briefs.

"Like I said, there's a trust issue here." There's a level of self-deprecation that makes me believe that it's not me he's worried about, but his own ability to keep his hands to himself—the hands he has tucked under his head.

"We can pretend like we're Puritans and use the pillows as a bundling board," I suggest.

"What the hell is a bundling board?"

"Like a log or sack you stick between two people before they get married. That way they can get used to sleeping with each other without giving up their precious V-cards."

"You remember the weirdest things, Hart."

My own heart skips a beat, as it does whenever he calls me by that nickname. Like I'm his heart. Like I belong with him. I force my gaze to the ceiling.

"I'm going to memorize a bunch of random facts so that my head's full of them. Maybe being *Jeopardy* champion should be my life's goal. I'll skip college, spend all my time memorizing trivia books, and win a million dollars on a game show."

"Okay," he says simply, as if my idea isn't the strangest thing.

"I think you'd say okay even if I said my plan was to learn how to swing on the trapeze and join the circus."

I feel him roll onto his side. I twist my head to see him smiling at me.

"First, swinging on a trapeze is sexy. Second, the circus is dope. Third." He reaches out and trails a hand over my hair. "Third, I love you, Hart. So yeah, if you want to join the circus or sell magazines door to door or work as a clerk at the mall, then I'm all for it. Whatever makes you happy."

He loves me?

Oh my God. He says the most unexpected things at times. My heart flips over, the butterfly house in my stomach feels like it just got shaken by a hurricane wind, and tears prick my eyes. I blink furiously to keep them back.

"You're just saying that so I invite you to be my partner in the circus act."

His thumb flicks under my eye to wipe away a stupid tear that escaped. "For sure. I need to be there if you're going to be swinging around in a leotard looking impossibly hot. I can't let the bearded lady or the lion tamer steal my girl."

Because he's Easton Royal and I have zero self-control, because my sore heart needs all the sun it can get, because I love him back, I throw myself into his arms and kiss him.

I meant it to only be a kiss, a quick peck even, but I can't stop. I kiss him and kiss him and suddenly my hands are finding the button on his jeans. My fingers are pulling down his zipper. My mouth is skipping across his jaw to taste his earlobe and then his salty neck.

He lets me do all of these things until he lies beneath me, naked except for a pair of black boxer briefs.

"You done?" he asks when even those are off.

"Not yet." My cheeks heat up as I admire him. *All* of him. He's beautiful in a way that I didn't expect him to be. I'm not a big fan of guy's dicks. Generally, I find them unattractive. I spend zero time online searching them up, but Easton? I can't stop staring at him—from his silky brown hair to his abnormally good-looking toes, Easton Royal is pure perfection. His chest is powerful, his abdomen is ridged. His thighs are strong and his legs are long. Every inch of him looks powerful.

His hand drifts down to clasp himself and he squeezes so hard, his knuckles turn white. "You're making me crazy, Hart. I'm going to last all of two seconds unless you stop looking at me."

"I can't help it."

He responds with an explosion of activity, flinging my shirt over my head, lifting me off the mattress enough to pull my pants off. There's the faint sound of fabric tearing, a curse, and then a satisfied "Finally."

He slows when I'm down to my underwear. His hands smooth over my hips in long, sweeping strokes. He maps my curves, my stomach, the arch of my back. His mouth moves from my lips to my jaw, down my neck and across my collarbone. He kisses the curve of my breast, the tip, and the valley between.

He reaches between us to roll on a condom. "You okay with this?" His eyes are hot and his color is high. His lips are swollen from my teeth and tongue.

I have never been so ready in my entire life. "Yes," I say with embarrassing eagerness.

He rolls over and positions me over him.

"Remember, go easy on me. It's my first time," he whispers before I lower myself.

I don't know if it's my first time or my fiftieth, but it doesn't matter because it's our first. He grits his teeth and sweat forms on his forehead. His fingers tighten on my hips and his entire body is tense beneath me. The cords of his neck straining as he grapples with his control.

"Hart," he gasps.

"East," I sigh.

Our nicknames for each other have corny meanings we can't ever give voice to because the cheesiness would ruin it. But here, in this moment, we can think them. We can explain them with our bodies. How he's my sun, my warmth, my guiding star. My East.

How I'm his soul, his purpose, his love. His Hart.

We take each other's breath and give it back until we're one unit, one heart, one body. It's erotic and intoxicating—a high that I never want to come down from. But he catches me as I spiral out of control. He clasps me against his broad chest, his warm arms gathering me close, whispering that he'll never let me go, never stop loving me, never, never, never, never.

CHAPTER THIRTY

Hartley

AFTER THE MOST THRILLING NIGHT of my life, I thought I'd be on cloud nine the next morning. But breakfast is kind of a gloomy affair. Everyone meets in the kitchen, eating various protein shakes, oatmeal and cereals prepared by their cook, Sandra. The lady is in her mid-fifties and is back after an extended vacation caring for her newly born grandchild. Ella and I set the table while the boys stagger down in stages. Sebastian is first. He takes one look at me, curses, grabs a smoothie and disappears. Sawyer is next. I expect him to follow his brother's path, but he takes a serving of oatmeal from the housekeeper and sits down at the breakfast table that overlooks the massive back lawn, pool, and ocean beyond.

With only about five minutes before we leave, Easton arrives.

"He's perpetually late," Ella murmurs.

We join Sawyer at the table. "He's cute, so I guess he can get away with it."

"He's right here," Easton grouses, dropping his hot self into the chair next to mine.

"He's not a morning person, huh?" I ask Ella.

"Not really. When I first moved in, I thought he'd make a good vampire since he stays up all night and sleeps during the day."

"If you want to know the truth—" I lower my voice. "I haven't seen his chest in the sunlight, so it's possible."

"Seriously. Right. Fucking. Here."

"I have," Ella declares. She points her spoon toward the pool. "And I'm sad to report there is no glitter going on."

"That could change. I've got this badass eyeshadow called Glitter Bomb and we could brush it on his pecs."

"Ohh, when it gets warmer, let's try that."

Beside me, Easton grumbles about how he should've never brought me here, but I know he's teasing. He woke me up in the best possible way and announced, even before we got out of bed, that it was already the most lit morning of his life. It was definitely the most active morning of mine.

And last night was... I can't even put it into words. Easton was so gentle and so amazing and... My cheeks heat up as I remember how slow he'd gone, how patient he'd been with me. Considering his reputation for being a bit of a slut, a part of me thought he'd be all about himself, but he hadn't been selfish at all. He'd been...amazing. My cheeks get even hotter.

We totally need to get a bed at the apartment and a big one at that. And I wonder if there are sheets that don't pull away from the bed? That would be nice.

Ella sighs, a long despondent gust of air that has us all turning toward her.

"What?" Easton asks.

This time I'm the target of the pointing spoon. "I recognize that morning blissed-out look. That used to be my look," she complains. "Thank God stupid football season is almost over and I'll get to spend some decent time with Reed."

Across the table, Sawyer pushes his bowl away. "Can we talk about something other than the two of you screwing my brothers?"

I turn scarlet and stammer, "We—I—there was—we didn't."

Easton reaches over and whacks his brother across the top of his head. "Shut up, you're embarrassing Hartley."

"What about me?" Ella asks in an aggrieved tone.

"Since when do you get embarrassed?" He pats her on the head, gets up and drops a kiss on the top of mine. "We better get going. Ella drives like a ninety-year-old grandma, so if we don't leave now, we'll be late."

"I drive the speed limit," she protests.

"Like I said, grandma style."

Ella tries to hit him, but Easton easily slides out of reach. The two chase each other around the kitchen as Sawyer and I watch from the table. Someday, Dylan and I are going to be like that with each other—comfortable and happy and loving.

I take the moment of privacy to turn to Sawyer. "I don't know if this will piss you off, but I'm sorry about the accident and your brother."

He drops his gaze to his nearly empty bowl and stirs the spoon aimlessly. I don't know what thoughts are buzzing through his head until he raises a pained gaze to meet mine. "It wasn't your fault and we both know it," he says in a low, resigned tone. "We were driving too fast. We were…distracted by shit going on in the Rover, so don't apologize anymore.

Seb will come around. We've just been dealing with a lot of…
stuff," he finishes.

I wonder what *stuff* means, but I feel like it's not my place
to ask. I'm just relieved that he feels that way. I don't want
Easton to be alienated from his family over me.

"You done?" I tip my head toward his bowl. "I'll take it to
the sink with me."

He nods and pushes it my way. He flicks an unhappy glance
toward the doorway, probably waiting for his brother—who is
likely waiting for me to leave before coming out. I hope he's
right and that Sebastian does come around, because this love
between East and me is so new that it wouldn't take much to
snuff it out completely.

On the way to school, I lean against the headrest and
listen as Easton and Ella chatter on the way to school about
Thanksgiving and the Christmas holiday and how they both
hope that State does terrible in its last few games so that Reed
doesn't go to a Bowl game. Easton says they should go to
Aspen, and Ella wants to go somewhere warm.

"It's the *winter*," she tells him as she drives about five miles
per hour under the speed limit. "And in the *winter*, people go
to warm places."

"No, in the winter, you go to snowy places because snow
only exists for a short amount of time, whereas there is always
someplace warm in the world," he counters.

"There is always snow at Everest," Ella proclaims.

"You can't ski at Everest." He twists in the seat. "Babe, back
me up here."

I flip one eye open. "Can't you ski year-round in Dubai? I
think I read that once."

"This is what you remember?" he says in a wounded voice. "You're supposed to be on my side. Make up shit that backs me up."

"Can't. Sister solidarity and all."

Ella raises a fist in acknowledgment.

"Sister what?" East exclaims. "What about this morning when I had my tongue in your—"

I fly forward and slap a hand over his mouth. He licks the center of my palm. I yelp and fall back.

"—in your mouth," he finishes, a wicked glint in his eye. "What did you think I was going to say?"

"Nothing. You were going to say nothing." I glare at him, but inside, my heart is doing little jumping jacks of happiness. I loved every single thing Easton and I did last night. And... yeah...I have zero complaints about his tongue.

"And we're here. Saved by the Astor Park bell," Ella announces as she turns into the school parking lot.

I'm not sure who was saved—Easton or me.

As the three of us walk up the wide sidewalk leading to the main building, the stares we receive are comical. Jaws drop, people stop walking, conversations abruptly cease. If eyes could fall out, the concrete would be littered with them.

East stops in the middle of the sidewalk, just below the stairs, and turns to face a stunned student body. I want to keep going inside, but his strong arm around my waist prevents me from escaping.

"Because I'm a helpful, giving man, I'm going to answer some questions for y'all before classes start so you can concentrate on your shit inside, instead of spending the class period making up your own stories. Yes, Hartley and I are together. Yes, my family is okay with that." He taps Ella, who nods. "Yes, Hartley still has amnesia and yes, I will beat the shit out of anyone who even makes her frown. If you make her cry, you'll have so many broken bones that it'll take an entire fleet of Chinese steel to put you back together."

He says all of this with a huge smile and a conversational tone, which is probably why it sounds chilling.

"Any questions?" he hollers.

The silence is deafening. Easton smiles wider, claps his hands together and says, "All right, then. Thanks for coming to my Ted Talk. See you inside."

He turns and urges Ella and me inside.

"Was that necessary?" I'm torn between embarrassment at what happened and embarrassment at myself for enjoying it so much.

"It was necessary," Ella answers for him. "Especially when Seb shows up. We want to show a united front. Last year, the Royals were kind of shambling around like zombies and the school went nuts. There was so much awful bullying going on until we stood up together as a team. It's always better for the sharks at Astor to know that the Royals will stick up for each other. Anyway, I'll see you at lunch."

She waves and jogs off, falling in beside a brunette who immediately hugs her.

"That's Val, Ella's best friend. You met her once before at the pier," East murmurs in my ear. "And that's Claire, my ex-girlfriend." He points discreetly to a delicate, doll-like girl looking in our direction with sad eyes. "I'm only pointing people out so that you won't be surprised. Let's see. You should meet Pash. He's my best friend outside my family." He looks around.

He does these things all the time—these off-hand, seemingly unimportant gestures that turn my insides to mush. A few minutes ago he announced his intention to throw the massive Royal mantle over my shoulders, and now he's anxious to share the smallest part of his life with me. He doesn't want me to feel left out.

I thread my fingers through the ones that are dangling over my shoulder. "I can meet him later. Tomorrow. We have class now."

He smiles at me, warming me from the inside out. My own personal sun.

The morning goes smoothly. Easton is in all of my classes. He admits that it was not a coincidence but that he finagled his way into them. I don't mind. It's nice not being isolated. There are plenty of stares in our direction, but East's big frame is a formidable shield.

When we go to lunch, he steers me away from the corner. "There are bugs there, remember?"

"Oh, right. Bran told me."

He scowls. "I told you, too, before Bran."

I turn to hide a smile. His little, petty jealousies are adorable. "Bran's a nice guy. You could be friends with him."

"I was friends with him until he tried to trespass on my territory," East mutters under his breath as he offers his ID card to the cashier.

"Your *what*?" I ask with a raised eyebrow.

"Our territory?" he counters in an effort to save himself.

I hand my cash over. "I don't think that's much better."

He pushes my hand down and gives the cashier his card.

"You can't swipe it twice," I remind him.

"Since when?" He points to the cashier. "Swipe it."

"Um…"The guy bites his lower lip. "We're not supposed to."

"Swipe it," East repeats, quiet but firm.

The cashier does as he's told, the transaction goes through, and we pick up our trays so the next student can be checked out.

"They wouldn't do that before," I tell East, omitting the detail that it was Bran who had offered previously.

"It's a stupid rule that no one enforces. They get paid, so what's the big deal." He stops at the table near the floor-to-ceiling plate glass window overlooking an athletic field. Ella and her friend Val are seated, as are the twins. Now that the two are together, it's harder to tell which one is Sebastian and which one is Sawyer, but I guess that the scowling face belongs to Sebastian while the pained one is his twin's.

I give them both a nod and a quiet hello. Sebastian pretends to gag when I sit down. It's awkward and uncomfortable for everyone, but I don't know if leaving would cause a bigger scene than staying.

My dilemma is momentarily interrupted by a drama playing out two tables away. My old pal, Kyle, stands next to the table where Felicity is seated with her squad. He has a tray in his hand and it's evident he wants to join them. It's equally obvious that Felicity doesn't want that. She places her purse on the empty space beside her tray.

"This is taken," she says.

"By who?" he challenges. "The seat's been empty for the last five minutes. Besides, you said I could join you."

"You must be kidding," she says in a loud voice dripping with disdain. "You're a sneed. We don't with sit with sneeds."

"Sneed?" I whisper to East.

"Needs-based student," he murmurs in my ear. "He must have a scholarship or something."

"That's a ridiculous-sounding insult. Like she stole that from Dr. Seuss or something," I hiss back.

He shrugs. "She's got money. She doesn't need to be smart or clever."

Over by Felicity, Kyle is turning deep red. My secondhand embarrassment meter is at an all-time high. I hate the dude for feeding me a bunch of lies, but this kind of school humiliation is awful.

"That's not what you said before."

"You must be joking. I would never invite a casual like you to eat lunch with my girls. Doesn't your father fix *cars* for a living? What if there's grease on your hands? Do you know how much Skylar's mom paid for that blazer? It's not the cheap synthetic that you're wearing. Skylar's is made out of virgin wool from a village in Spain. You'd have to fix like a million cars to be able to even have the right to breathe on that wool, so just"—she makes a shooing gesture—"go."

It's so rude that I gasp. I tense and start to rise to my feet. Easton grabs my right hand and Ella grabs my left. Together they hold me in my seat.

"This isn't your fight," East warns. "Those two have issues to work out and none of them have anything to do with you."

"He's right. There's a time to fight and this isn't one of them."

Any other day, I might have listened to their warnings. But as Kyle stomps out of the dining hall, something about the satisfied smirk that curls Felicity's lips triggers my temper. I shrug Easton and Ella's hands off and shoot to my feet.

"No," I tell them. "She can't keep getting away with this shit."

Before they can offer more objections, I march up to Felicity's table. She's about to take a sip from some fancy soda bottle with a label written entirely in French. Of course she drinks imported soda. Of course she does.

Gritting my teeth, I snatch the bottle out of her hand. She screeches in outrage, and her eyes blaze when she realizes I'm the culprit.

"What the hell! Give that back!" Her arm thrusts out angrily.

I hold the soda out of her reach. "What gives you the right to treat people like that?" I growl.

She blinks in confusion. Seriously? Has she actually *forgotten* what she *just* did to Kyle?

"Kyle?" I prompt. "How dare you treat him like he's a piece of garbage under your shoe?"

Understanding dawns on her face. Then she bursts out in gales of high-pitched laughter. "Are you serious right now, Wright? What do you care how I treat that loser? Do you realize how easy it was to get him to agree to mess with your poor broken head?" She laughs again. "Cost me less than I pay my drycleaner to take care of my uniform." She gestures to her white shirt and pristine blazer.

"You mean *this* uniform?" With a big smile, I tip the bottle and pour it all over Felicity.

There's one long beat of silence.

Then I hear Easton's familiar chuckle.

And Felicity's horrified shriek slices through the lunchroom. Another scream quickly follows, this one from her friend Skylar, who ends up being collateral damage. Some of the fizzy red liquid has splashed her magical virgin-wool-from-Spain blazer, and she claws at the lapels, tears filling her eyes.

"*My blazer!*" Skylar wails.

"You *fucking* bitch!" Clothing stained red and soaking wet, Felicity jumps to her feet, her hand flying out in an attempt to slap me. But it doesn't reach my face, because there's soda all over the floor now, and her designer pumps slip on the puddle.

She goes toppling forward and lands face-first on the shiny floor.

Laughter breaks out in the cavernous room as everyone watches her try to get up, but to no avail. She's slipping all over the place, getting up and flopping back down, like some ridiculous comedy act.

I give the gathering crowd a murderous glare and hold up my hand to silence the laughter. My intention wasn't to embarrass Felicity or make everyone laugh at her. That would be no better than what she did to Kyle, who I don't even like! But a point needed to be made.

"You are *not* better than us, any of us," I snap at her. "Just because your family can buy and sell mine a hundred times over, just because you and your stupid friends aren't here on scholarships and have seven-figure trust funds, doesn't make you better than anyone. And it doesn't give you the right to humiliate people, or use them, or 'mess with their heads.'" Anger bubbles in my throat. "I swear to God, Felicity—if I ever see you pulling that cruel superiority shit on anyone ever again, I'll do a lot more than spill a drink on you." I give her a menacing glower. "I'll kick your fucking ass."

There's a familiar snicker. *Dammit, Easton, I'm in the middle of my tough girl act here.*

He must sense my irritation, because he steps forward and says, "Remember when Ella dragged Jordan Carrington by the hair through the school?" He beams at Felicity. "Well, Hart will do twice that damage."

"Damn straight," I confirm.

Felicity finally manages to stand up, but she's still wobbling precariously on her heels. She glares at me, then at Easton, Ella, her own friends, and everyone else that's looking her way with unrestrained laughter.

She opens her mouth as if to say something, but then she wisely slams it shut, brushes past me, and flies out of the room.

"Holy shit," Ella's friend Val says once Felicity is gone. "That was *badass*, Hartley!" She holds up a hand for a high-five.

I slap her palm, a blush creeping into my cheeks as other students come up to high-five me or gush about how awesome that was.

There's one person, however, who doesn't seem at all impressed by what I've done.

"Gee, she spilled something on some bitch," Sebastian Royal says mockingly. "What a hero!"

"Seb," Sawyer cautions.

"No." The angry twin slices his hand through the air. "Who gives a shit that she told Felicity off? I can't believe I even have to be around this bitch. It was bad enough that I came down to breakfast in my own house and she was sitting at my table like she didn't ram her car into the side of my Rover, nearly killing me, my brother, and our girlfriend—"

"Ex," Sawyer cuts in.

Sebastian ignores him. "—*girlfriend* who doesn't even talk to us anymore. But now she sits at the family table at Astor Park, too? And she gets treated like some kind of hero? Don't you guys even give a shit that I was in a fucking coma because of her?"

"Seb, man, don't be like this," Sawyer pleads.

"I see you've turned into a pussy since the accident," his twin sneers. "I'm telling you, either you get rid of this bitch or you'll be rid of me." He jerks out of his chair and storms out of the lunchroom.

"He doesn't mean it." East turns to me, brushing a hand down my back.

A prickle of uneasiness follows the path of his palm. It doesn't feel right to accept comfort from him. I don't deserve this.

"I—I have to use the restroom." I jump to my feet.

"Wait, Hart—"

"Let her go," I hear Ella say to him.

As the third person to run out of the lunchroom in as many minutes, I'm sure I look ridiculous, but sitting in there with guilt pressing me into the tiles was worse. I don't know how I can make it right to Sebastian, but I can at least start with an apology. I gave one to Sawyer this morning, but I've never been able to offer one to his twin. Words aren't much, but they can be a start.

I jog down the halls trying to look for him but come up empty. I slow to a halt near a sign that says "Men's Locker Room." I press my ear against the door and hear a squeak of sneaker against tile.

Taking a deep breath, I knock. "Sebastian? It's Hartley Wright. Can I talk to you for a minute? I want to apologize."

There are a few more squeaks as someone walks closer to the door.

"Thank you," I say, and then let out a small scream when the door whips open and I see Kyle Hudson instead of Sebastian Royal.

"You owe me an apology, too," Kyle snarls.

I jump back. "Why do I owe you one?"

"Because you exist, you stupid bitch."

Man, I'm getting tired of being called a bitch. First Sebastian and now Kyle? And to think, a few minutes ago I was *defending* him to Felicity.

I could fire back an insult, but what's the point? He'd only call me a bitch again, which, as I just said, I'm tired of. So I turn my back and walk away.

Or try to.

A meaty hand with fingers as thick as hotdogs lands on my shoulder and whips me against the lockers. I land with a hard thud that momentarily leaves me breathless.

"You're free game now, you know. The Royals stick together, so Easton Royal is going to kick you to the curb." Kyle approaches menacingly.

I look around for something to rip off the walls and bash over his big head. "You bring your dick near me and I'm going to cut it off."

He shoves me again. "Like I'd stick my Johnson in your dirty pussy. Forget it. But here's a little preview of what life's going to be like for you until graduation day."

I don't see his fist coming. It's something I never

expected. I thought he'd try to maul me, stick his tongue down my throat. I thought he'd flip my skirt up and I had my knee ready to go. I never in a million years thought he'd hit me.

The punch—powered by the anger of a two-hundred-and-fifty-pound boy who's feeling humiliated and impotent—strikes me right in the gut. I fold over, the contents of my lunch flying out of my mouth. The blow takes my breath away and drops me to my knees. I gasp for air.

Out of the corner of my eye, I see a loafer rear back. *He's going to kick*, my mind screams a warning. I curl up into a defensive ball and try to roll out of the way. I don't make it in time and the hard toe of his shoe strikes my side. Through a haze of tears and pain, I try to figure out how to get out of this. Where's a safe place? A classroom? Is there a classroom nearby? *Come on, Hart! Get up*, I scream to myself.

It hurts to move, though. I hear laughter and then a shuffling sound and then more voices that are abruptly cut off.

"What the *fuck* is going on here?" Easton's bellow practically shakes the halls.

Above me, Kyle stutters, "H-h-hey Easton. This bitch tripped and fell. Probably wanted to suck my dick, but I told her no thanks."

There's a blur of motion that I can't make out, followed by two bodies crashing to the floor next to me. I hear the sickening sound of flesh hitting flesh. I croak out something, like "stop" or "help" or "no." No one pays a lick of attention to me. I struggle to my feet, using the locker handles to pull myself upright. I cradle an arm across my side, wondering whether my intestines will fall out if I let go.

The sound of the fight attracts attention. Students gather at the end of the hall.

"A hundred on Royal."

"No one's taking your bet."

"How about a hundred on Hudson lasting five minutes?"

"Okay, that one I'll consider."

"What's going here? Stop! Move aside." A squat, heavy-set man wearing plaid pushes his way to the front of the crowd.

Easton's on top doing his level best to drive Kyle into the floor. The boy is motionless on the ground. His face is covered in blood, as is Easton's fist. A real worry grips me that Easton's done some kind of irreparable harm to this boy. Kids have been put into prison for assaulting other students.

Ignoring the pain, I scramble over and grab his arm as he pulls back to hit Kyle again.

"Easton," I moan. "Please."

He drops his arm and looks at me. What he sees must be shocking, because a terrible expression transforms his face. He bares his teeth. "I'm going to kill him," he says.

"No! I don't care about him, but I need you with me." The idea of my sun being taken from me is too awful to contemplate. I'd rather endure a thousand kicks to the stomach than for that to happen.

"Mr. Royal. Enough of this. One more punch and I'm suspending you. I don't care how much your father has donated to this school."

"Easton," I beg. "Please."

His stiff arm bends a tiny amount. I press my mouth to his elbow and whisper my plea against his skin. "Let's just go. You paid him back. I promise. You paid him back."

"Fuck. All right." He curls his arm, bringing my head to his shoulder. He bends his head and rests his cheek against my hair. "I'm stopping for now, but I swear to you that if he touches you again, he will be picking his testicles out of his teeth until graduation."

"Fair exchange," I say, but I doubt Kyle will be back.

Easton plants another tender peck on my forehead before getting to his feet. "How's the stomach?" He bends over to inspect me, pulling up my shirt.

I fight to keep it down since we have an audience of about fifty students staring excitedly in our direction. "I've felt better."

"I want to take you to the hospital."

"No, really, I'm okay."

"Mr. Royal, you need to step into my office right now."

Easton barely looks the man's way. "I'm taking Hartley to the hospital to check to see if she has any internal bleeding. If she died because you kept her from care, it'd probably be a big-ass lawsuit."

The administrator's already thin lips flatten into a non-existent line. "Fine, but first thing in the morning, I expect all three of you there."

"Sure thing." Easton has no intention of keeping that appointment, and as for me, I'd rather be expelled.

We get into a small tiff over whether I'm going to the hospital—which I refuse—and whether he carries me out of the school—which I also refuse.

"It's embarrassing," I tell him as I bury my face in his chest.

"This is some heroic shit I'm doing. It's not embarrassing," he states.

"You're not the one being carried down a hall while a

couple hundred students are watching." There's one student, in particular, whose gaze I don't want to meet again. The malicious satisfaction on Sebastian Royal's face as Easton was lifting me into his arms isn't a sight I'm going to forget soon.

"Nah, everyone's in their classrooms."

"I can hear them. No one is in their classrooms." There's been a steady buzz of noise from the moment East picked me up. "You're a bad liar."

"They will be. Ella, can you get the door?" There's a clink of metal against metal as the front doors are pushed open. "Thanks. I'll see you at home."

"Are we still on for tonight?" Ella asks anxiously.

I have enough energy to give her a thumbs up, but East has to raise my hand high enough over his shoulder for her to see it.

"Toss me your keys, little sis. You can grab a ride home with Sawyer."

Somehow he manages to catch them without dropping me.

"You could have opted for the hospital. I would've let you walk then," he rumbles as he makes his way toward Ella's convertible.

"No, you wouldn't."

"You're right. I wouldn't. I promise that if I get beaten to a pulp by someone two times my size, you can carry me around as much as you want." He bends his knees and somehow manages to open the passenger's door without dropping me. He slides me inside and buckles me in, pressing another sweet kiss to my forehead.

"We're going to the apartment, right?"

He pauses before closing the door. "I thought I'd take you home."

How do I explain, in a nice way, that I think his brother might smother me with a pillow? "I'd feel better at the apartment. It's cozier there."

His brows furrow in suspicion, but my not-so-fake moan of pain convinces him to agree. "Apartment it is."

No matter how hard I try, I can't keep Sebastian's face out of my head. He hates me. I don't know if it's because of the accident or because of what happened after the accident, but it's the ugly truth. That causes me so much more pain than Kyle's fist in my stomach. I can heal from the punch. I can heal from the kick. I can get over a nasty word from Felicity's mouth.

I don't know that I'll get over losing Easton. I'm not ready for my world to be dark again.

But what are my options? I can't separate East from his family. They're a unit. A puzzle that only looks right when all the pieces are slotted into place together.

"You're thinking about something so hard that it's going to slow the car down. What is it?"

I could lie to him. That'd be easy. Or maybe that's the coward's way out. That way I can always say to myself that Easton didn't fight for me. That way I can be the victim. Which is bullshit. I hate being the victim. If my memory loss gave me a new chance at life, then I shouldn't color my future with lies and self-pity.

"Your brother doesn't like me much."

"So you saw him?"

I roll my head toward East. "You, too?"

He clicks his tongue against his teeth. "Hard not to. Look, Seb's a few days out of waking up from a coma. He probably shouldn't even be at school. The boy's as weak as a kitten. A hard wind is going to take him down. All of that combined with Lauren breaking it off is making him feel down. Give him time to come around."

I could do that. I could also fall deeper in love with Easton—so deep that it'd feel like a part of me was torn away when we broke up. Or I could run now in self-preservation. That's the opposite of being a victim. Running away is the smartest option to take when faced with danger. I'm sure I read that somewhere.

"I can't remember events, but I remember feelings. There was a strange unfamiliarity whenever I was with Kyle. Felicity invoked fear. So did my dad. When I thought of you, I always got this warm glow. When I try to press into the endless black box that I think my past is locked into, there's this deadness. Like I'm standing in the middle of the desert and there's no one around and there hasn't been anyone around forever. I yell as hard as I can for as long as I can until I have no breath, but there's no response. There's not even an echo. The sound's swallowed up. That's loneliness, and when I think hard about the past, that's what I remember. I don't want that for you."

"What about you? What do you want for you?"

God, why is he asking me such hard questions? "What I want for you and what I want for me don't seem compatible at this point."

"So is your answer for us to break up?" His voice is even, almost unconcerned. His hands are loose around the wheel and his shoulders show no signs of tension. Whereas I'm as tight as a knot.

"I don't know what the answer is. Maybe we wait. We wait until Sebastian comes around."

"He has a brain injury. That's why he's fucked up. I read about it the other night. It's actually super common for people with brain trauma to turn out to be angry bastards for no reason. He may never come around. What then?"

I don't answer him, because like I told him before, I don't have an answer. At least not one that I'm willing to say out loud.

CHAPTER THIRTY-ONE

Easton

"I CAN'T BELIEVE THE PRINCIPAL just let us walk out like that," Hart says as I pull up next to the curb in Ella's tiny car.

"Headmaster Beringer's spineless. My dad's bought him off a ton of times. Last time was when Ella slammed Jordan Carrington around at school. Jordan deserved it. She and her friends cut a girl's hair, stripped her naked, and taped her to the side of the main building."

Her jaw falls open. "What?"

"Astor Park used to be a madhouse."

"Used to be?"

"Sure. We're using flags on flagpoles now instead of people taped to the wall. That's progress. Hold on. I'll come get you." I hop out and round the car's front to get to Hartley. Kyle's punches have literally taken the wind out of her sails, because she's still struggling to get out of the car when I reach her.

"Come on, babe. Let me help you."

She sits back on the seat with a sigh of frustration. "I'm still going to the park tonight."

"We'll see," I say noncommittally. The girl's as weak as a kitten. I don't see her going anywhere but the bathroom. There's no point in arguing much about it on the street, though.

I slide my arms under her body and lift her into the air. She doesn't weigh much. I don't think she's eating like she should.

"Can you get the food?" I nod toward the paper bag full of soup and grilled cheese that we stopped to get on the way here.

She reaches out, wincing at the effort.

"I can walk," she asserts feebly.

"We already had this fight at school." I grip her closer and climb the stairs. I have to lower her to ground when I reach the top to unlock the door. Despite her repeated assurances that she's fine, she keeps a hand at my waist for balance. I don't point it out to her.

Once the door is open, I pick her up again and carry her into the apartment, not letting her go again until I reach the sofa.

I pause before setting her down. "Do you need to use the bathroom?"

"I would rather Felicity tape me to the side of Astor Park than to have you carry me to the bathroom," she declares, the flinty look in her eye telling me she's not kidding.

"Okay." I leave her on the sofa and fetch our dinner. "I should've put the coffee table together." I gesture toward one of the flat-packed boxes that's supposed to turn into a wood and glass table.

"Nah, the floor's good for me." She slides off the cushions.

I watch her carefully for signs of pain, but she doesn't show any signs of distress. Her appetite is good, too. She gobbles up her grilled cheese, practically drinks her soup, and then leans back against the sofa, enjoying an after-dinner Diet Coke and a couple of leftover soup crackers.

There's something satisfying about feeding someone you care about. Watching her eat so happily is filling me up in ways that food can't touch. I trace my eyes over the small bridge of her nose, her straight eyebrows, her full, round cheeks. I never had a type before. I liked all the girls—the rich, prissy ones; the sassy, sexy ones; the round, happy ones. As long as they wanted to get down, I was there with them.

But now, if I close my eyes and conjure up my ideal girl, it's Hart's face that pops to mind. She might not be perfect for anyone else, but it doesn't matter because she's perfect for me.

"Do I have something on my face?" she asks, touching her cheek.

"No. I like looking at it."

She ducks her head in embarrassment. "Stop it."

"No."

"Seriously, you're making me uncomfortable."

"Nah. You're embarrassed but you don't need to be. You're beautiful." I stretch out on an elbow and drink the other Coke.

"Did you pour vodka into your can?" she asks suspiciously. "Because you're talking like you're drunk."

I slosh the liquid around in my can. Remarkably, I haven't felt the urge to drink lately. Too much shit has been going down. "No, but even if I was, they say that drunks only speak the truth."

She scrunches her nose adorably. "Is that really a saying?"

"It is now. Easton Royal declares it so."

She throws a pillow at my head. I bat it aside and lunge

toward her. She screams and tries to dodge me, but I'm too fast. I catch her up in my arms and bury my face in her neck, inhaling her sweet scent. She's warm and soft and *right*.

What do I need alcohol for? I've got the best drug right here. I capture her mouth, sweeping my tongue inside. My world spins at the taste of her. Her fingers dance around my shoulders unsure of whether she can touch me. When they finally land, the rope that she unknowingly snuck around my heart tightens even further.

Shit, I love this girl. And because I love her, I draw back. She needs to rest, not be mauled by me. I draw my finger over her forehead and down her soft cheek. "I'm going to put the bed together," I say huskily.

She nods, blinking like a baby owl. I force myself upright and walk over to the mattress and the frame that I abandoned because I didn't have the right tools. I need a bolt tightener, which my little pink set didn't come with. I kick the metal frame to the side and pull the mattress down to the floor.

"Have you ever done this before?" she asks, curling up on her side.

I avoid looking at her because the temptation to climb all over her is way too great. Instead, I root through the bags, looking for the sheet set I bought with the help of one of the store clerks. "No, but how hard can it be?"

Five minutes later, I've worked up a big sweat, taken off my dress shirt, and still not succeeded in getting the damn sheet to stay put. But at least my mind is off my dick for the moment.

"How does this even work?" I ask in disgust, holding up a large piece of fabric that Hart told me was a fitted sheet—in between her sniggers of laughter.

"I'm torn between wanting to help you and enjoying the show," she teases, but gets to her feet and takes the bedding out of my hand.

I watch as she bends down, her round ass waving like a red flag in front of me. I turn away. Whenever I wanted to feel alive, I'd fight, so I know what it's like to be punched in the gut and how your ribs can ache for hours—even days—after. I enjoyed the pain, but nothing lights me up like being with Hartley. Past me was an idiot.

"I'm done," she announces. "It's safe to look again."

I swing around to find her lying on the bed. She stretches her arm across the mattress. "This is a big bed," she says, looking at me under her eyelashes.

My blood heats up. It's hard keeping my hands off her, especially when she looks like she'd like to sink her teeth into my chest.

"I like a lot of space." I struggle to get under control. She's injured, I remind myself and toss a blanket over her. Her Astor Park skirt is riding up and the flash of thigh is making me sweat. As I lower myself onto the mattress, I bite my inner cheek and hope the pain keeps my dick under control.

"You're still staying home tonight," I whisper into her hair, drawing her into my arms.

"We'll see."

I doubt this is a battle I'm going to win, so I content myself with holding her tight, digging my thumbs into her tense back, rubbing a gentle hand over her sides, tangling my legs with hers. She presses her sock-covered feet against my shins and tucks her head against my shoulder. I rub her from neck to butt and back again until her breathing evens out and her body slackens against me.

My pants are tight, the arm tucked under her frame is going numb and it's becoming uncomfortably hot, but I wouldn't move for all the money, planes, and booze in the world.

AT NINE, ELLA SHOWS UP at the apartment in my truck, which is big enough to fit all three of us. Her Audi convertible is too small, so it'll have to stay out on the curb. I make a mental note to toss Jose a hundie to keep an eye on the car, make sure no street punks try to mess with it.

"You're in a bad mood," Ella remarks when I let her in.

"No. I'm…" I don't know how to describe it. Ever since I saw Hart get punched by Kyle, I haven't felt right. Cuddling with her all day, as nice as it was, didn't succeed in easing my nerves. I want to call tonight off, but this might be our best—and last—chance to nail Hartley's dad and save the case against Steve.

I can't let either of these girls down. Especially Hart. Last night she handed her trust over to me. Fully and completely. But that comes with a lot of responsibility. The urge to protect her at all costs was strong before, but now it's a mantra that repeats itself on every beat of my heart.

"I'm worried," I finally say.

"We're just taking pictures."

"Right." But her words don't reassure me.

Upstairs, Hart stands inside the door, wringing her fingers together. Ella, dressed in black from head to toe, her bright golden hair tucked inside a black beanie, surveys the place slowly. Hart's braced for insults over the size, the condition, the mattress still sitting on the floor and not in a bed frame.

Hart's anxious because she doesn't want Ella to insult our apartment. I realize she doesn't know Ella's past.

"This is dope," Ella says, and drops onto the sofa. "But why are you living here and not with your parents?"

"They kicked me out," Hart answers stiffly.

"Damn." Ella whistles. "I didn't know parents did that. Was it because you were dating Easton? I mean, he is offensive and all, but I figured parents liked him."

"Thanks a lot, little sis." I cuff her lightly on the top of her head before making my way to the fridge, appreciating her attempts to make Hartley comfortable. I grab two sodas and pop one open for Hart and another for Ella.

Hart's still standing just inside the door, all wide-eyed and amazed.

"She doesn't know where you came from," I explain to Ella. "She's been too busy researching her past to bother with yours."

Ella takes a sip of her soda before replying. "That's kind of nice, though. Can I keep her in the dark?"

I level her a look.

She sighs. "Fine. I came here a year ago. Gosh, has it only been a year, East?"

"A long, terrible year, Ella," I tease.

She gives me the finger in return. "A year ago, Callum found me stripping at a nightclub and brought me here. They hated me at first." She points at me. "They were mean to me. Kicked me out of their car in the middle of the night and made me walk home."

"We followed you," I growl as Hart's wide eyes swing to me.

"You *left* her and made her walk home? In the dark?"

I clear my throat. "We made it look like we abandoned her, but we had eyes on her the whole time."

"Easton Royal, I can't believe you'd do that."

"It was my brother's idea!" I argue.

"You should've stopped him," she counters, looking adorably outraged. At least she's not hiding nervously in the corner.

"You're right." I reach over and grab her wrist and haul her over to sit on my knee. She perches on the end of it like she's afraid contact with my groin is the same as putting on a porn show for Ella. "Good news is that Ella forgave everyone and is now playing hide-the-salami on the regular with my older brother."

Hart snickers. "Really?"

Ella reaches over and punches me in the arm—hard. "I forgave you for past sins, but not the ones you're currently committing." She turns to Hart. "Yes, really. Reed and I overcame a lot of bullshit, but we're together now. The problem is that my sperm donor keeps popping up like one of those whack-a-moles or villains at the end of a scary movie who you think you kill but don't. It's not just that he tried to kill me, but that he blamed a murder on Reed, and that he's trying to get away with it. The man's dangerous. He can't get off." Ella's chin juts out, readying more arguments in case Hartley objects.

"I agree," is Hart's response. Her lips tilt up a tiny bit at the corners. "And I thought my dad was bad."

Ella is relieved. "So when do we leave?"

I pull out a piece of paper and hand it to Hart. "After Hart does these."

She jumps up. "What's this?"

"What is it?" Ella slides over to peer at the list of exercises.

"It's a physical readiness test. You can go when you pass all of these elements." Hart and I spent an hour arguing over whether she was going with us tonight.

"You have got to be kidding me," she squawks.

I fold my arms across my chest. "Not even a little. If you want to crawl around in the forest and spy on your dad, then this is the price of admission."

"I told you I don't hurt anymore."

"And I told you I didn't believe you."

We glare at each other.

"Ten burpees?" Ella says, plucking the list from Hartley's fingers. "When would she be doing burpees tonight?"

"She might have to jump up and run. She might have to hop a fence. She might have to leap over a log. These are all exercises designed to simulate duck-and-cover and escape maneuvers."

"I'm going even if you don't take me with you, so short of tying me up and stuffing me in a closet, I'll be lying on the pine needles right next to you in less than an hour."

I throw up my hands. I knew this was a losing argument, but I had to try. I stomp off to the front door where Ella left a bag. How did I fall for someone twice as stubborn as Ella? I grab a few items and return to Hart, thrusting them into her hands. "Ella brought these for you. Why don't you change and we'll go case the joint."

She hops into the bathroom to change.

"You're going to burn a hole through the door if you stare harder," Ella says.

"You didn't see her get punched in the stomach." That image is going to stick in my memory for a long time.

"We women are hardier than we look." Ella flexes a non-existent muscle in her arm.

I don't want to get into an argument, so I keep my grumbles to myself. Hart exits the bathroom, pulling the hat over her head.

She stops short, registers my concern and comes over to pat me on the shoulder like I'm a five-year-old who lost his toy down a storm sewer.

"I'm going to be okay," she reassures me.

My eyes fall to her wrist. "Don't do anything dangerous. We're only there to take pictures to add to the audio we recorded and the text message you received. Nothing more."

She gives me a smart-ass salute.

"You, too," I remind Ella, who jumps up to stand beside Hart.

"Aye, aye, Captain."

"You two are real clowns, aren't you?" I sigh. I should've never introduced them. "Let's go, Thing One and Thing Two."

"Does that make you the Cat in the Hat?" Hart mocks.

My response is to swat her ass as she passes by on her way out. She finds this hilarious and so does Ella. They crack sillier and sillier jokes, quoting lines from Dr. Seuss books, which somehow Hart recalls.

But as each mile passes, their laughter gets quieter and less frequent until it's way too quiet in the cab of the truck. I glance over and see the two girls gripping each other's hands. Nah, I don't regret introducing them. I wish they'd found each other sooner. They have a lot in common and, after tonight, I think they'll need each other more than ever.

"Ready, Things?"

Hart gives a nervous bob of her head while Ella's jaw hardens. I wish the two could forget what happens tonight. Whatever the outcome, they're both going to be hurt by the actions of their dads, and that sucks hard.

"I'm going to drive down the road a bit. Are you two okay with walking?"

"Yes," Ella replies and immediately jumps out when the vehicle stops. Hart tumbles out after her.

I grab the camera from the glove compartment.

Outside, Ella's hopping from one foot to another. "Come on," she hisses and gestures for us to hurry.

As soon as I clear the door, she's jogging down the road. Hart and I hustle to catch up.

"Let's go this way," Ella says, pointing to a low wooden fence that surrounds the entrance to the park that sits about a city block ahead of us.

Concern for Hartley tugs at my gut, but she climbs over the fence without so much as a wince. I relax. Maybe she wasn't lying about not being sore, after all.

We skulk into the woods, careful to avoid stepping on branches that might give us away. Thankfully, the ground is mostly grass and weeds. It's dark, with the canopy of trees blocking the half moon. Out in the parking lot, a few lamps light up the paved space. There are no cars here at all.

Did we miss them? Did we come on the wrong day?

"Hart—" I start.

She waves her hand furiously. "Shh. Get down. Someone's coming."

Headlights flood the entrance to the park. Ella and I drop

to the ground. The camera digs into my breastbone. I hope our dark clothes hide us well enough. The first car is a familiar silver one. It's the perfect car for a clandestine meeting. Electric cars make almost no noise. If it weren't for the lights, we would've missed it. Steve parks his Tesla on the far end of the lot, just beyond the last pool of light.

"We need to get closer," I whisper.

The girls nod in agreement. We all get to our feet and make our way through the woods until we're just off the edge of the parking lot. We drop to our knees just in time to see another car drive in.

"That's my dad," Hart says.

"Where's Callum? Or the guys he hired?" Ella hisses.

"No clue." I look around. "Maybe over there." I point to the other side of the lot where a concession stand and a bathroom sit in near darkness. I can't make anyone out. My attention veers back to the cars.

The two men climb out and then stand about twenty feet apart. It reminds me of a bad Western movie. Maybe they'll shoot each other. That'd solve a lot of problems.

I give myself an internal slap. Neither of these girls need to see their fathers die. *Get it together, East.*

"We need to get closer," Hart says in a hushed tone.

She starts to move, but I drag her back. "You can't. They'll see you."

"I want to hear what they're saying."

"Wait. Something is happening. East, get the camera."

I pull it out and point it toward the men. Too bad I don't have a mic. It's hard to see much detail in the green wash of the night-vision lens. I begin to have second and third thoughts that pictures and audio and messages are actually going to do anything. Hartley's dad has obviously been selling his services for years. At least three times, if not more. Even if we get this evidence, won't he get free? Won't he conveniently lose it?

I shift the lens back to Steve, who walks to the back of the Tesla and pops the trunk. Shortly after, Hart's father appears in the frame. They both lean in.

"Are you getting this?" Ella tugs on my sleeve.

"Yes."

I crawl forward on my elbows to get a better shot. I snap a few pictures of them peering into the trunk. This is shit evidence, I decide. Pictures of people looking into vehicles are not going to carry an ounce of weight. We need something more. I need a photo of the bag and the men in the same frame. I inch closer.

"Gold bars?" Hart's dad half shouts, or at least he's loud enough that his voice carries to us. "I can't convert this. I told you I wanted cash."

"My accounts ... frozen ... case is over," Steve replies. He points to the gold as if it's normal to be storing gold bars in the back of a Tesla.

Mr. Wright curses and then stomps off. I hold my breath. Is the deal falling apart over this? How stupid is Hartley's father? He could easily take those bars to a broker and exchange them for cash if that's what he wants. My earlier feelings of dread come roaring back.

"I have cash," a third man announces.

Everyone startles.

Steve digs into his coat pocket. Mr. Wright stumbles backward in surprise. Behind me, I hear two shocked gasps.

I'm too stunned to move or make a noise.

"What the hell are you doing here?" Steve exclaims.

My own father steps forward. He holds out his arms, a black bag in each of them.

"I'm here to offer you a deal, Steve. You don't want to go to prison, but if you're free, Ella isn't going to be able to sleep one solid night on her own. I can't have that." There's a pause. "I owe you a lot. You're my best friend…but my kids are more important." Callum sets one of the bags down and then walks across the lot and drops another bag. Raising his voice so everyone can hear him, he says, "In that bag is a new identity and enough cash to set you up nicely. I'll wire you money once a month so that you can live however you want, as long as it is far away from Ella. All I want in exchange is the recordings I know you have of each and every conversation you had with Wright."

Hart's dad makes an angry noise in his throat. No one pays him any attention.

Callum points to his feet. "This one is just cash. This is for you, Wright. It's a down payment on the five-million-dollar bonus you will be paid for successfully prosecuting Steve O'Halloran."

During my dad's show, the two girls have crawled up to join me at the edge of the lot.

"What the hell is he doing?" Ella hisses.

Dad's pitting the two men against each other, but I don't know what option he wants. Me, I want them both to suffer. Where's *that* solution? I want bag number three.

Time slows as two terrible people consider their options. I count my heartbeats as the seconds tick by. Beside me, Ella becomes motionless. I don't think she's even breathing. Hart grips my shoulder. It *really* is like a scene out of a bad Western. A semi-hysterical laugh catches in my throat. This is ridiculous. I half expect a banjo to start playing in the background.

Mr. Wright clears his throat. "I'll take the money."

"The hell you will." Steve dips his hand into his coat pocket and out comes the gun.

One of the girls gasps. I push their heads down, but it's too late. All three men's heads swivel toward us.

"Goddammit, Callum. What have you done?" Steve growls. The barrel comes up and I jump out of the hiding spot.

Bone-deep fear spurs me forward. Steve took my mom. He's not taking my dad, too.

CHAPTER THIRTY-TWO

Hartley

I NEVER HEAR THE SHOT, only its echo in the park. I don't see my father fall, because my attention is focused on Easton sprinting toward his dad. I don't register that it's my dad who cries out in surprise and not East or Callum or Ella, until Ella's high-pitched "Mr. Wright!" jerks me out of my trance.

"Dad…" I stumble toward him where he's lying on the ground.

He hasn't moved since the gunshot. His hand is flung over his head, reaching for that bag of money.

"Dad." I fall to my knees beside his body.

Relief hits me. He's still breathing. His chest is rising and falling. But he's grimacing in pain, and there's blood around his mouth. I never wanted this. I never imagined that this is how it would turn out. I thought I'd get evidence. I thought there would be newspaper articles and lawsuits and legal filings. I did not believe there would be guns and violence and blood. I tug my sleeve over my fingers and try to wipe it off.

"You're going to be okay," I whisper. I fumble inside his

coat pocket, looking for a phone. Blood pulses up with every breath he struggles to take, slicking my fingers. "I'm going to call the ambulance. They'll save you."

His hand clamps over my wrist in a surprisingly strong grip. His fingernails dig into the scar. "You got me killed," he spits at me.

My heart lurches. "You don't mean that." I twist out of his grip and press down on the wound.

He gasps in pain. "If you had kept your mouth shut...I wouldn't be here. I should've broken...more than your wrist... Should've pushed you harder at the hospital."

"P-pushed me?" The hospital? Is he talking about the night I fell and hit my head? I suddenly feel queasy.

His harsh laughter is cut short by a cough. "You tripped... with help."

Tears burn my eyes. Oh my God. My father is the reason I lost all my memories? *He* did this to me?

"I never wanted you kids... None of you...none of you..." he repeats in labored breaths. "A burden, all three of you girls. A worthless, money-sucking burden."

He rolls over painfully onto his stomach, pushing himself along the pavement until the bag is in his grasp.

"Stop moving," I order, gathering my wits and scrambling after him. He's too weak now to push me away. I pull him onto his back and scream over my shoulder, "Help me! My dad is shot. Help me."

"Don't...want...help." He tries to pry my fingers off his chest, where the blood is burbling up like a small fountain. "Leave me to die...worthless...child."

"Come away, Hart." Strong hands grip my shoulders.

"Dad's called an ambulance. Someone will be here soon."

"He's hurt, Easton. My dad's hurt." But he's more than hurt. His eyes are staring sightless at the sky. His chest has stopped moving.

Easton pushes my face into his shoulder so I stop staring at my dad's dead face. "I know. I'm sorry."

I cling to him as my father's terrible admissions ping around in my head. I wish my memory loss began today. A kid shouldn't have to hear that her father wanted her dead, that if he could rewind time, he would've hurt her worse. Hot tears scald my cheeks. He got what he wanted. His words, his confession, his rejection are tearing me to pieces.

"It's going to be okay," East murmurs into my hair.

But the cold sound of a bullet being chambered tells a different story.

"Easton, my boy, come over here by the rest of the family."

We both look up to see the ugly barrel of Steve's gun pointed in our direction.

"What are you doing?" Easton growls, immediately stepping in front of me.

"We're going to resolve this by ourselves. You, me, your dad, Ella. I never would've hurt you, Ella. You know that, right? You're my daughter. I needed to scare Dinah and you happened to be there."

"You pointed a gun at me, just like you're pointing it at Easton!" Ella exclaims.

"No. It's pointed at Ms. Wright. I wouldn't hurt Easton, just like I wouldn't hurt you. Callum knows this, don't you, friend?"

"Steve!" Callum yells. "Stop this."

Steve responds, low and unintelligible. Or maybe I just can't hear because panic and horror have filled my head.

"You're going to have to shoot me to get to her." Shoulders rigid, Easton spreads his hands out.

"No. No more," I snap. I've reached my blood and guts limit. I've cried all the tears I have in my body. I can't take another moment of this drama. "Stop this. Mr. Royal, put a stop to this," I beg Easton's dad.

Callum springs into action, rushing toward Steve, who swings around reflexively. I'll never know if he pulled the trigger intentionally or whether it was in reaction to a threat, but the bullet flies out anyway.

"*Dad!*" East screams.

"*Callum!*" cries Ella.

I shout in horror.

Because it's not Callum whose body jerks as the bullet finds a target. It's not Callum who staggers backward in shocked pain. It's not Callum who collapses with his hand pinned to his side.

It's not Callum.

It's Easton.

Ella and I lunge toward him, but it's Callum who catches his son.

"My God, what have you done?" he howls to Steve.

Ella's father tries to take a step, but his knee folds underneath him. "No." The declaration comes out on a hoarse shudder. "No," he repeats.

"Call it in," Callum orders to no one or everyone.

"I already called the ambulance for Mr. Wright," Ella says quickly.

"*Call them again!*" Callum screams.

Terrified, Ella can't move. I clench my fist and realize I have my dad's phone in my hands. I dial emergency, but I don't take my eyes off Steve. The gun's still in his hand.

"What's your emergency?"

"Gunshot wound to the stomach," I babble. "Gunshot wound. Winwood Park."

"Ma'am, there's already an ambulance on the way to that location."

"There's an ambulance on the way," I repeat, dropping the phone to the ground. I want to go to East, but I'm afraid of Steve. He has a trapped look on his face. He's already shot two people. I don't think he's going to stop there.

"Goddammit, Steve. Why?" Callum's eyes are flooded with tears. His fingers are getting stained with the same dark red that mine are covered in. "I gave you that bag. You could've taken it and walked away."

"I would've gone to jail. I can't go to jail!" His eyes are wild, his voice shaking. "I just wanted to get rid of the Wrights. I knew you and I could work it out. I didn't want this to happen. You have to believe me. I wouldn't have ever hurt Easton. He's my son."

If I had any breath inside me, I'd have gasped.

"No," Callum says, strong and loud. "In every way that matters, Easton is my son. He has always been my son."

"He's not," Steve insists. "Maria and I, we were carrying on and off for a long time. She was lonely and I comforted her."

"Do you think I'm a fool? I always knew. Of course I fucking knew." Callum shakes his head. "Easton's a carbon copy of you. Not in looks, but everything else."

"He's not your son," Ella bursts out. She spears Callum with a glower. "Easton's nothing like that...that...monster."

Callum's tone gentles. "You're right, sweetheart," he tells her. "East isn't entirely like him. My boy has a heart. He cares, deeply, about others." His gaze briefly flicks toward me before returning to Steve. "But the addictions, the rashness, the thoughtlessness he can't always control, the mood swings. That's all you, Steve."

Rather than deny it, the other man nods.

"That's why I never questioned Maria," Callum says. "I loved Easton like he was my own, because he *is* mine. He's *my* son. I don't fucking care that you share the same DNA. He's mine and you're not going to take him from me."

Sirens blare in the distance, growing louder as help gets closer. I swing my eyes toward the road in relief.

"They're coming," I say quietly.

Steve's head comes up. He knows the walls are closing in.

I tense. Can I jump him? Can I kick the gun out of his hand? I have to do something. I'm not going to lose one more person without a fight. So I rise onto the balls of my feet and ready myself.

"Use me, Steve," Callum pleads. "Take the money and take me hostage. We'll get you out of here. Just leave my kids alone."

"How did it come to this, Callum? How did our perfect lives come down to this shabby park and a bag full of money? We're supposed to be kings. We're Royals." Then he barks out a horrible laugh. "No. *You're* Royals. I'm just the hanger-on. I'm a shit friend. An even worse dad. I slept with my best friend's wife. I let him raise my kid. I abandoned my other one. But I killed to protect you. I killed that woman to protect you."

"I know you did," Callum replies. He draws a shuddering breath. "I know you never meant any harm. That's why I'm begging you to go and not do any more damage."

Steve shakes his head. "I won't last a day in jail. Not a day. Cover his eyes, Callum. I love you. I really do."

He raises the gun to his temple, and before I can reach him, he pulls the trigger.

Ella screams.

Callum breaks down.

I collapse on the pavement next to Easton.

"We're going make it through this," I whisper to him. "I promise. I promise."

I keep repeating that even as he's strapped to a gurney, rolled into the ambulance and driven away. I repeat it to Ella, who grips my hand so tight that my fingers become numb. I say it all the way to the hospital, during the long wait through surgery, until he finally wakes up hours and hours later and grins at me with his crooked, devastating smile.

"We're going to make it through this," he says, laying his hand over mine. "I promise."

CHAPTER THIRTY-THREE

Hartley

"I feel like I live here," Easton says crossly.

It's only been three days since the surgery, yet the way this boy complains, you'd think it was four years ago. I'm so used to his grumblings that I don't bother looking up from my textbook. "Good thing your name is on the building."

He laughs and then groans. "Stop saying funny things. It hurts to laugh."

I mock gasp. "Who would've imagined that your stomach would hurt after getting one of your kidneys removed?"

He sighs. "You still pissed?"

I lower my voice and repeat his words back to him. "'Don't do anything dangerous. We're only there to take pictures.'"

"Okay, so maybe I was a little reckless."

I peer over the top of my book. "A little? That's like saying yesterday's twelve-inch rainfall was a sprinkle."

He grunts a non-response and then pounds his head on the pillows. "Now I know why Seb wanted to leave immediately. I think I'm getting sicker each minute I spend on this bed.

Shouldn't I be up, moving around? Doing physical therapy or some shit?"

"I don't know, Doctor Royal. Since you're the expert, why don't you tell me?"

"Were you always this sarcastic or is this a new thing developed for my torture?"

"New thing developed for your torture," I answer.

He pats the side of the bed. "I think your torture would be more effective if you were closer."

I set my calc book aside. "Is that right?" I glance toward the door. The last time the nurse caught me lying in bed with him, I almost got thrown out. Only his haughty reminder that he was Easton *Royal* saved me. Wealth has its privileges.

East makes room for me, wincing lightly as he moves. "I think the VIP suites should have bigger hospital beds," he whines.

I climb onto the sheets and tuck my hand under my head. "I don't think they're meant for two people."

"Yeah, well, maybe if the beds were bigger and a guy could sleep with his girlfriend, he'd heal faster."

"I'll drop that in the suggestion box before I go to school in the morning."

He runs a finger across my forehead. "I appreciate that."

We stare at each other. We've spent a lot of time since he woke up just staring at each other, memorizing each other's features. We're both so grateful to be alive. I stop his hand in its trek across my forehead and bring his fingers to my mouth. I lace our hands together and clasp them to his heart where I can feel the steady beat of his lifeblood moving through.

It's odd, because my life is divided into halves, but the demarcation line isn't when I lost my memories. It's before the park and after the park. Before the park, I had no answers. Now I'm full of them, but the knowledge doesn't make me feel better. Before the park, I seriously considered breaking up with East because his brother Sebastian was so opposed to us being together. After the park, I've decided that only an act of God will sever East and me. And even then, I think I'd fight heaven or hell to be back by Easton's side.

Easton presses a kiss to my knuckles. "I'm sorry for everything." *Everything* being that his dad killed mine.

"Me, too." When Mom came to the hospital, she was full of fire. She was going to sue the Royals. She was going to send everyone to jail. I think she meant me, too. I explained to her about the evidence we had against Dad for the bribes, and she shut right up.

Dad's crimes will eventually be exposed. The police found a USB drive in Steve's pocket that had a full accounting of Dad's shady deals—not just with Steve, but with many others, including Mrs. Roquet. Steve had done that for insurance, in case my dad double-crossed him. There really is no honor among thieves.

"How's Astor Park holding up?"

"You're a hero. I think they're going to hold a celebration in your name. Ella is telling everyone how you threw yourself in front of a bullet to save me, your dad, her, and maybe even all of Bayview." I pat his cheek. More seriously, I add, "No one knows the stuff Steve said at the end."

"I don't care," he replies. "I think having a near-death experience can clarify what's important. Callum's raised me since birth. He never once let on that he knew I wasn't his biological son—but blood doesn't amount to much here, does it? Steve only cared about himself. And the fucking coward killed himself because he didn't want to go to prison. What a jackass." He chokes out a broken laugh, because it hurts him more than he wants to admit. "Seriously, though, I know who my family is. Gid, Reed, and the twins are my brothers. Ella's my sister. Callum's my dad. Maria's my mom. And you, you're my heart."

I blink to keep the tears at bay. You wouldn't think I had any more since I've done nothing but cry buckets since I woke up in the hospital with no memory.

"I saw Dr. Joshi in the hall. He asked me how my memory was and I told him it's still shit."

"Yeah?"

"He said I'd probably never regain all my memories."

"How are you feeling about that?"

"Surprisingly okay. I mean, maybe in a year I'll break down in the middle of the college cafeteria in distress, but for now I'm okay with it all. Dylan's safe. You're alive. That's all I want."

We sit there for a ridiculous amount of time, just smiling at each other, because it wasn't so long ago that this simple pleasure might have been taken from us forever.

A knock at the door has me jerking away and East frowning.

"Who is it?" he growls.

"Me."

I look up to see one of the twins standing by the door.

"Seb," Easton says warily.

"I'm going to go and get us an ice cream treat," I say hastily.

East doesn't want to fight with his brother, but I know he'll go to the mat for me. Which is the last thing I want.

"Wait, actually. I'm here to talk to you," Sebastian says to me.

"About what?" East sits up and pins a glare on his brother.

"I'm going to apologize. Got a problem with that?" Seb juts his chin out in irritation.

I hurry over and drag a chair next to the one I'd been sitting in. "Please, come in." I laugh nervously at my own arrogance. "That's stupid of me to say. Like you can't come into your own brother's room." I rush over to the closet where I've been keeping a small stash of contraband items like Cheetos, sour candies, and Reese's Peanut Butter Cups that I feed to Easton in between his regular, terrible hospital meals. "Want something?"

"No." Seb shakes his head. "Can you just...come over here?"

"I love you, Seb, but just because I'm in this hospital bed doesn't mean I can't kick your ass for mistreating Hart."

"Easton!" I cry in dismay. "Just let your brother talk."

"Yeah, let me talk, asshole." Seb jerks the chair back and drops into it with a huff. "Sit." He points to the extra chair. "Please," he tacks on.

I do as he asks.

"I'm sorry," we both say at the same time.

On the bed, Easton laughs and eases back against the pillows. "This might be the most entertainment I've had since Hart dumped that drink on Felicity and then we all watched Felicity slipping and sliding in a puddle on the floor like an idiot."

"Shut up," Seb snaps at the same time I cry, "Easton!"

He makes a show of zipping his lips shut.

"I'm sorry, Sebastian. I'm so sorry for what happened to you. If I could change things, I would."

He nods slowly, a frown marring his high forehead. "Yeah, I'm sorry, too." He drags a hand over his mouth. "Look, I shouldn't have said what I did before. Sometimes there's a thick cloud in my head and the pressure builds and builds. I try to keep it in, but when I do, it just gets worse. I know I shouldn't say half the shit that I do, but it comes out anyway. I can't stop it and no one—*no one*—gets it."

He peers at me with desperate, pleading eyes and I experience a kinship so acutely that I might as well be inside his head. He's been changed irrevocably. He's not going to be able to reclaim who he was before. He can't, and maybe I'm the only one who truly gets it. Our heads are so fragile, but our hearts are even more delicate.

When he says *no one*, he's referring to his twin. The two of them have been cleaved in half. Sawyer's responding by never wanting to leave his brother's side, whereas Sebastian is trying to figure out where he belongs in this mad world.

I want to wrap my arms around this poor lost boy and hug him, but I know he'd hate that. All I can give him is affirmation that he's not wrong to feel the way he does, that he's not a bad person for changing.

"I know," I say. "You're not the same Sebastian you were before and you never will be. And that's okay. It will be okay."

He firms his lips and nods once and then again. He swipes a hand across his eyes and gets to his feet. "Good talk, Wright. See you around."

I turn to find Easton gnawing his bottom lip in concern.

"He'll work it out," I assure my boyfriend. "But we have to

let him do it on his own."

"Dumbass," Easton mutters affectionately as I climb in next to him. "We don't care if he's a surly asshole. We're just happy he's alive."

"He knows that. It's coming to terms with his changes that's the hard part." I snuggle close, careful not to bump his surgery site.

He rests his chin on the top of my head. "And you. Are you having a hard time coming to terms with everything? Your mom was screaming at you over the phone."

"You heard that, huh?"

"It was hard not to," he admits.

I sigh and rub my nose against his chest, inhaling his warm, male scent. "She's afraid. Her whole life is going to be dismantled. She had dreams of joining the country club and hosting teas with the first ladies of Bayview. Now she'll be lucky not to be stoned at the gas station."

"I'd rather be stoned at the gas station than drink weak piss with Felicity's mom," Easton declares.

"Anyone in their right mind would take the gas station over Felicity's mom. There are hotdogs at the gas station," I remind him.

"Good point. Nectar of the gods right there." He chuckles and then groans. "Fuck, don't make me laugh." He tips my chin up. "I'm going to take care of you. My dad will, too. He's not going to leave you out to dry. You're a Royal now."

He seals this promise with a kiss.

Being a Royal doesn't mean that my last name is the same as Easton's or that I live under the same roof or wear the Astor Park Prep badge on my clothes. It only means that there's a tribe of people who welcome me, and a boy who loves me. If I can accept that, then I'm a Royal.

Steve O'Halloran never understood. He never realized that he was in Callum's heart all these years, receiving love and forgiveness and acceptance despite all his sins. He kept searching for fulfillment and never found it—not in the money, the cars, the danger. He slept with Maria Royal, not because he loved Maria, but because he loved what Callum had. A family of big strong boys who were fiercely loyal. Who loved with their whole beings. Who fought for everything they believed was right and good and worthwhile in this world.

I could let myself be sad about my loss of memories. I could spend years bemoaning that my father never loved me, that my mother is more interested in her money, and that it might take a while before my sisters learn that we're on the same side. If I did that, I'd turn into a Steve or a Felicity or a Kyle, where the hate takes up so much space in my heart that there's no room left for joy.

Instead, I can be a Royal and open my heart up to receive all the precious love that Easton wants to shower on me. So I wrap my arms around the sun and let him warm me from the inside out.

I'm a Royal because I'm loved by Easton Royal.

There's nothing more pure and wondrous in the world than that.

CHAPTER THIRTY-FOUR

Hartley

"They're ready for you, Hart!" my sister Dylan yells from the bottom of the stairs.

"I'll be right down," I holler back.

"I'll finish this," Easton tells me. "You go on."

This being the making of the bed that was delivered earlier this morning. Dylan and I live with the Royals now, which is the most surreal thing in the world. But we didn't have anywhere else to go once Mom and Parker moved to Virginia. The scandal was too much for either of them to endure. To Mom's credit, she tried, but as more and more of Dad's cases were revealed to be frauds and convictions were expunged, she couldn't take it anymore. After the first of the year, she packed up everything. Parker followed shortly after.

Fortunately, Callum offered to take both me and Dylan in. As Easton said, we were Royals—or at least Callum and everyone else treated us as such. At first, we stayed in the main house, but both Dylan and I are loners, and I think Callum recognized that we would be more comfortable in our own space. So he cleaned out the huge area above the detached garage, which had been used for storage before. Then he hired a contractor to turn the space into an apartment for us.

East has been cracking the whip over this project, which served the dual purpose of proving that he's becoming a responsible adult and ensuring we finally have some privacy, because I've refused to leave the apartment to sleep in his bedroom while my baby sister is here.

He's taken to sleeping on the sofa many nights. I'll admit, it makes me feel safe. Both of us are taking a year off before we go to college. I want to spend time with Dylan, and East's been allowed back in the air. He told me he doesn't care if he ever goes to college. I gave him a book about engineering in hopes he'll change his mind.

Within the addition, Dylan and I each have our own bathrooms and bedrooms along with a sweet kitchen and small dining area. There's even a small deck built off the back, and if you lean around the corner, you can see the ocean.

"You should go, too. You're the man of honor," I remind him.

"It's best man," he insists. "How many times do I have to remind you people that my role is Best. Man."

"Whatever you say, man of honor," I tease and then run off so whatever punishment he has in mind can't be meted out. I trip down the stairs, cross the cobblestone courtyard, and slip through a side door and into the Royal mansion.

I grew up in a big house, but the Royal place is on an entirely different level. Just like how their life is on an entirely different level. It's very glamorous, but anyone who knows the Royals knows that all of that richness came at a price.

But today we're not going to dwell on the past. Today is a day of celebration, a day to look toward the future.

I don't have all my memories back. There's a spot in my life that's just a big hole. But if I had to start new, this seems like the right place to do it. Easton says that I kissed him first on the top of the Ferris wheel, and that in keeping with tradition I kissed him first again. I think what he was trying to say was that I am the same person today as I was a year ago and that the loss of my memory hasn't changed me.

I made mistakes in the past. I should've never left Dylan, although when I was fourteen and she was ten, I didn't have a lot of options. She promised me that Dad never hit her, but she didn't deny that he was emotionally abusive. He mocked her illness and didn't take her seriously. Mom was embarrassed by her. All those anxieties only served to worsen her condition. She didn't want to take medications because she wanted to pretend she didn't need them. That way the criticisms of our parents wouldn't stick.

She's so much better now. The Royal brothers have taken her under their wing, spoiling her rotten. But Easton's been the best of all because he told her that he felt the same way. He validated her feelings and helped her accept that her bipolarity was just like a physical illness. She adores him. I think she'd throw me into the ocean if she had to choose between the two of us.

Easton battles his own demons. Sometimes when he has a stressful day, I know he wants a drink. His hands will tremble. His eyes will flit all over the room and then he'll have to go do something, whether it's laps in the pool, a run along the beach or, if Dylan isn't around, I can exhaust him in other ways.

The weather is just on the cusp of getting hot, but there's a sweet afternoon breeze coming up from the ocean. It's a perfect day for a wedding.

I make my way past the dining room that seats fourteen and across the marble floor under the crystal chandelier that sparkles so brightly it could rival the sun. The long room in the front has been transformed into a beauty parlor. Callum hired an army of staff—caterers, waiters, hairdressers, makeup artists, musicians. I feel like half of Bayview is here prepping for this event.

"Oh good, you're here. I was just about to come and get you." Dylan prances over. Her long hair, so similar to mine, has tiny braids around the crown. A crystal and enamel floral headpiece sits just behind those braids, and around her neck is a simple necklace with the same enamel flowers.

I suspect the jewelry is worth more than some people's cars. Callum Royal throws money around as if there's a printing press in the basement. And there's no point in putting a stop to his generosity. Easton says it's because it makes him feel less guilty and that if I have any compassion I'll accept all these gifts with a smile.

It's easier to do when they're showered on Dylan, because she deserves the world.

"You look beautiful," I tell her.

"I know." She twirls in a circle, her skirt flying up. "Your turn now."

I give myself over to the team to dress me, perfume me, do my hair and makeup and slip red-soled shoes onto my feet. Next to me, Ella's best girlfriend, Val, gets the same treatment while Savannah, Gideon's girlfriend, plays UNO with Dylan.

The wedding planner sticks her head in the room. "If everyone is ready, can you take your places?"

The four of us make our way outside onto the vast lawn that overlooks the endless sea. Dylan and I take our seats in the front row—the row designated for family. My sister slides her hand beneath mine. Our finger lengths almost match. I glance up in surprise. Dylan's growing up. I hadn't realized it before when she was spinning like a top before me.

My attention is diverted when Easton walks up from behind the floral arch with his oldest brother behind him. I nearly swallow my tongue. Easton Royal in a tux should be illegal. I wonder how many other women in the audience are getting pregnant just from looking at the two Royal brothers.

"You're disgusting," Dylan whispers.

I dab a finger at the corner of my lips. "Am I drooling?"

"Not yet." She sniffs with disdain. "But any second now I expect your eyes to fall into your lap. Can you act with some self-control? Both of you are an embarrassment."

Both of us? I look up to see Easton staring at me like I'm his favorite dish and he hasn't eaten in two weeks. I blush.

Dylan nudges me. I nudge her back.

"No, I can't act with any self-control." The smile that breaks across my face is uncontrollable, but Dylan is saved from any further antics when Bruno Mars' "Marry You" starts playing.

The entire congregation rises to watch Ella Royal stroll down the center of the aisle looking like a fairy princess come to life, decked out in a tightly-bound satin bodice with tiny sleeves and a huge ball gown skirt that appears to be made of a thousand layers of tissue-thin silk. Her blonde hair is caught up in a delicate bun at the base of her neck. Around her head she wears a diamond tiara, and a train floats so far behind her that if you stretched it out, it might reach the house several yards away.

Reed Royal stands opposite Easton in a dark tux and snow-white shirt, but it's the pure love shining from his Royal-blue eyes that captures everyone's attention.

I like to think of myself as not overly sentimental, but I cry during the wedding. It might be a remnant of last winter's trauma when my father was killed, when Easton was shot, when he endured a long and painful recovery from his kidney transplant.

But it might be out of happiness. That I'm alive. That Dylan's with me. That Easton's as healthy today as he ever was. That his sister and his brother are marrying even though neither of them is even in their twenties. Reed proposed at Christmas and to everyone's surprise, Ella said yes. She did so with a lot of caveats, though. She was going to college. Then she was getting a job. They would live only on the money the two of them made. Reed agreed with everything. She could have said that she wanted him to wear the dress and I think he would've said yes.

I think she was ready because she'd lost so much—her mother, her father. I'm clinging extra hard to Dylan these days, much to her dismay.

I'm not the only one who cries, though. Dylan weeps. So do Val and Savannah. I swear I see Gideon wipe his eyes. Callum doesn't bother to hide his tears. And all those claims about mascara being waterproof are bullshit. Every single female looks like a damned raccoon.

After the ceremony is over, the army of folks who were hired to make us look beautiful in the first place descend on the wedding party and fix us up so we can take pictures and party during the reception looking perfect once again. Easton gives a hilarious and embarrassing toast recounting how Ella became part of the family.

"Reed swore up and down that he didn't like her, but then he'd go sit outside her bedroom waiting for her to come home every night," Easton reveals, which makes both his siblings blush for different reasons. "He was like her own personal guard dog."

Reed shrugs and makes a woofing sound. Ella turns even redder. And the redder she gets, the louder the crowd roars. When Easton is done teasing them, Gideon stands up and then it's the twins' moment to turn up the heat.

When the toasts are done and the champagne kisses are performed, the DJ cranks up the music, filling the massive lawn with heavy dance beats. Dylan hops from foot to foot, anxious to get out on the dance floor. She scans the crowd, looking for a partner. Her gaze stops on the twins, who are seated at a table a couple feet away.

"This is pretty cool, right?" Dylan asks them.

Seb nods. Or Sawyer. I can't tell them apart anymore. They're both sarcastic, charming, and dangerous. They've broken more hearts in the last five months than I thought was humanly possible. It's almost like they're in a contest to see who can bed and leave the most girls in Bayview before they're seniors. But they're kind to Dylan, as evidenced by the fact that they aren't saying something bitingly sarcastic about their barely twenty-year-old brother and their teenage foster sister getting married, and so I can't fault them.

She gives them a sweet smile. "And the music is lit."

They nod again.

"And everyone's happy."

Another nod.

Her smile widens even more. "Four years and it'll be our turn."

I blink at the random statement. Four years? What is she babbling about now?

"Four years?" One of them raises his eyebrow.

"Our turn?" The other one is slightly panicked.

"Yeah, I'll be eighteen then."

"So?" says the one with the upturned eyebrow. The other twin, the smart one, is half out of his chair and looking ready to flee.

"So that's when we'll get married," Dylan announces.

I nearly swallow my tongue. The boys exchange a look, the kind where they have an entire conversation about how inappropriate my sister is. They both get to their feet.

"We'll have it here just like Ella, but with more flowers. I like roses."

I slap a hand across Dylan's mouth. "She's kidding," I assure the twins.

She pushes her wet tongue between my fingers.

"Ugh, yuck, Dylan."

"I'm not kidding," she declares. "I'm going to marry them when I'm eighteen."

"Which one?"

"Duh," she says. "You can't split them up."

And then she flounces off, leaving the three of us staring after her with shocked expressions. At least...*I'm* shocked. I'm not sure I can read the twins' faces. No. I don't *want* to read their faces. Deliberately, I turn away. I didn't see anything there, I tell myself. Nothing is there.

Easton appears at my side to stick a champagne flute in my hand. "Do you want the real stuff or is grape juice okay?"

"This is good." I take a sip of the sparkling juice and let the bubbles tickle the inside of my mouth. I'll worry about Dylan in four years, I decide. No need to share what just transpired with Easton. He'll lock Dylan in the carriage house and not let her out. This is a phase. She'll grow out of it. I hope.

"I never thought I'd be giving a toast at a wedding or that I'd drink juice in celebration." He crinkles his nose.

"Both are perfect. You make a good man of honor."

"Best. Man."

I grin, take another sip, then turn my attention to the dark water lapping quietly against the sand.

"What are we doing out here?" Easton asks, resting his chin on the top of my head.

"I'm making a memory."

"Ahh." He wraps his arms around my shoulders. "I think it'd be a better one if we took your dress off."

I shiver, but it's not from the cold. "My sister did say earlier we should get a room."

He places a hot kiss on the side of my neck. "Dylan's the smartest girl I know."

Smiling broadly, Easton takes my hand and leads me across the dance floor, under a floral arch, onto the cobblestone courtyard and up the stairs of our home to make a new memory.

ACKNOWLEDGMENTS

Special thanks are owed to Jessica Clare and Meljean Brook who read and re-read this book and helped make it what it is today.

All errors are ours, of course.

And thank you to all the readers who so passionately love the Royals. We hope that you enjoyed reading these books as much as we enjoyed creating them.

Stay tuned for our next adventures.

STAY CONNECTED

We promise to only send an email when it's really important. Stay connected with us by liking Erin Watt's Facebook page for updates and fun teasers!

LIKE US ON FACEBOOK:
https://www.facebook.com/authorerinwatt

FOLLOW US ON GOODREADS:
https://www.goodreads.com/author/show/14902188.Erin_Watt

ABOUT THE AUTHOR

Erin Watt is the brainchild of two bestselling authors linked together through their love of great books and an addiction to writing. They share one creative imagination. Their greatest love (after their families and pets, of course)? Coming up with fun--and sometimes crazy—ideas. Their greatest fear? Breaking up. You can contact them at their shared inbox: authorerinwatt@gmail.com

CPSIA information can be obtained
at www.ICGtesting.com
Printed in the USA
BVHW07s1928290618
520451BV00002B/2/P